THE DEUCE OF DIAMONDS

Roaming Reynolds and Texas Joe find themselves helping out a couple of old ranchers who are being plagued by rustlers. Reynolds suspects that local cattle baron Griff Tyson, owner of the Deuce of Diamonds spread, is behind the trouble. But Tyson is quite a gunfighter himself, able to shoot playing cards out of the air. Will Reynolds and Joe prevail against him?

CHARLES M. MARTIN

THE DEUCE OF DIAMONDS

Complete and Unabridged

LINFORD
Leicester

First published in Great Britain in 1938 by
Ivor Nicholson and Watson Limited
First published in the United States by Greenberg

First Linford Edition
published 2021
by arrangement with
Golden West Literary Agency

A catalogue record for this book is available
from the British Library.

ISBN 978–1–78541–953–9

Published by
Ulverscroft Limited
Anstey, Leicestershire

Printed and bound in Great Britain by
TJ Books Ltd., Padstow, Cornwall

This book is printed on acid-free paper

TO CATH

My wife and pard, who has ridden many of the Western trails with me in good times and bad. Cath knows the old outlaws and peace officers of the Old West as I do — and calls both 'Friends'

I dedicate this book with love to the best cook in the world, and my saddle-pard.

Like Always,
CHUCK.

1

Roaming Reynolds knew that trouble was riding to Paradise on the same trail that had brought Texas Joe and himself to the little cattle-shipping town in Summit Valley. They had crossed vast open ranges green with sacaton and buffalo grass, sure signs of plentiful water the year around. There would be work enough for cow-hands in such a country, but still the feeling of trouble persisted.

Roaming had a premonition that could not be explained in words. His right hand automatically loosened the heavy gun on his leg of riding crimp when they turned in a dusty winding street and headed towards a cluster of buildings. He stopped at a hitch rack and anchored his tall roan with trailing reins when he swung from the saddle.

He smiled with the corners of his mouth when the lanky young cowboy copied him move for move. Neither said a word as they settled their shoulders against the front of the General Store to feel the pulse of Paradise. Something was wrong, but range land usually settled its own difficulties.

Texas Joe was a range veteran of just past sixteen, but he spotted the trouble as quickly as his older companion. His light blue eyes flicked briefly over the faces of half a dozen men lolling in the shade and came to rest unhesitatingly on a pair of strangely contrasted riders, nearest the door. His thin lips moved slightly in a deep bass whisper that only Roaming Reynolds could hear.

'Them two, pard. They're fixin' to cut a rusty on the big waddy inside!'

Roaming Reynolds eased his six feet of bone and muscle against the adobe wall and nodded imperceptibly. His narrowed blue eyes were studying the pair without seeming to be interested. Strangers minded their own business in high Arizona, if they were saddle-broke and knew their way around. They kept their eyes open and their mouths shut, and the tall cowboy did both as he cuffed his Stetson low over his eyes.

Whatever they had in mind, the two riders by the door were getting ready for action. One was a huge fellow with the shoulders and arms of a giant. His companion was short and slender, not more than five feet five in his high-heeled boots. Both were watching a rider coming up the winding street, and the older cowboy drew a deep breath when he saw that the newcomer was a pretty girl.

The other men were also watching the girl with carefully veiled indifference that told of expectant interest. Light calfskin *chaparejos* over worn Levi's tucked down in polished hand-made boots. Wool shirt open at the neck and caught with a silk bandanna. Smooth skin richly tanned by sun and wind to mark her for a daughter of the great out-of-doors.

Dark eyes flashed a brief glance at the tie rail before the girl reined in at the only open space beteen two cow-trained jugheads down at the end of the line. She swung down like a cowboy to fasten

3

her *mecate* with a slip knot, and held her chin high as she attempted to pass the big puncher and his waspy companion. She stopped abruptly and stepped back when the big fellow fiddle-footed to bar her way.

'Just a minute, Bobbie Zander,' he growled roughly.

'The big Augur sent me in with a message for you and yore Pa.'

The girl curled her lips scornfully. 'Keep your hands off me, Butch Cawdorn,' she answered sharply. 'I came here on business of my own which does not concern you.'

'That's what you think,' Cawdorn sneered, and winked at his pard. 'Griff Tyson figgered you and yore old man would both be interested.'

The girl shrugged a shapely shoulder. 'I am not interested in any message from Griff Tyson or anyone else on the Deuce of Diamonds,' she answered with biting contempt.

The blue eyes of Roaming Reynolds flicked briefly to the brands on the jugheads that now pocketed the girl's spirited sorrel. A figure 2 in a lengthwise Diamond burnt on the left shoulder. The brand on the girl's sorrel was a Lazy L. Funny that, and her name Zander.

The hoarse voice of Butch Cawdorn growled savagely in a tone that sent the hand of Texas Joe reaching toward the old gun on his lean thigh. Then the lanky cowboy stopped the move and waited.

'The boss said you was to keep yore stock away from Big Springs, and he don't aim to tell you again. We took that water for our Deuce of Diamonds critters. What I said like wise goes for Lafe Lassiter and that over-growed chip of his!'

The girl caught her breath when a square-shouldered cowboy stepped out from the store and headed straight for Butch Cawdorn. Taller than the Deuce of Diamonds rider and nearly as heavy in the shoulders and arms. Not more than twenty-two, but his dark eyes were glittering with anger when he pushed the girl gently aside and faced the sneering bully. This was the play Texas Joe had seen coming up.

'Big Springs is open range,' the cowboy announced huskily, 'and since when did Griff Tyson start making war on women?'

'Since her old man and yores commenced moving stock on our range,' the bully growled deep in his chest. 'Now you high-tail it before I come uncorked and snap the rough out of you!'

The girl stared at the two men and bit her lip. A frightened expression leaped to her dark eyes when she stepped forward and touched the young cowboy on the shoulder.

'Please go, Manny,' she pleaded softly. 'Can't you see what they are doing? They have the trap all baited, and they were just waiting for you to spring it!'

Manny Lassiter shook his big shoulders stubbornly. Blinding anger flashed across his smooth tanned face when Butch Cawdorn laughed sneeringly. His big hands knotted suddenly into ham-like fists as he started for the Deuce of

Diamonds man, but the latter slapped down his gun and got the drop, Lassiter stopped his charge and stared into the muzzle of the cocked .45 while his dark eyes blazed with an anger he could not control.

'Put up that iron and meet me like a man,' he growled in a choked voice. 'You've threatened me for the last time, Butch Cawdorn!'

'Watch him, Shorty,' and Cawdorn spoke over his shoulder to the waspy gunman who had fanned out to one side. 'You heard what the salty hairpin said!'

Shorty Peters twitched his thin shoulders and flicked his right hand. A gun appeared like magic, and his voice was a thin whisper that twanged like brass when he gave his pard the go-ahead.

'Take him, Butch. He's asking for it!'

Roaming Reynolds lowered his head to hide the expression in his watchful eyes. But Cawdorn split his thick lips in a grin to show broken yellow fangs in the corners of his big mouth. The heavy gun disappeared in his cut-away holster, and his worn vest bulged when he hunched his shoulders to ripple the muscles of his broad back. A chuckling laugh rumbled from his deep chest when Bobbie Zander tried to pull Manny Lassiter away.

'I only aim to cripple him some, lady,' he boasted. 'He made his bet, and I don't aim to let no feller draw back his chips when he goes on the prod and calls my hand.'

Manny Lassiter shook himself free from the restraining hands of the pleading girl. His left fist lashed out to rock the sneering bully back on his rounded heels, while Texas Joe set his lips and narrowed his light blue eyes to watch Shorty Peters.

Butch Cawdorn took the blow with a grin. Then he lowered his head and charged like a bull with both arms flailing. Lassiter was crowded against the tie rail before he could side-step, and a heavy right-hand swing nearly tore the head from his shoulders. The Lazy L cowboy buckled his knees and clinched to save himself, and for a moment he hung on desperately and tried to clear his brain.

Not a man under the board awning made a move to interfere. Butch Cawdorn swung his big shoulders and tore loose from the grip of his victim. His heavy fist crashed across with killing force when Lassiter was just out of reach, and the cowboy went to the ground like a sack of barley. The girl screamed when his opponent rushed in with right boot kicking at the unprotected face.

'Roll, cowboy; roll!'

Texas Joe forgot himself and screamed the advice with his changing voice breaking on a high note. The bully had every ounce of his two hundred pounds behind the heavy boot that was swinging forward to maim his victim. The girl covered her face with her arms and screamed just as a gun roared throatily. Butch Cawdorn fell on his broad back when a bullet tore off the high heel of his right boot before the blow could land.

'Hold it, Shorty!'

Texas Joe growled the warning

viciously, crouching across the gun in his grimy right hand. The little gunman had whirled like a flash with thumb dogging back the hammer of his Colt when he saw Roaming Reynolds bucking the smoking gun down in his hand. His thin face hardened when he saw the half-grown boy holding the drop on him.

'I'll remember, Button,' he snarled hoarsely.

'You better draw out yore chips!'

Texas Joe bristled and dared the little gunman with his blazing eyes. Shorty Peters thought quickly and dropped his weapon, and. Roaming Reynolds holstered his Peacemaker with a grim smile.

Broad shoulders hunching forward, the tall cowboy walked stiff-legged across the baked ground like a dog on the fight. He stared down at the bully while ridges of muscles knotted around his jaws to frame his tight-lipped mouth. Butch Cawdorn rolled over and came to his feet with a roar of rage, and his beefy face twisted horribly when he saw Texas Joe against the wall with finger itching to press trigger.

Then he turned his head and saw Roaming Reynolds watching him intently. He trembled like a bucking horse that has been stomped into the ground, and his voice was thick with venom when he finally controlled himself.

'You bought chips in a closed game, feller,' he rasped hoarsely. 'You and yore pard is both strangers,' and he shrugged his heavy shoulders. 'Drop or no drop, I'm inviting you to go for yore cutter!'

Roaming Reynolds did not even glance at Texas Joe. He knew the lanky cowboy; a pard to ride the river with. His blue eyes held steady on the face of Butch Cawdorn for a brief moment. Then:

'I always buy chips in a stack-up,' he answered softly. 'I saw you and yore pards deal the cards off the bottom of the deck, and you're lucky I didn't kill you when you aimed to kick that big Lazy L waddy to death, and him out cold. Now you deal yoreself a hand if you feel lucky.'

Not once did he raise his deep drawling voice while he tallied the failings of Butch Cawdorn. The bully spread his fingers wide and crouched forward to shadow the handle of his gun, while Roaming Reynolds waited and watched with a slow smile on his craggy face.

Shorty Peters husked a warning before the bully could slap down for his gun. 'Hold yore hand, Butch! That jigger could kill you before yore hardware cleared leather. He's a gun-slammer from the way he wears his tools, and if he wants action so bad as all that, I'm the gent what can bring it to him!'

Texas Joe held his hand and watched the face of his tall pard. Roaming Reynolds was smiling grimly. Smiling with the eager light of hell blazing in his deep blue eyes, while his gun-hand ached and the long fingers throbbed with anticipation. Like Peters had read the sign, he was a gun-fighter.

Butch Cawdorn's face began to pale slowly. He swallowed noisily and bobbed his head with relief when his little greenish eyes flicked down to the titled handle on the tall cowboy's right leg. Reynolds's weapon was slung low, with the tie-backs holding the moulded holster for a speedy draw when a fraction of a second meant the difference between life and death.

Manny Lassiter lay under the tie rail without moving, and the girl held a little hand to her heart and moaned softly, unable to speak for the fear that gripped and paralyzed her vocal chords. And then Butch Cawdorn broke the silence.

'Take him, Shorty,' he whispered, and tried to wet his thick lips with a burning tongue that scraped across the dry membranes like a snake looping through the sand.

Roaming Reynolds smiled frostily and turned to face the crouching figure of Shorty Peters. Except for the smouldering fires burning deep in his blue eyes, there was no expression on his tanned face. While the men along the wall held their breaths and tensed their muscles to get away from the line of fire.

Texas Joe sighed jerkily and felt his hand stiffen. It always did that when his tall pard took the play. Roaming was fast

13

with his tools, but he always gave the other man more chance than Texas Joe figured he deserved. And then Shorty Peters rumbled deep in his corded throat.

'Take him, Shorty,' Butch Cawdorn whispered hoarsely.

Roaming Reynolds dropped his right hand suddenly and flicked his wrist with the same movement. Shorty Peters stopped his clutching fingers when he stared into the muzzle of the leaping gun and realized that he had been out-speeded.

'It wouldn't be a fair shake, Shorty;' and the voice of Roaming Reynolds was tinged with regret. 'You don't stack up against fast company.'

The little gunman growled softly. 'You pulled a sneak to copper yore bet!'

Roaming Reynolds tightened his jaw and relaxed almost at once. 'You and him step across yore hosses and make tracks while you still got yore health,' he advised softly, and jerked his head toward the Deuce of Diamonds horses at the rail.

Shorty Peters glared savagely while his lean jaws worked with impotent anger. He was rated fast with a hand-gun, and faster still with a throwing knife, and he begged for the chance to match speed with this blue-eyed stranger who had taken the play away from him on what he considered a gun-sneak.

'Holster yore cutter and draw me evens,' he pleaded earnestly. 'A gent can't die but one time, and I got you faded nohow!'

Roaming Reynolds stared into the glittering little eyes, and his face hardened when he lowered the hammer of his Colt. For a moment he was tempted to accede to the gunman's request, but he thought better of the impulse and shook his head.

'I don't often give a jigger but one chance to draw on me,' he drawled softly. 'You better take that chance and get long gone before young Lassiter rouses 'round. And take yore pard along with you before I cut his horns for what he tried to do to the lady!'

Shorty Peters glared and mumbled under his breath. Butch Cawdorn was edging toward his horse, and he pulled the tie rope and mounted up before speaking.

'Better pile on, Shorty,' he rumbled hoarsely. 'This gun-slinging pilgrim holds high hand right now, but he ain't met up with the boss or the Ramrod yet. He won't last long in these parts, I'll tell yuh man!'

'Long enough, you boot-stomping maverick,' Texas Joe interrupted coldly, and his eyes squinted with contempt when he stared at the bully. 'Had it been me throwing lead yore way, I'd have cen-tred plumb on yore brisket 'stead of yore heel. I don't get soft-hearted none that-away, and you and him start travelling like Roamin' said!'

Reynolds smiled slightly and glanced at his pard. Texas Joe was crouching over his old .45, his thin face twisted into a scowl. Old for his years, but every man there knew that he meant just what he said. And all the while he stared at Shorty

Peters like a cat watching a mouse.

Peters stared back for a moment before shrugging his thin shoulders. Keeping his hands high, he slid around the rail to get to his horse. He hit the saddle with one flying leap, grapped the whangs with his left hand and held the horse with a tight grip.

'I ain't forgetting you, Button,' and his voice was a savage promise.

Texas Joe spat derisively. 'Any time, you busted flush,' he sneered nastily. 'You and me is just about of a size!'

Butch Cawdorn was edging away, and Shorty Peters scratched with both feet to rocket his claybank down the dusty street. Texas Joe holstered his gun and shook his head with disappointment.

'You should have pulled that little jigger's stinger, Roamin',' he complained bitterly. 'You and me is going to have trouble with that outfit shore and certain.'

'Mebbe not,' Reynolds murmured carelessly. 'But yo're bound to run into grief one of the days unless you lean to keep down yore mad. I thought for a minute he was going to call yore hand, and him under a double drop.'

'I should have let him have it when he tried to turn his gun on you,' the lanky cowboy growled. 'Right after you shot the heel from that big killer's boot.'

'You don't know that them two is killers,' Roaming Reynolds answered reprovingly. 'You and me is strangers here while them two is old hands.'

Texas Joe smiled. 'Don't never take us long to get acquainted,' he answered more quietly.

The tall buckaroo remembered then and turned to the big cowboy on the ground. Manny Lassiter came to his feet with a rush, swung his head from side to side while his eyes tried to locate Butch Cawdom. The girl caught his arm and steadied him, and her throaty voice brought the light of reason back to his dark eyes.

'Stop fighting yore head, Manny. I warned you not to fall into the trap they set for us.'

The big cowboy was breathing deeply and rubbing a welt on his jaw. His eyes were still dazed and blinking, but he tried to wrench free from the girl.

'They've gone now, Manny,' she told him. 'Butch Cawdom would have killed you with his boots if Mister Reynolds hadn't stopped him when he did. It was terrible!'

'Reynolds?' and Lassiter turned slowly to stare at his rescuer. 'Yo're new in these parts, ain't you?' Roaming Reynolds nodded. 'Just passing through, you might say,' he answered slowly. 'Me and my pard just finished a job of work over yonder in the Strip.'

Manny Lassiter squared his big shoulders, and his eyes brightened with sudden recognition. 'Yo're Roaming Reynolds who cleaned up that outlaw spread Eagle Dupree was rodding?'

'Me and him,' Texas Joe interrupted to explain. 'I was making a hand on the M. T. spread for old man Mormon Tucker when Roamin' signed on as gun boss. It didn't take long to do what had to be

19

done, and I reckon you know the rest.'

Roaming Reynolds frowned, but Texas Joe swelled out his chest and rubbed the handle of his old gun. Grinned impudently when the tall buckaroo nudged him roughly with his elbow.

'Take a hitch in that loose jaw of yore's, Button,' Reynolds growled. 'You talk too much with yore mouth.'

Texas Joe backed away with a scowl twisting his thin face. 'There's been a heap of talk going on here since we rode into Paradise,' he countered sullenly, 'and it ain't much like you to throw off yore shots like you done.'

'Get yore hoss,' Reynolds said softly. 'I know you, feller, and yo're itching to ride down trouble. Better wait until it catches you up.'

Manny Lassiter flushed and rubbed a big hand on his right leg where his gun should have been riding. Roaming Reynolds followed that hand with his eyes and frowned. Texas Joe snickered, and the Lazy L puncher sucked in his breath and rubbed his chin.

'How come you ain't dressed proper, with war riding out to meet you from that Deuce of Diamonds spread?' Reynolds asked bluntly. 'And both them other hands heeled to go?'

'I'm a cattleman, not a gun-fighter,' Lassiter growled resentfully. 'I ain't had time to practise none with a hand-gun since I took over as Ramrod for Dad four years ago.'

'You mean to say you rod a riding crew in a country like this without something to back you up?' the tall buckaroo persisted. 'With notch-whittling killers like Butch Cawdorn and Shorty Peters on the loose?'

'We ain't had any trouble to speak of up to now,' the big foreman muttered. 'And my boys have been too busy riding to work up much speed with six-guns.'

'And you see what it brought you,' Texas Joe interrupted dryly. 'Them Deuce of Diamonds hands had plenty of time to keep in shape.'

'They got a big crew,' Lassiter growled, and then, raised his head. 'Thanking you for what you done, Reynolds,' he said huskily, as though the words came hard.

'I'm thanking you too,' Bobbie Zander echoed softly. 'I just stood there powerless to move, and I thought he was going to kill Manny. And then Shorty Peters would have killed you if Texas Joe hadn't been watching him close.'

'What I was trying to tell Roamin',' Texas muttered. 'But he tells me I'm only a button what ain't man-growed!'

Roaming Reynolds smiled and slapped the lanky cowboy on the shoulder. 'I'd rather have you at my side than any man I know,' he said quietly. 'You know that, Joe, but you got to quit fighting yore head when you get in a tight.'

'Looks like Lassiter is in one,' the cowboy muttered.

The Lazy L foreman nodded vigorously. 'Like he said, Reynolds,' he admitted. 'You looking for work?'

'Yes,' the girl added and touched the tall buckaroo on the arm. 'I know you are a cowboy from your rigging and gear.'

Roaming Reynolds turned his head

22

and studied the girl with range-wise eyes. He could see the smooth shine on her chaps where a rope had burned when she had hip-leaned after snaring her saddle horse. Tiny high-heeled boots peeped out from under deep cuffs, and a battered grey Stetson was pushed back to show curls of copper-red. He tore his eyes away from her pretty face to answer Manny Lassiter.

'I dunno,' he drawled slowly. 'What kind of work you got in mind for me and Joe?'

'Cow work, of course,' Texas Joe sneered quietly. 'We seen plenty of cattle on the way down here from the Strip.'

'What I told you a while back still stands,' Reynolds answered sternly. 'Now you button that loose mouth of yores while me and him talks,' and he raised his eyes to stare at Lassiter.

'Anybody can see that yo're tophand with hosses and cattle,' Lassiter answered slowly. 'But I wasn't thinking so much about that.'

'Yeah? Give a name to what you was

thinking,' Reynolds prompted.

'The kind of work you know best,' Lassiter snapped suddenly. 'Griff Tyson has done declared war, and I'll pay you a hundred a month and shells. Half that to the Button if he wants to sign on to lend you a hand!'

Roaming Reynolds remained silent while his eyes turned to watch Bobbie Zander. She was leaning forward with lips parted, waiting eagerly for his answer. The tall gun-fighter frowned and shifted his eyes from her face.

'I dunno,' he hesitated, and glanced at Texas Joe.

'Took!' Texas Joe squared his thin shoulders and stalked forward to shake hands with the Lazy L foreman. 'How far out is this outfit yo're roddin'?'

'Just a minute, pard,' Reynolds interrupted. 'Did you hear me say we were signing on?'

Texas Joe grinned slyly. 'Reading the sign in yore face, I saw the answer before I spoke,' he answered positively. 'Special after what them two gunnies 'said about

Griff Tyson and that gent he called the foreman.'

Manny Lassiter stepped up and offered his hand. 'It's a long twelve miles to the Lazy L,' he said quietly. 'Reynolds, I want you to meet Bobbie Zander of the Bar Z Bar. I'm thanking you the best I can for keeping that Cawdorn bully from messing up my face with his boots.'

Roaming Reynolds nodded and swept off his hat.

'Howdy, Miss Bobbie,' he drawled softly. 'Looks like we're going to be neighbours for a while.'

'Then you will accept the job Manny offered,' the girl answered quickly, and stepped forward to grip his hand. 'I don't know what we would have done if you hadn't interfered when you did.'

'My pard said we'd take the job, and I most always back him up,' the tall buckaroo answered gravely. 'Looks like we find the kind of work we like best no matter where we roam.'

Texas Joe cut in slyly. 'That's how come him to get his handle,' he chuckled. 'He's got the restless foot worse than any hand I ever saw.'

Manny Lassiter nodded. 'We heard about that ruckus up in the Strip,' he said thoughtfully. 'And we figgered you'd stay on there with Tucker after the offer he made you.'

Roaming Reynolds shifted uneasily. 'Our job was finished up there,' he muttered soberly. 'And when we get through doing what we signed on to do, me and Joe usually drifts along to see what's over the hill.'

'Reckon we will be here a right smart spell of time,' Texas Joe added, 'that Deuce of Diamonds is some outfit from all the signs we saw.'

'It's big,' Lassiter admitted with a frown. 'But the Lazy L ain't exactly a little outfit,' he added proudly. 'If Dad was younger …'

Roaming Reynolds remembered where he was and glanced at the men under the wooden awning. They looked away when his blue eyes briefly scanned each face, and the tall buckaroo nudged

Texas Joe when the boy was about to speak.

'Save it, Joe,' he warned. 'Too many ears here in Paradise, and mebbe the boss better tell us the whyfors about this war while we're riding toward the Lazy L.'

'Good idea,' Lassiter seconded. 'I've got the mail, and I put in my order for supplies.'

He was still shaky when he untied his big bay and pulled himself to the saddle. Bobbie Zander mounted her sorrel lightly and rode ahead with the big Lazy L foreman.

'Don't talk too much, Joe,' Reynolds warned softly. 'But keep yore eyes open in case we run into them two. Shorty Peters picked you for his gun- handle shore as sin.'

Then he gigged his tall roan after the pair ahead, and Texas Joe nodded his head silently and came up to rub stirrups with his pard. Once more they were hired to do the kind of work they knew best.

2

Bobbie Zander led the way down the dusty winding street, and Manny Lassiter rode beside her in thoughtful silence. Roaming Reynolds and Texas Joe caught up at the edge of the little cattle town. Then the tall buckaroo reached for his gun and jacked the spent shell from the cylinder, and his blue eyes were questioning while he thumbed a fresh cartridge in the loading gate.

'This Griff Tyson of the Deuce of Diamonds,' he drawled softly. 'How come him to swing such a wide loop in these parts?'

'Cash money,' Manny Lassiter answered bitterly, and glanced at the girl. 'The rest of the outfits built up their spreads from scratch, but Tyson had money enough to buy in when he drifted up here, three years ago.'

'Like yonder,' Reynolds drawled, and pointed to a herd of grazing cattle. 'He's running white-faced stock the same as Lazy L. Can't tell 'em apart until you get close enough to read the brand. Seems to me it would make quite a problem come calf branding.'

'The big Lazy L foreman nodded and his face was gloomy. 'That's just it,' he growled. 'Dad sold him some yearling heifers for foundation stock at a good price, and our calf gather has been slipping ever since.'

'It's the same on the Bar Z Bar,' the girl added. 'We've been breeding up our stock, but Griff Tyson is the only one who is making any money. Now the Deuce of Diamonds sends us warning because we moved our shippers over here to Big Springs where we could keep an eye on them. We all need the money beef round-up will bring.'

'That's what a feller raises cattle for,' Reynolds remarked. 'And it's up to every one of them to protect his own interests.'

'You mean rustlers, Miss Bobbie?' Texas Joe interrupted to ask. 'You figger this here Tyson gent is raising his calf tally too fast?'

The girl stared at Texas Joe with a frightened expression in her dark eyes. 'It pays to be careful how you talk out loud in these parts,' she warned. 'But you have said what the rest of us have only been thinking. It don't seem natural for all of us to lose money, while one man makes a large profit in the same business.'

'Seems to me old man Lassiter would do something about it,' Joe muttered.

Manny Lassiter stood up in his stirrups and shaded his eyes against the morning sun. 'That's Dad yonder,' he grunted, 'and unless I miss my guess he's making medicine with old Ely Zander of the Bar Z Bar.'

Roaming Reynolds had also been watching the two men up ahead. He recognized the elder Lassiter from his resemblance to Manny, tall and powerful, with tremendous strength in his broad shoulders.

The other man was no larger than Shorty Peters, and the longhorn moustaches drooping at each sde of his mouth were wagging angrily while he pointed at a cow and her calf.

'Them two are making war talk,' Reynolds said briefly. 'You all better high-lope yonder if you want to keep them from going on the prod. They're just about to lock horns if you ask me!'

Manny Lassiter and the girl jumped their horses forward and raced across the rolling grassland. Reynolds waved Texas Joe to the rear, and he fell in beside the lanky cowboy and shook his head for silence.

'Me and you is Lazy L hands now,' Joe growled sullenly. 'We usually fight for the iron that pays us our wages.'

'Use yore eyes and take a hitch in yore jaw,' Reynolds muttered softly. 'Hell is due to pop soon from what I gather.'

He rode stirrup to stirrup with the boy and reined to a stop several paces away when Bobbie Zander and Manny Lassiter swung down to the grass. Old Lafe Lassiter was past sixty, but the only mark of age was in his heavy white hair.

Now he glared at Ely Zander while he called his son's attention to the weaner calf standing close to an old white-faced cow.

'That's where our get has been going,' he shouted hoarsely, and his deep voice boomed like an echo in a well. 'Take a good look at the scab burns on that weaner yonder and pass yore opinion!

Manny Lassiter stared at the calf and raised accusing eyes to the face of old Ely Zander. Zander was past fifty, and his clothes were sizes too big for his lean frame. He resembled a knotty pine that has weathered the high mountain storms of many a hard winter, and all his movements were cat-like and jumpy. No trace of fear showed on his seamed face or in his wide grey eyes that glittered under heavy, shaggy bros.

'That brand has been vented,' Manny Lassiter muttered slowly, and continued to stare at Ely Zander. 'you can see where the Lazy L has been made over into a Z with two bars added. And dang poor venting at that.'

Bobbie Zander leaped at him like a panther, and her dark eyes flashed angrily. 'Don't you dare say anything like that about Dad,' she stormed. 'That's the same thing as calling him a rustler!'

'He is a rustler,' Lafe Lassiter boomed. 'You mebbe could fool a cowboy when it comes to brands, but you can't fool the old cow herself. She always knows her own calf no matter how many are running loose. Look at them two yonder.'

All eyes turned toward the old cow an her calf. Both were white-faced, and the calf was trying to suck while the cow whipped her hips around to escape its efforts. Finally the cow gave up the battle and stood quiet while the calf satisfied its hunger.

'Our calf,' Lafe Lassiter muttered angrily. 'You can't fool an old cow.'

Roaming Reynolds broke the deadlock. when he reached for his rope and caught the calf in a small loop. Then he came hand over hand down the tight rope and flanked the little animal while Texas Joe tied off three legs and turned

33

the calf over where they could study the brand.

'Hold yore mad, men,' the tall buckaroo advised softly. 'There ain't no profit in flying off the handle until we see how come and figger the why-fors.'

'We ain't asking for help from saddle tramps,' Ely Zander snapped truculently.

'You might need some help before long,' Roaming Reynolds answered softly, and straightened up to stare at the little old warrior. 'The way I see it, both you and old Lafe is at war with this Deuce of Diamonds outfit.'

'That's our business, and I never laid eyes on you before,' the little man shouted. 'What's your handle, and what's yore business here in Summit Valley?'

Dad,' the girl reproved. 'You don't give anyone time to explain things. Meet Roaming Reynolds and Texas Joe, his pard. They saved Manny and me a heap of grief back in Paradise this morning.'

'That's right, Ely,' Manny Lassiter nodded gravely, 'Butch Cawdorn and Shorty Peters baited a trap for me right in front of the store. They waited until Bobbie rode up, and Butch stopped her while he was talking loud enough for me to hear what he said.'

Both the old cattlemen widened their eyes and stared at young Lassiter. 'Keep on talking,' Zander growled.

'Cawdorn said Tyson sent both our outfits warning to keep our stuff away from Big Springs,' Manny continued, and a flush of shame spread over his face.

'Manny didn't have a gun on him,' the girl explained quickly. 'He came out to help me, and Butch Cawdorn knocked him down and was going to kick him to death when Roaming Reynolds took a hand and shot the heel from the big bully's boot. Texas Joe covered Shorty Peters when that little gunnie tried to back up his pard.'

Ely Zander stared at the tall buckaroo and tugged at his cowhorns. Manny Lassiter drew a deep breath and turned to his father.

'So I hired Roaming Reynolds and Texas Joe to ride gun-sign on rustlers,'

35

he explained frankly. 'Want you to meet old Lafe, Roaming.'

'T'meetcha,' Reynolds grunted without offering to shake hands. 'About this brand-blotting now.' He turned his eyes on the two old cattlemen. 'You got no call to get yore hackles up, neither one of you.'

'He called me rustler,' Zander growled savagely.

'And I ain't backing up one little step,' Lafe Lassiter answered quickly. 'I made my bid and I'm letting it ride.'

Roaming Reynolds held up his hand between the pair. 'Somebody done that job for a purpose,' he announced firmly, 'somebody who don't like neither, of you gents.'

'It was a Lazy L to begin with,' Old Lafe muttered.

'You can see the scab where that L has been made over into a Z, and then two bars throwed out, one on either side. It's as plain as the whiskers on that old He's face.'

Ely Zander went into a crouch with his

hand clawed above his gun-handle. 'Me or you,' he growled deep in his chest. 'So I'm a rustler at my age!'

Bobbie Zander stepped in front of the angry little man while Manny Lassiter laid a big hand on his father's arm. And while they glared at each other, Texas Joe went to his knees beside the calf and traced the brand with a grimy finger.

'Cast yore eyes this-away,' he said dryly. 'The brand has been vented, but that altering was done with a running iron or a ring one. Personally I'd say some waddy used a saddle ring account of them curves he had to work out on the L.'

Ely Zander stiff-armed his daughter to one side and faced the big cattleman belligerently. 'You made a bet and yo're letting it ride,' he growled hoarsely. 'Make yore play, you old mossy-horn!'

Old Lafe Lassiter glanced at the brand and scratched his white head. Then he sighed and glanced at his neighbour with a rueful grin on his weathered face.

'Sorry I fit my head that-away, Ely,'

he rumbled softly. 'After knowing you for better than twenty-odd year, I might have knowed you wouldn't have no part in venting a brand no matter how the sign read.'

'Time you was getting some sense,' the little cattleman snapped. 'You like to got yoreself shot apart calling me out of my name that-away!'

The two oldsters glared at each other until Roaming Reynolds took the play to save another clash. 'That's just what somebody wanted you to do,' he stated quietly. 'If you two gents commenced fighting each other, you wouldn't have no time to watch anybody else. Reading it that-away, what does it spell to you gents?'

Ely Zander dropped his hand away from his gun and stared at Lafe Lassiter. Then he shifted his eyes to study the brand on the calf, and his voice was a savage rumble when he rubbed the handle of his old gun.

'Spells War to me with a captal W,' he began jerkily. 'That there is some of

Griff Tyson's sneaking tricks, and he figgered on me shooting old Lafe becuse he knows I can't match Lafe pound for pound in a skull and knuckle ruckus!'

Roaming Reynolds compared the two old warriors and smiled. Ely Zander would weigh perhaps a hundred and thirty while Lafe Lassiter would crowd the beam at two hundred odd. Both were of the breed who would never admit defeat as long as they had life. He smiled again when the two moved together as if by common consent and gripped hands across the tied calf.

'You should have drilled me, Ely,' Lafe Lassiter growled, 'for shooting off my head like a danged yearling that-away. Don't know how you held yore gun in leather.'

'I'd have done the same thing my own self in yore place,' Ely Zander snapped back, but his eyes softened when he gripped Lassiter's fingers. 'Looks like we owe something to yore new gun-boss yonder.'

Old Lafe Lassiter turned his grey

eyes on the buckaroo. 'I know you now, Roamin',' he grinned. 'Yo're the salty hairpin who helped old Mormon Tucker clean out that Strip over in Antelope Valley. You got any ideas about this ruckus from what you ve seen so far?'

'I got ideas, but that ain't proof,' the tall buckaroo answered slowly. 'That's clumsy venting yonder, and any cattle inspector would see it in a glance. Manny was telling me that both yore outfits is shy on yore calf tallies. Might be best for me and Joe to kinda ride the outside circle for a few days while we keep our eyes skinned.'

'You work it any way you see best,' Lafe Lassiter agreed. 'We run to the brakes back yonder, but you and Joe has proved that you can take care of yoreselves. Just wanting to add my thanks to Manny's for what you did back there in Paradise.'

Roaming Reynolds shrugged. 'Forget it,' he muttered. 'But from what Shorty Peters let out, they don't aim to let it drop there,' and he wrinkled his blue eyes into a grin.

'Shorty Peters,' Joe muttered, and snugged his gun down tight. 'If that runty bantam makes another play at me, I aim to do my talking through smoke!'

'You'll do some thinking first,' Reynolds corrected dryly. 'It don't pay to go off half-cocked with a gent like Peters. He knows what it's all about and next time he won't be taking any chances of losing.'

'I don't fight to lose my own self,' the lanky cowboy muttered, and then he raised his head and stared. 'Hossbacker coming yonder,' he warned quietly. 'Pointing this-away.'

Lafe Lassiter took one quick look and turned to the tall buckaroo. 'That's one of Griff Tyson's men,' he muttered. 'Ramrod McCall from the way he rides; foreman of the Deuce of Diamonds, and all-fired fast with a six-gun.'

Roming Reynolds was studying the approaching rider intently. 'You and Miss Bobbie hit yore saddles and fog it away like you was on the prod,' he suggested to

Ely Zander. 'If Tyson baited this trap, it's best to let him believe that yore outfits don't want no truck with each other. Hit the high spots, old-timer. I want to listen close while Lafe gives this gent howdy!'

'I ain't never run yet,' Zander growled sulkily. 'Too dang old to larn now!'

'Dad,' the girl pleaded. 'Don't you see that Roaming is trying to help us? The least we can do is to let him work out his ideas. Now hurry before Ramrod McCall gets any closer. We might spoil the whole thing.'

Old Ely continued to grumble, but he stepped spryly to his horse and swung up like a young puncher. Then he spurred after his daughter while the four Lazy L men hunkered down on their boot-heels around the hog-tied calf. Manny Lassiter spoke softly to Roaming Reynolds and acted as though he had not seen the oncoming rider.

'Ramrod McCall is *segundo* to Griff Tyson,' he explained in a whisper. 'He's a tophand with hosses and cattle, and chain lightning with a hand-gun. Strong as an ox, and a man-killer with his fists.'

Roaming Reynolds nodded carelessly, but the fires of battle began to glow deep in his blue eyes. An expression of content softened his face when gunspeed was mentioned. Then the lean jaw ridged over with muscle to tighten his mouth.

'I'd figger him that-away,' he murmured. 'He ain't so big as some, but well put together. All whalebone and whang leather; built both for speed and endurance.'

'And he's got brains,' Manny added. 'You watch and listen when he begins to talk.'

Texas Joe shifted restlessly and chewed on a straw while he watched McCall from the corner of his slitted eyes. His face was openly hostile, and the tall buckaroo smiled and drawled a soft warning to his young pard.

'Get a poker face, Texas. You want that feller to know offhand that we're on to their game?'

Texas Joe twisted angrily and straightened out his thin face. Only his eyes betrayed his emotions now, and he reached down carelessly and loosened the gun in his scabbard. Then he leaned over and began to trace the scab burns on the weaner calf.

'Like you said, Roaming,' he muttered. 'But if this Ramrod is salty like Manny claims, I'd let my gun do most of the talking was I in yore place!'

'Which you ain't,' Reynolds reminded gruffly, and began to make range talk. 'Now, you take this here new burn,' he continued more loudly, 'you can see where it's been run over the brand you slapped on during calf round-up.'

'And it's vented Bar Z Bar,' Manny answered in the same loud tones. 'Looks mighty funny to me.'

Roaming Reynolds levered to his feet and stretched his arms when the Deuce of Diamonds foreman came over a little rise and stopped his gelding while he stared at the four men.

'You talk to him, Lafe,' Reynolds whispered without moving his lips, and turned slowly to study the newcomer.

Ramrod McCall came up fast and sat his horse back on its haunches when he neck-reined to complete his showy entrance. His hard face marked him as an old-young man, perhaps thirty-five, with every one of his years spent in the stern school of frontier experience. His flicking grey eyes took in the whole picture at a glance and rested longest to study Roaming Reynolds.

The tall buckaroo returned the scrutiny impassively while he balanced his weight on widespread boots. Ramrod McCall was the first to look away.

'Morning, Lassiter,' he said to old Lafe. 'Saw you hunkered down over this-away. Thought I'd lope over and satisfy my curiosity.'

'Howdy,' the old cattleman muttered. 'I noticed you looking when you rode up.'

'Looks some like you come up on rustlers,' McCall answered without hesitation.

'Looks that-away,' the old cattleman answered grimly, and watched Texas Joe pull his tie and throw, off the pigging string. 'We been losing considerable stock lately and before that, and now I aim to do something about it.'

McCall nodded and ran his eyes across the circle of faces. 'There's only one way to treat rustlers,' he remarked quietly. 'Reckon you know the only cure.'

'Reckon I do,' Lassiter grunted, and played with the end of a rope.

'Griff Tyson will be glad to hear about this brand-blotting,' McCall said, indicating the calf struggling to its feet. 'We don't want no trouble, but Griff ain't running the Deuce of Diamonds for his health. He had good health when he rode up here to buy in summit Valley.'

'So I noticed,' Lassiter muttered, 'and his health has been getting better right along.'

Ramrod McCall leaned forward a trifle in the saddle. 'Meaning what?' and his voice was hard and metallic.

Lafe Lassiter stared for a moment and shrugged his wide shoulders.

'What Tyson does is his own business

when he's raising cattle for the beef market,' McCall pointed out. 'If you don't want any help, you don't have to get yore hackles up!'

'Nor hindrance,' Lafe Lassiter said levelly. 'Manny was telling me bout the message Tyson sent into Paradise by them ringy riders of yores!'

Ramrod McCall was only medium tall, but his muscular body radiated the strength that was reflected in his craggy face. He never smiled, and his unusual calmness contrasted strangely with the blinding speed he could demonstrate when necessary.

A long-barrelled, single-action .45 Colt was laced low on the right leg of his bat-wings, and his hand was on his hip just above the handle when he turned his eyes to stare at the tall buckaroo. Then he jerked his head at old Lafe.

'New hands?'

Lafe Lassiter shrugged. 'Yeah,' he drawled slowly. 'This here tall jigger is Roaming Reynolds. The button is Texas Joe, his saddle pard. Both of 'em on the

Lazy L payroll. Boys, make you used to Ramrod McCall, foreman of the Deuce of Diamonds.'

Ramrod McCall nodded slightly. 'I've heard about them two,' he said softly. 'Shorty Peters was fanning his bronc down the hind legs when I met him yonder coming from town.'

'Seems to me like he mentioned you before he left town so sudden,' Reynolds answered carelessly, and allowed his blue eyes to wander up and down the Deuce of Diamonds foreman from peaked Stetson to the bench-made, calfskin boots.

McCall's eyes narrowed slightly. 'I don't know what Shorty told you, but I'm giving you warning, feller,' he answered softly. 'Strangers ain't welcome in Summit Valley, special when they pull gun-play out on the Deuce of Diamonds.'

'Yore outfit was strangers when you rode in here, three years ago,' Lassiter answered dryly, to prevent Reynolds from talking.

'And we paid cash for what we wanted,' McCall snapped. 'You, Reynolds,' and his voice was edgy, 'you and the Button better straddle yore kaks and light a shuck over the hills.'

Roaming Reynolds sighed softly and shook his head. 'Sometimes me and Joe stops for a spell of time here and there,' he murmured in his quiet drawl. 'Being free, white, and full-growed up, me and him ain't asking for no advice. That tell you anything?'

The foreman showed no surprise. 'Not much, and you and him is getting the advice regardless,' he clipped. 'You drew yore iron on Deuce of Diamonds help, and Shorty Peters aims to get you sometime when you can't pull another gun-sneak. Aside from that every man on the spread is backing up his play!'

Roaming Reynolds straightened slowly and locked glances with the man in the saddle, no expression on his hard, tanned face when his voice purred softly.

'Meaning yoreself, McCall?'

McCall tightened his lips and sat perfectly still. Then his right hand flicked down and sideways in a blurring flash. of speed. He stiffened and loosened his fingers on the half-drawn gun when his eyes stared into the tunnel of Reynold's Colt. His face twisted with anger when Texas Joe hoorayed him with open contempt.

'Mebbe you can call that a gun-sneak like yore runty pard done,' he sneered. 'Ramrod McCall faded on the pass when he tried to run out a pair of harmless saddle tramps!'

The Deuce of Diamonds foreman fought his anger with all the force of his will. He sat and stared until the anger left his face; Manny Lassiter glanced at his father and smiled.

'Was I on the ground it would be different,' McCall grunted, and his voice was low with disappointment.

'Ain't yore hoss trained to stand ground-hitched?' Texas Joe asked dryly. 'Or mebbe you got yoreself glued to the saddle to keep from buckin' off?'

McCall set his lips. and, ignoring the lanky cowboy, he stared at Roaming Reynolds. 'Be seeing you some more, you slick gun-passer,' he almost whispered.

Old Lafe Lassiter interrupted with a smile. 'Reckon you will, Ramrod,' he chuckled. 'Roaming and his pard is working for Lazy L. You might tell the same to yore boss when yo're doing the rest of yore telling.'

'I'll tell him,' McCall growled, and his eyes were hard and bright with rage. 'What he said about Big Springs still goes for you and old man Zander!'

Lafe Lassiter swelled his big chest and hunched his white head forward. His hands were clenched into fists that cracked with the effort he made to control his temper. When he finally spoke his voice was booming and hoarse.

'Big Springs is open range or I'd have had that water for my own long ago. My stock stays where it is if we have to fight all the gun-totin' punchers on the Deuce of Diamonds to keep them there. I reckon you understand my wawa, feller!'

3

Ramrod McCall held his horse perfectly still while he stared at old Lafe Lassiter. Roaming Reynolds nodded his head approvingly. He knew that any man who could control an animal with such ease could also control his own emotions. Texas Joe stared at the Deuce of Diamonds foreman, but the latter ignored the lanky cowboy and focussed his attention on the old cattleman's weathered face.

'My men do what I tell them to do,' he stated arrogantly. 'And I reckon you know why.'

'Yeah, yore men,' the old cattleman emphasized.

'But my men don't pay no mind to threats like you sent in, and I reckon you know why.'

McCall backed his horse away a few steps. Only his thin lips tightened sneeringly and his grey eyes swung coolly from face to face like a card player's getting ready to make a bet. His glance came to rest at last on Roaming Reynolds and stayed for a long moment.

'I'll tell Griff,' he said shortly, and then his voice cracked like dry leather. 'Like I said, Reynolds, I'll be seeing you through smoke!'

The tall buckaroo holstered his gun and nodded carelessly. 'When yo're on the ground,' he agreed, as though nothing had interrupted his train of thought. 'And you might remember that a hot saddle ring slows up a gent's hand.'

Ramrod McCall stiffened in the saddle and locked glances. 'Meaning just what?' and his voice was thin and deadly.

Roaming Reynolds shrugged and allowed the corners. of his mouth to tilt. 'Meaning that you can swing down to the ground right now if yo're feeling lucky,' he drawled softly, and his blue eyes were smouldering with challenge. 'I don't booger worth a hoot, so make yore play or get long gone!'

For a moment the Deuce of Diamonds

foreman fought the impulse to empty his saddle. No trace of fear was noticeable on his hard face, but he showed the reason why he was *segundo* to Griff Tyson when he counted guns and wisely shook his head.

'I never crowd my luck,' he answered softly. 'And I come right out and say what I have on my mind instead of making riddles.'

'We run across one right here,' the tall buckaroo reminded, 'and we figgered we made out the answer.'

McCall swung his eyes to glance at the calf and took a deep breath. 'I'll remember what you said about that saddle ring,' he promised grimly. 'I'll look you up when I make out the answer.'

He wheeled his horse and rammed home the steel to rocket across the rolling mountain pastures. Manny Lassiter watched him ride his spurs until a rise hid horse and rider, and then he turned to Reynolds with a question in his dark eyes.

'You mean McCall vented that brand?'

he asked slowly, and shook his big head doubtfully. 'I don't like him none, but he packs the sand to play his hand out open.'

'The feller who changed that brand wore a Deuce of Diamonds studded in his right heel,' Reynolds answered quietly. 'Yonder is the fire where he dragged the calf on the end of his rope. If you look right close you can see that heel-brand plain.'

Young Lassiter walked across to the charred ashes and leaned over to study the soft loam. His father watched him; read his face before the big cowboy reported his findings.

'It was Griff Tyson,' Manny almost shouted. 'That's his own private mark, and he'd kill the man who tried to copy him!'

'That's what I wanted to know,' Roaming Reynolds answered with a grim smile. 'McCall will tell Tyson what I said about that hot saddle ring, and once more he will figger he has us fooled. How many hands do they carry on the Deuce of

Diamonds payroll?'

'Eight, counting McCall,' old Lafe growled. 'Every one of them the same breed as Shorty Peters and Butch Cawdorn. I dunno, Roamin'. It shore is a fightin' outfit!'

'And they all got something to fight with,' Reynolds almost sneered. Then his voice changed suddenly. 'You gents wear yore hardware after this,' he said sharply. 'And carry a saddle-gun under yore fender when you ride away from the spread.'

His eyes rested longest on Manny Lassiter, and the big cowboy twisted uneasily and dug a little hole with the toe of his boot. Resentment showed plainly in his dark eyes when he glanced at the long-barrelled gun in the tall buckaroo's holster.

'Like I said back there in Paradise, I'm a cattleman, not a gun-hawk,' he growled. 'It takes practice to keep your hand in.'

'You better practise up or you won't have any critters to look after,' Reynolds answered dryly. 'Griff Tyson is out to get both the Lazy L and the Bar Z Bar for himself if he has to kill off the lot of you to do it. After this every man gets himself fully dressed with his hardware close to his hand.'

'Seems like we could get us a little law,' Manny Lassiter muttered stubbornly. 'That's for why we pay taxes.'

'You ought to be packing the law on yore leg,' Texas Joe interrupted quietly, his mouth showing the contempt he felt while he stared at the Lazy L foreman's empty leg. 'Six-gun law is the only kind them jiggers knows anything about, and right now they figger to make what they need.'

Lafe Lassiter scratched his jaw and nodded. 'The Button is right,' he agreed quickly. 'After this every hand on the Lazy L goes loaded. You can pass that word along, Manny.'

He stiffened suddenly when a sharp voice barked from the little rise just ahead. 'Sky them dewclams, the lot of you! First man that reaches for a gun is due to kick hot ashes in hell!'

'Ramrod McCall,' Manny Lassiter gasped, and raised his big hands high over his head. 'We might have knowed it!'

Roaming Reynolds turned slowly and lifted both hands when he saw the Deuce of Diamonds foreman covering them with a rifle. McCall was flanked by Butch Cawdorn and Shorty Peters, and the little gunman was grinning like a wolf as he sighted down the barrel of his Winchester. Butch Cawdorn leered, six-gun in his big fist.

The three men rode slowly forward. Ramrod McCall and Shorty Peters swung down while Butch Cawdorn held the drop, after which the bully stepped off and holstered his gun, his little eyes fastening in a stare on the face of Roaming Reynolds.

'Gun-slammer, eh?' he taunted, and unbuckled the heavy belt which he hung carefully on the horn of his saddle. 'And you figger yo're pretty fast the way you told it.'

Roaming Reynolds widened his eyes. 'You ought to know after this morning,' he remarked softly, and watched the big man continue his preparations. 'You and Shorty both,' he added dryly.

Butch Cawdorn scowled and started to roll up his sleeves. Thick muscular arms covered with coarse black hair. Arms that could break a man's back, and had done so several times. Yellow teeth gleaming in the corners of his loose mouth when he spoke again.

'Me and you is going to settle up for what you did to me this morning, feller,' he announced hoarsely. 'Now you shuck that gun-belt before Shorty forgets himself and does you a meanness!'

Roaming Reynolds lowered his hands slowly and unbuckled the heavy gun-belt around his lean hips. There was no expression on his tanned face except for the smouldering flame deep in his narrowed blue eyes. Texas Joe growled under his breath like a wolf cub, but it was Manny Lassiter who made the first open protest.

'You can't do that, Cawdorn,' he blurted. 'You outweigh Reynolds by forty odd pounds. I ain't satisfied, and I'll take you in his place.'

'You tried to take me this morning,' the big puncher grinned evilly. 'Now this jigger is going to get what I aimed to give you when he bought chips in a closed game. He had his warning, and he thought it was bluff.'

Texas Joe continued to growl in his throat. Butch Cawdorn swung his eyes briefly and ground his teeth : spoke over his shoulder to the Deuce of Diamonds foreman.

'Watch them three, Ramrod. And even the odds if any one of them makes a play.'

'I'm watching that salty Button yonder,' Shorty Peters murmured softly. 'If he so much as wags a flipper, he never will be no older than he is right now.'

Texas Joe straightened his thin shoulders and turned squarely to face the little gunman. 'You talk too much with yore mouth,' he sneered. 'Mebbe you'd like to take me like yore pard is aiming to do for Roamin'? You and me is just about of a size!'

'Take a hitch in yore jaw, Joe,' the tall buckaroo growled softly, and threw his gun-belt to the ground. Shorty Peters refused to be turned aside. 'I'll take you,' he promised grimly. 'But it can wait until you lose some of yore nerve. You ain't never seen a skull and knuckle ruckus till you see Butch work a hombre over.'

Roaming Reynolds smiled coldly and ignored the little man. 'You ready, Cawdorn?' he asked softly. 'Ready to give me that working over while yore pards copper a tinhorn play?'

'I been ready ever since I left Paradise this morning,' and Butch Cawdorn pulled his head down between his thick shoulders. 'Come and get it!'

The laziness fell away from the tall buckaroo like a worn slicker. His boots flashed in the grass when he danced in and ripped two jolting lefts to snap the bully's head back on his thick neck.

Butch Cawdorn grinned and weaved forward like a shambling bear, and his opponent crossed with a looping right that started from his hip.

The Deuce of Diamonds man rocked back on his heels without giving ground. Roaming Reynolds stepped back with surprise written on his tanned face. He had expected Cawdorn to drop, and his arm was numb from the force of the last blow.

'Work on his belly, pard,' Texas Joe shouted and scowled when his deep voice changed on a high note. 'He can't take it downstairs,' he growled in his lowest bass.

Shorty Peters swung his rifle to cover the Button. 'One more peep out of you and I aim to cut yore comb,' he threatened savagely. 'You ain't seen even the beginning up to now. Take him, Butch!'

Manny Lassiter was clenching his big fists until the knuckles cracked. His shoulders were weaving and rolling in an effort to help the tall buckaroo, and Ramrod McCall chuckled to call attention to the Lazy L foreman.

'It hurts Lassiter as much as it does you, Butch,' he sneered. 'Get in there and polish that saddle tramp off.'

Butch Cawdorn shook his head and advanced slowly.

His left arm pistoned out and rocked Roaming Reynolds off his balance, although the tall buckaroo caught the blow on his forearm. He side-stepped and jabbed with his right; sharp-shooting at the little eyes gleaming at him like those of a maddened boar.

Roaming Reynolds retreated until a gun-barrel pressed against his back. 'Stand up and fight like a man,' and he recognised the voice of Ramrod McCall.

Butch Cawdorn saw his advantage and set himself for a rush. Roaming Reynolds took a chance and side-stepped like a flash, just as a hoarse, barking voice rasped through the breathless stillness.

'Drop them rifles, gents!'

Shorty Peters stiffened without turning his head. Then he glanced at Ramrod McCall who was caught off balance when he had turned to follow Roaming Reynolds. McCall opened his fingers slowly and allowed his saddle-gun to drop to the ground.

'Shuck it,' he told the runty gunman. 'You know old Ely Zander as well as I!'

Shorty Peters dropped his long gun and turned to face the little cattleman in the over-sized clothes. Old Ely had a rifle in his hands while Bobbie Zander sat her saddle easily with a cocked .45 covering the Deuce of Diamonds foreman.

'Another sneak,' Peters growled under his breath. 'We might have knowed it.'

'Two sneaks,' Zander corrected grimly. 'We just eased in to give you tinhorns a run for yore money.'

Butch Cawdorn grunted and began to weave in to make his fight. 'Damn yore guns,' he roared, and glared at Roaming Reynolds. 'I'll crack yore blasted neck before I get through!'

He lowered his head and charged like a maddened bull. The tall buckaroo stepped forward and jabbed rapidly with his left fist. He side-slipped like a dodging steer, hitting and getting away before Butch Cawdorn could grip him in his powerful arms.

The Deuce of Diamonds puncher stopped at last and glared out of his one good eye. Then he shuffled slowly forward and came uncorked like a bucking stallion. His right fist whistled across with all his weight behind the blow, and Roaming Reynolds turned his head while his left jabbed to jolt the bully off balance.

Cawdorn grunted and raised his head for a bare instant. His eyes turned glassy when his opponent brought a right up from his boot tops and found the unprotected jaw. Reynold's arm dropped to his side from the force of the blow, but he smiled grimly when Cawdom buckled his knees and pitched forward to fall on his face.

The big man bounced and rocked back on his heavy chest. Texas Joe forgot himself and leaped high in the air with his heels cracking together.

'My turn now,' he shouted, and

crouched toward Shorty Peters. 'I'm coming, you runty sidewinder!' Shorty Peters tightened his thin lips and moved in with the promise of hell in his little eyes. Old Lafe Lassiter leaned forward with a grin on his weathered face, while Ramrod McCall watched and waited with a gleam in his grey eyes.

Texas Joe jumped the little gunman before Roaming Reynolds could interfere. He hit his enemy all sprawled out, and the ground was blurry with legs and arms when Shorty Peters went down and tried to roll. The lanky Button was clawing and kicking like a yearling colt, and he yelled like an Indian when the little gunman levered with his legs and kicked himself clear.

The youth landed on hands and knees and ripped right back before Shorty Peters could get to his feet. Swinging like a windmill, the saddle-toughened young cowboy battered the little gunman with rights and lefts that cracked like pistol shots.

'Fight him, Shorty,' Ramrod McCall

called softly. 'He's wore himself plumb out.'

Texas Joe turned his head and snarled like a wolf. 'I ain't even started yet,' he boasted hoarsely, and leaped high to crack his heels again.

Shorty Peters caught him coming down and kicked out with his right boot. Texas Joe grunted when the blow took him high in the groin. Then he made a flying tackle and bull-dogged Peters to earth, and when the dust cleared some he was working his man over with no thought to the rules of fair play.

Shorty Peters was flat on his back. Texas Joe reached down and grabbed the stunned gunman by both ears. After which he proceeded to batter the bobbing head on the ground until Roaming Reynolds jumped forward and pulled him from the limp body of his foe. Texas Joe was still fighting blindly when his tall pardner shook him until his teeth rattled.

'Snap out of it, you locoed yearling. You know better than to kill a man when he's down!'

'Let me at him,' the Button shouted hoarsely. 'I aim to work him over with my boots for pulling a sneak, like him and his pards went and, done!'

'I don't pard up with no gent like that,' the tall buckaroo said coldly, and shoved Texas Joe away. 'You and me is all through until you can learn to quit fighting yore head.'

Texas Joe scowled for a moment and then raised his eyes to stare at Roaming Reynolds. A. wide grin split his thin lips as he nodded his head. He walked across to Shorty Peters who was trying to sit up, and helped the little gunman to his feet.

'Sorry I hit you when you was down, feller,' he muttered. 'Now that yo're up on yore feet again ...'

His right hand blasted out and landed flush on the little gunnie's jaw. Texas Joe stepped back and watched Shorty Peters fall face forward, and he was still grinning when he walked stiff-legged up to Roaming Reynolds and held out his hand.

'Never hit a gent when he's down,' he

repeated gravely. 'I'll remember what you said, pard!'

The tall buckaroo smiled in spite of himself. 'Thought I heard a gent remark that you was about all wore out,' he remarked softly, and gripped Texas Joe hard. 'Nice going, feller.'

Ramrod McCall stood perfectly still without moving a muscle of his craggy face. Only his grey eyes seemed alive when he spoke softly to Reynolds.

'Shifty, you and yore pard,' he said tonelessly. 'Neither one of you could stand up and fight like men.'

'You ever hear that old one about a gent who fights and runs away,' Reynolds asked quietly. 'And I took it you were a cowboy.'

He smiled slowly when he saw the frown of uncertainty edge in to change the Deuce of Diamonds foreman. 'More riddles,' McCall grunted.

'You wouldn't bust up a good horse if a bull charged you,' Reynolds explained patiently, and blew on his skinned knuckles. 'You might tell that to Butch when he gets over his sleep.'

'He'd have had you in another minute,' McCall growled, 'when that old mossy-horn edged into the play!'

'Like you did,' Reynolds reminded. 'You had yore gun in my back, trying to hold me like a hog-tied steer while yore pet bull gores him to death. Looks like yore bull lost.'

Ramrod McCall shrugged. 'Butch will get over it,' he answered carelessly, and then his eyes changed. 'That little play you put on with old Zander and his gal had me fooled there for a minute,' he said slowly. 'Now that you've tipped yore hand, the Deuce of Diamonds will know what to do about it.'

Roaming Reynolds nodded soberly. 'Figgered you would,' he agreed. 'And what you said makes good sense both ways around. Is that clear, or would you call it another riddle?'

'Clear enough,' McCall grunted, and took a backward step toward his horse.

'One minute,' Reynolds barked. 'Now that we understand each other, it might be a good idea for you to lend them pards of yores a hand.'

Ramrod McCall shrugged. 'They'll rouse 'round,' he answered carelessly. 'I've done the same to both of them myself. Serves them right for not doing what they were sent to do this morning.'

'Yeah, that's right,' Reynolds grunted. 'They was told to kill Manny Lassiter, and both Joe and me knew it when we saw them baiting their trap. What the Deuce of Diamonds outfit calls square shooting.'

His low tones cut the Deuce of Diamonds foreman like a lash. Ramrod McCall flushed angrily and then wiped the expression of anger from his face, while his grey eyes wached the tall buckaroo for the next move.

Roaming Reynolds reahed for his gun-belt, strapped it on, and fastened the tie-backs without removing his eyes from McCall's face. Old Ely Zander rode do the slope with his daughter and stopped in front of McCall with rifle cradled against his lean hip. His vest and grey pants flapped in the wind, and his long moustaches shook angrily when he said his say.

'Me and Bobbie seen you high-tailing it back here when we cut out for the Bar Z Bar. I catch any more of yore gun-slinging hands running my iron on Lazy L critters, I aim to leave 'em lay out for the kiyoties and buzzads. You tell Griff Tyson what I said and tell it straight!'

'Send yore gun boss over to tell him,' McCall answered softly. 'Griff would like to meet him.'

'I ain't hard to meet,' Roaming Reynolds cut in quickly. 'And I'd admire to ride over and give him the word.'

Manny Lassiter stepped forward and faced McCall with jaw thrust out. 'If any word went to the Deuce of Diamonds,' he said hotly, 'it would come from the Lazy L. Not that Reynolds wouldn't deliver it, but from now on we know what to do.'

'You ain't made much of a hand doing it,' McCall sneered, and looked the big cowboy squarely in the eyes.

'So far we've done right well figgering

out traps,' and Manny Lassiter turned his head when Roaming Reynolds touched his arm lightly.

'Pay him no mind,' he advised with a shrug. 'He will bust his breeches getting back to Tyson with excuses along with his news.'

He was surprised when the Deuce of Diamonds foreman nodded agreement. 'Like you said, Reynolds. I'll tell the big Augur just how the play worked out.'

He scanned the ring of faces briefly and reached for his bridle reins ; swung up to the saddle and waved a hand carelessly.

'Be seeing you some more,' he promised.

Ely Zander swung his rifle around and growled hoarsely. 'Yo're taking yore pards with you, McCall. And tell 'em both to stay away from Big Springs if they want to keep their health.'

'Tell 'em yoreself,' McCall grunted, and pointed with his left hand.

Butch Cawdorn was sitting up, rubbing his jaw. He saw McCall in the saddle, and he pushed up on his thick legs and weaved unsteadily when he made for his horse and reached for the reins. Then he saw Shorty Peters trying to sit up. He staggered over to his pard and set him on his feet.

'Easy, Shorty,' he muttered through thick, bruised lips. 'That banty moss-horn is holding the drop.'

'And I aim to use it,' Ely Zander growled softly, 'the first time I catch either of you two around Big Springs.'

Butch Cawdorn steadied himself against his horse and turned his head to stare at Roaming Reynolds. He muttered softly under his breath and pulled him-self to the saddle, and Texas Joe grunted and lowered the hammer of his gun.

'Fog it, you two,' Ramrod McCall ordered sharply, and touched his own horse with the spur. Lafe Lassiter watched the three ride away with a frown on his heavy face.

'Sometimes shooting square has its drawbacks,' he muttered irritably. 'Was me in their boots, some one would have to boot-hill the lot of us. Obliged to you for riding up when you did, Ely.'

'Thank Bobbie,' the little cattleman answered. 'She seen McCall meet them two hands of his just before we reached the Bar Z Bar. So we grabbed our guns and come boiling back here when we saw them three heading this-away. Reckon we better lope over to the Lazy L with yore crowd to make medicine.'

4

Texas Joe brought up his horse and jumped the saddle. Old Ely Zander grinned when he saw the skinned knuckles, and then he chuckled with amusement.

'That was quite a working over you gave Shorty Peters, Button,' he praised warmly. 'I never see a prettier knockdown in a fairly long life.'

'Shorty won't fight with his fists next time,' Manny Lassiter warned softly. 'And Shorty is right handy with his cutter.'

'With which I ain't no creeping snail my own self,' Texas Joe growled fiercely. 'Likewise, I ain't never learned to throw off my shots none.'

Roaming turned his face to hide a grin, flushed when he caught Bobbie Zander winking at him. He twisted uneasily when the girl rode up beside him. She put a hand on his arm and shook her head when he was about to answer Texas Joe.

'He was wonderful,' she whispered, 'and he only followed your example when he challenged Shorty Peters with his hands.'

'Reckon he did at that, ma'am,' the tall cowboy answered honestly. 'But he ain't had enough seasoning to go up against an old hand like Shorty Peters. You see, ma'am, I don't want to lose my pard. Me and him have done a heap of things together lately.'

The girl pointed to her father and old Lafe Lassiter riding up ahead. The two old-timers were staring at the deep waterhole where a perennial spring was gushing from the rocks. Manny Lassiter frowned and rode up to join his father, and the girl turned to Reynolds and shook her head soberly.

'That's Big Springs,' she explained. 'Looks like some of those Lazy L steers have wandered away. The Deuce of Diamonds outfit lies back there in Wild Horse Canyon.'

'Wild Hoss Canyon,' Reynolds repeated, and scratched his head thoughtfully. 'That's right close to the badlands bordering the Strip if I remember rightly. Long rocky pocket big enough to hide a sizeable herd of steers.'

'We better see what's up,' the girl answered, and kicked her sorrel into a lope.

Reynolds followed her close with Texas Joe bringing up the rear. Old Lassiter was grumbling in his deep voice, and he turned to Reynolds waving a gnarled hand at the grazing cattle.

'Two-hundred-odd head gone since last night. That makes upward of a thousand head we've lost the past two years.'

'Funny thing, too,' his son added. 'There's nearly that many more Deuce of Diamonds critters here now than there was the day before yesterday.'

Reynolds studied the cattle carefully; rode closer for a better look at the brands. Texas Joe was right beside him, but he stopped his young pardner before he could speak what was on his mind.

'Quiet,' he grunted. 'You and me will do our talking later on when we are alone. Use yore eyes right good now, but keep still about what you see.'

'I see plenty from where I sit,' the boy muttered.

'Look and see some more,' Reynolds rapped sharply.

Texas Joe scowled and then he nodded slowly when he caught the warning in his pardner's eyes. 'Got you, feller,' he murmured. 'Some of them critters has been on the move, and they travelled fast from the looks of them.'

Roaming Reynolds turned slowly when the three cattlemen quartered their horses. Lafe Lassiter set his jaw grimly and watched the face of his new hand. The tall cowboy answered the inquiring look with a nod of his head.

'Looks like Griff Tyson is cutting a rusty on you, Lafe,' he remarked quietly. 'He had his riders run yore stuff back in the scab rock while he brought down his own. That-away it puts taller on his critters and takes it off of yores.'

'That's the way me and Ely figgered,' Lassiter agreed. 'And not only that, Roamin'. It bottles us off from getting back there to make our beef gather after them steers is finished for market on good grass.'

'It might do it if Big Springs wasn't open range like you said,' Reynolds argued quietly. 'That being the case, you can make your gather providing yore men fight for the brand that pays them their wages.'

Lassiter allowed a worried look to flit briefly across his face. 'They'd fight,' he muttered. 'But they wouldn't have much chance against Tyson's hands. I know it, and Griff Tyson knows it too.'

'You can't tell,' the tall buckaroo answered dryly. 'Me and Joe will take a ride across Kanab creek before we light off at the Lazy L. Tell the Cooky to count us in for grub tonight, and don't worry none, I have good reasons of my own.'

Manny Lassiter started to speak and thought better of it. Reynolds rode back to Texas Joe and jerked his head toward the distant hills. The lanky Button grinned and fell in beside him, and they rode in silence until they were well out of sight. Then the youngster edged in closer and rubbed the handle of his six-gun.

'Griff Tyson is changing them brands, Roamin',' he drawled. 'You remember that blind valley we got into, back yonder, when we angled down from Vermillion Cliffs?'

Reynolds nodded approval. 'That's using yore eyes, Joe,' he praised softly. 'I knew you would get it, but I didn't want you blurting it out back there to worry old Lafe with the news. You remember the brand on that herd of white-faces we found bottled up in that pocket?'

'Deuce of Diamonds,' the young cowboy answered promptly. 'Mostly long threes and fours, well fleshed up and prime for shipping.'

'Yeah,' Reynolds agreed. 'Only we didn't know the lay of things at the time, and we got to slip back there for a closer look before we start something that might be a mistake.'

Texas Joe shrugged impatiently. 'This here waiting bogs me down sometimes,' he growled. 'Right now we both know the answer, and it's just a waste of time reading the same sign twice.'

Roaming Reynolds smiled tolerantly. 'That's just the difference between a yearling and an old hand,' he pointed out. 'Up here, where every man carries his own law, it pays to be sure before you talk too loud. Let's get back in those hills.'

Increasing the pace, the two rode back in the twisting coulees until they came to a brawling creek. Texas Joe pointed to the opposite bank where a trickle of water led back into the brush. Then he worked his horse into the water and crossed on a sandy ford packed hard by the feet of many cattle.

'Two hosses crossed here recent,' he told Reynolds, who was reading the sign for himself. 'What you reckon now, Roamin'?'

'We better ride easy from here on,'

and Reynolds gigged his horse to follow a dim trail through the brakes. 'Like as not them two is going to ride outlook on that canyon just in case the Lazy L gets suspicious and starts running down sign.'

'Rustler sign,' Joe muttered. 'You as good as said so yoreself.'

Roaming Reynolds walked his horse through the underbrush and came to a sudden stop when giant rocks loomed up ahead to mark the mouth of the hidden canyon. He held up his hand for silence when Texas Joe came closer, and the two sat their saddles while they peered through the leafy branches at a pair of riders just disappearing through a narrow pass.

'It's Butch and Shorty,' Texas Joe whispered excitedly. 'Them two didn't lose any time getting back here, Roamin'. Like they had orders from the boss man.'

'We done enough to them two for one day,' Reynolds murmured. 'But I'm glad we saw them first. You and me will live a while longer.'

'I dunno,' Joe muttered, and his grimy hand slipped down to his gun. 'We ought to do something about it now that we got a chance.'

The tall buckaroo shook his head. 'I'll slip in there on foot and see what I can see,' he whispered. 'You wait back here to cover me in case I run into grief. Use yore head now, feller.'

He dropped from the saddle, grounded his reins, and worked slowly through the dense brush like a shadow. A moment later he slipped through the narrow pass. For a moment the Button frowned through the leafy branches, and then he was out of the saddle to follow Roaming Reynolds.

'Always taking chances,' he growled softly in his throat. 'Someday he will take just one too many!' The tall buckaroo rounded a bend and flattened against a slab of rock to listen with head cocked forward. The faint whisper of hoofs came from up ahead, and he loosened his gun and removed the spurs from his boots. He made no more noise than a stalking

Indian when he again moved forward.

The two Deuce of Diamonds riders were up to something shady. Shorty Peters was riding carelessly up the trail with no attempt at concealment. His big pardner. had disappeared, and Reynolds stoppd suddenly in an effort to place him. And when he did, it was too late for him to do anything about it.

A lariat circled down from above and pinned his arms before he could slap for his gun. Reynolds was jerked to his haunches when Butch Cawdom hipleaned heavily against the rope to spill his catch. The Deuce of Diamonds man laughed hoarsely.

'Got yuh,' he gloated. 'Shorty saw you following along back there just as we shagged into the brush!'

Roaming Reynolds got his feet under him and levered up like a flash. Cawdom grinned and jerked back to spill him on his shoulders, and the tall buckaroo shook his head to clear away the cobwebs. A grating laugh snapped his head up again, and he laid on his side and stared at the little gunman.

'Let him have it now, Shorty,' the big puncher snarled viciously. 'They won't ever find him way back here, and the rest of those Lazy L rannies will be easy with this gun-boss out of the way for keeps.'

'The boss wants to talk to him,' the little gunman muttered angrily, and Reynolds could see him fighting with the desire to even the score. 'You think we could get away with it?'

'Who's going to tell?' Cawdom growled. 'You been wanting the chance, and you won't ever get a better one.'

Shorty Peters lifted his eyes slowly when a slight scraping sound came from the mouth of the pass. The little gunman froze with his hand above the butt of his gun when he saw Texas Joe crouching toward him with thin shoulders hunched forward. Reynolds was on the ground between the two, and Shorty dropped his right hand to make a flashing draw.

Butch Cawdom grinned like a wolf on the kill and eased off on the rope, waiting to see that sliding gun explode into flame. Reynolds had seen the shift in the gunman's eyes, had heard the slight scraping behind him. That would be Texas Joe coming in to take the play.

He held his breath until a gun blasted behind him just before Shorty's gun cleared leather. The little gunman jerked back across the cantle of his saddle and slid to the ground, his horse wheeling and bolting up the narrow, twisting trail through the rocks.

Shorty Peters bounced on his shoulders and flattened out not far from the tall buckaroo. Roaring echoes bellowed back from the rocks, interrupted by a high pitched yell.

'Fight that twine, pard!'

Roaming Reynolds had made himself thin on the ground when Texas Joe blasted over his head. Nearly every gunman will trigger a shot away after he has been hard hit, and the tall buckaroo held his place until the snarling voice of Texas Joe whipped across the pass. He rolled swiftly with both arms spreading the loop just as Butch dragged his six-gun and threw a shot which plunked into the ground where Reynolds had been lying.

Texas Joe was around the outcropping and coming up fast. His tall pard came to his knees with right hand striking down for his holster; found familiar wood and made his draw with thumb dogging back the heavy hammer against the pull of his trigger finger.

Cawdorn caught the bucking gun in his big hand and brought the smoking Colt down in a panic of haste. A slug took him high in the shoulder and jerked the gun from his hand, but he came rushing down the rocky trail to take his man bare-handed.

Reynolds had no time to get to his feet. His eyes burned like flame in his craggy face when he thumbed back and dropped the hammer for a centre shot. Butch stumbled and pitched headlong even as his thick arms were reaching for a grip.

Texas Joe bounced out of the rocks with a scowl of hatred on his thin, grimy face. The old gun in his right hand followed the big Deuce of Diamonds puncher until the huge body quivered to a stop.

'Thought he had you that time, Roamin',' he panted, and held his gun ready until a hoarse rattle announced that the fighting days of Butch Cawdorn were over. 'It took a lot to make him lay down and roll over!'

'He would have had me if you hadn't yipped when you did,' and Reynolds reloaded his gun automatically. 'Now you can see why I told you to cover my back. Butch roped me like a yearling bull when I come cat-footing it through that cut back yonder aways.'

The younger cowboy's eyes brightened with happiness at the implied compliment. These were the things he lived for, and he followed Reynolds move for move in jacking out the spent shells and reloading his old Colt.

'You reckon them shots of ours will bring down the lightning?' he asked hopefully, and glanced back at the mouth of the narrow pass.

'Too far from the Deuce of Diamonds spread,' his companion muttered.

Texas Joe stared at Reynolds as he searched the bottle-neck opening with a frown on his tanned face; shifted his head and continued to scan both sides of the pass.

'You hunting for something?' Joe barked sharply.

Roaming Reynolds nodded and pointed to a sandbank where the winter rains had washed a passage for flood water in a shallow crevice. Texas Joe leaned forward to look, and then he got his companion's meaning.

'Bring up the horses,' Reynolds ordered briefly. 'We can't let them two lay there. No telling how long before some of their crowd ride in here, and we don't want 'em found right now, regardless.'

'Shore,' the youngster grinned. 'You mean we're to drag them corpses yonder to that little wash and cut the bank down on top of them. I'll get the broncs right up, and we can boot-hill them two pronto.'

He came back riding the roan and leading the tall buckaroo's horse. Roaming Reynolds took down his rope and looped the little gunman's heel. Made fast to Butch Cawdorn when Joe shook out his coils and took a dally around the saddle horn. Then the two horses rolled their eyes and did their part of the work.

The gruesome task was finished a few moments later and the tall buckaroo kneed his horse up the twistin trail and stopped when they rounded a bend and came to a high drift fence of adlers and mesquite. He turned in the saddle to study the back trail, and then followed the faint marks of cloven hoofs to the fence.

'We'd have missed that if they hadn't made a drive last night,' he remarked, and swung down to the ground. 'Now, I wonder?'

'There's a gate there, pard,' Texas Joe declared positively. 'You can see where it drug on the ground when they swung it back. Let me get my rope on that chunk of greasewood sticking out there by your right hand. I know dang well I'm right.'

He built a finicky loop while Roaming Reynolds stepped up to his saddle; made his cast and sat his horse down as though he were snaking a steer out of a soak-hole. The drift fence parted at the end and swung back slowly, and Reynolds waited until his companion put his roping horse to the pull and closed the big brush gate after them.

'You remember, there was a stake-and-rider fence at that west end where we rode in,' he said thoughtfully. 'We'll go out that way just in case somebody heard our thunder back yonder where we met them two.'

Texas Joe pointed at the cattle grazing down in the heavy grass. 'Was me, I'd cut one of them critters out of the herd and stretch him for a look,' and he glanced at Reynolds for approval of the suggestion. 'They're still too boogery to tell much by just riding among 'em.'

The tall buckaroo stared at the grazing cattle and nodded slowly. 'Good idea,

Joe,' he agreed. 'Take that big steer over yonder by himself,' and he pointed to a three-year-old, grazing in a little pocket. 'Get his head, and I'll take his heels.'

He reached for his maguey while Texas Joe lined his horse for the steer and coiled his rope. The loop snaked out to circle the big horns when the animal stopped grazing and threw up his head with a snort of surprise. Roaming raced up when the rope tightened and dabbed his twine behind the kicking heels. Set his horse back when the steer went down, and Texas Joe backed his roan away to stretch the two ropes tight.

The lanky Button hit the ground and raced forward with hands fumbling for the hogging string around his lean middle. Passed his loop over a foreleg and drew the two hind legs up to make a three-bone tie. After which he sat down on the thrashing head while his tall pardner slid down and high-heeled across to study the Deuce of Diamonds brand.

Then he looked at his companion with a question in his eyes. Texas Joe nodded his sandy head positively.

'Just what I was thinking my ownself,' he grunted. 'She ain't clean enough for a branding iron. that there's an old burn, and the rest of it was done with a running iron and a saddle ring. You reckon we can prove it, Roamin'?'

'We got to prove it before we do what has to be done,' the tall buckaroo answered quietly. 'A gent could find himself a lot of grief in this country making bad guesses.'

He stared again at the brand and levered to his feet. His right hand flashed down to his holster, and the gun exploded to drive a slug into the steers brain. Texas Joe climbed down sheepishly when the thrashing head lolled to the ground. Roaming Reynolds reached to the back of his belt for his skinning knife, and he motioned for Joe to throw off his ties.

'What you aim to do?' the boy demanded. 'Slow-elk us some fresh beef?'

'Don't be funny,' Reynolds grunted

coldly. 'You can always tell a vented brand on a green hide if you know how to look,' and he made his slashes to outline the Deuce of Diamonds burn.

Texas Joe scratched his head and watched. 'New wrinkle on me,' he muttered. 'Who you aiming to show it to?'

Roaming Reynolds continued to slit the thick hide. 'We'll take this back and keep it until the cattle buyers and Inspector ride into Paradise for round-up,' he explained. 'All the proof we need.'

Texas Joe threw off the last rope while the tall buckaroo finished his skinning job. After which he caught the heels and dragged the dead steer back into a pocket grown high with arrow weed, while Roaming Reynolds held his bit of hide up to the light and nodded with satisfaction at what he saw.

'You think they will find this critter?' Texas Joe called.

'The coyotes and buzzards will clean it up in a day or two,' Reynolds answered carelessly. 'Let's get along toward the upper end before night catches us up.'

The grazing herd paid little attention when the two mounted their horses and rode slowly toward the upper end of the long valley. They came to timber line where the air grew colder, and crossed several small streams fed by snow water high above.

'This would be a swell place for a gent to settle down,' Texas Joe said musingly. 'Looks like we will have to do it one of these days, pard.'

Roaming Reynolds turned his head and studied the young face. 'Yeah,' he muttered. 'What brought that up so sudden?'

'Well, a gent wouldn't want to stay back here by his lonesome,' Joe answered with a grin. 'I was thinking about Bobbie Zander and the way she looked at you back there in Paradise this morning.

Roaming Reynolds rode closer and blocked the trail. 'Don't try none of that fancy hoorayin' on me, feller,' he warned sternly. 'And you might remember yore manners about women, if you got any to remember.'

'Don't get yore hackles up,' the boy said quickly. 'Dang it all, Roamin', I was only thinking out loud. If I don't talk to you, I might just as well talk to myself.'

'You've got us into a heap of trouble before this because you talked too much,' the tall cowboy muttered, and started his horse up the trail. 'Swing down and drop a couple of those bars.'

Texas Joe stared at the broad back and swung from the saddle. He removed a section of the stake-and-rider fence, replacing it again when Reynolds rode through with the two horses. The sun was slanting down behind Vermillion Cliffs when they again crossed Kanab creek and headed for the Lazy L.

'I got a queer feeling,' Joe said suddenly. 'It's spooky as all get out, up here in these high hills.'

Roaming Reynolds shrugged. 'Sometimes you spook mighty easy,' he grunted. 'Mebbe you feel the hair raising up on the back of yore neck?'

'Gwan,' the Button almost snarled. 'I've seen you in the same fix many's the time,' and he unconsciously raised his hand to smooth the hair at the back of his head.

Roaining Reynolds watched the thin face for a moment and nodded slowly. 'I get what you mean, pard,' he muttered. 'Like someone was watching you from cover. When you feel that-away, it's a right good time to watch close and not do too much talking out loud. Sound carries quite a ways up here.'

'You take back yonder,' Joe muttered. 'Neither one of us expected to meet up with them two so soon,' and his grey eyes narrowed. 'I had the same feeling back there when I emptied my saddle to follow you.'

Roaming Reynolds raised his head and scanned the surrounding hills. They were on the edge of the Kanab forest, watered by the cold waters of the brawling creek. A thick growth of pine covered both steep banks, and the tall buckaroo frowned af the stillness.

Not a bird in the trees to quarrel at their intrusion. Usually the jays warned against strangers, but now the forest was strangely still. The two riders glanced at each other, and neither heard the muffled sounds of a horse's hoofs on the thick pine needles until a tall black thoroughbred minced out of a bosky to block the narrow trail.

Texas Joe grunted and threw his mount back on its haunches with his hand sweeping down for his gun. Roaming Reynolds continued on without speaking, but his blue eyes were watching the long-fingered hands of the tall rider sitting the hand-tooled saddle cinched to the thoroughbred.

His eyes narrowed and became smoky while he studied the stranger. The striking face was darkly handsome in an arrogant way that spoke of power. Straight nose above thin lips ; topaz eyes that stared steadily without winking. Expensive clothes and fifty-dollar Stetson. But it was the low-thonged gun on the right leg that held the tall buckaroo's interest.

The ivory-handled .45 was tilted out

in a hand-moulded holster that had been fashioned by the hands of a master who knew his tools. A light of admiration flickered briefly in the eyes of Roaming Reynolds, and when he raised his glance, he saw the same light of understanding flame and then pass to chilly indifference in the eyes of the broad-shouldered stranger.

Texas Joe was staring belligerently with hand on his gun, making no attempt to conceal his dislike for the man blocking the trail. Lips twisted into a sneer when he remembered and held his tongue. Roaming Reynolds would do the talking.

'You are Roaming Reynolds,' the tall man stated quietly. 'I recognized you from what I heard about yore get-up.'

'Same here,' Reynolds nodded. 'Yo're Griff Tyson. I could tell it from yore riggin' and gear, and from the way you wear yore tools.'

Tyson nodded. 'And the Button is Texas Joe,' he stated pleasantly. 'Glad you came into the valley, the both of you.'

5

Roaming Reynolds smiled and waited for what he knew was coming. 'You mentioned tools,' Tyson continued softly. 'No one but a gunfighter would use that expression.'

'That's right,' Reynolds agreed without hesitation. 'We both speak the same language, and we both know it.'

The topaz eyes narrowed momentarily when Griff Tyson stared at holster and gun on the tall buckaroo's right leg. Checked the tilt of the handle against the fighting jaw of Roaming Reynolds as competitors will do when weighing their chances. Then the peculiar eyes changed swiftly when their owner decided against immediate conflict.

Roaming Reynolds smiled coldly. He had been reading Tyson's face, and the change of expression had not fooled him. The Deuce of Diamonds owner was not afraid; every angle of his fighting body expressed the utmost confidence in himself.

'We both know it,' he repeated softly. 'So I thought I would ride down and make a little talk with you.'

'And you made it,' Reynolds answered soberly. 'Me and Joe will be riding along now, Tyson. You see, we signed up to make a couple of hands on the Lazy L.'

Griff Tyson shrugged carelessly. 'You only arrived this morning,' he pointed out. 'You have only worked a few hours, and I'll double what you are getting and save us both trouble.'

'Me and him ain't dodging trouble,' Texas Joe interrupted coldly, 'Roamin' told you we was riding for the Lazy L.'

The Deuce of Diamonds owner smiled and raised his eyes to study Texas Joe. 'You have the makings of a man, Button,' he answered lightly. 'I'd advise you to curb your tongue until you get your growth.'

Texas Joe gigged his horse closer, and his thin face twisted into a scowl of anger. 'I've done purty well so far,' he snapped viciously. 'I mind one salty gent who picked me for a button, and right now he looks like a soiled deuce in a dirty deck!'

'Shut up, Joe,' Reynolds warned sternly. 'You talk too much with yore mouth!'

The boy turned to stare at his companion, and Roaming Reynolds tried to pass a message with his eyes. Texas Joe nodded sullenly and dropped his glance, and Griff Tyson nodded approval.

'I saw Shorty Peters early this afternoon,' he said softly. 'I also saw Butch Cawdorn, which was one of the reasons I decided to give you two jiggers a job with the Deuce of Diamonds. From now on Shorty and Butch will stay back in line camp.'

'Reckon they will, Tyson, but like I told you, me and Joe is busy with a job of work right now. Like always, we aim to stay with it until we finish what we was hired to do.'

'This job of work,' Tyson answered slowly, 'it might not be so easy as you think. Throwing in with me might be a lot healthier.'

Roaming Reynolds shrugged. 'Like you said,' he admitted, 'healthier for some other fellers.'

The ranch owner stared at the tall buckaroo until he had finished speaking. Then he turned his horse until his broad back was to the puzzled partners. Reaching into a vest pocket, he produced a playing card and flipped it in the air. His right hand swivelled down with effortless ease, and the card flipped over and fluttered down.

Texas Joe blinked and stopped his reaching fingers when a throaty roar blasted out from Tyson's hand. The smoking gun was holstered again before the pasteboard settled to earth, and then Tyson turned back to face the wondering cowboys.

'Hand that card to Reynolds,' he barked at Joe.

'He might find it interesting.'

The youngster obeyed the sharp order instinctively, and he slid from the saddle to pick up the card. It was the Deuce of Diamonds with one pip partly shot out, and he shuddered as he passed the card to his tall partner. A smile crinkled the corners of Reynolds's mouth when he pointed to the bullet hole.

'You didn't get that spot clean,' he complained softly. 'And not only that, but there's two spots on that pasteboard.'

His left hand flipped the card away carelessly. A double roar blasted the stillness of the pine woods to twist the card in flight. Griff Tyson started for his gun when Reynolds made his flashing pass, but he stopped his hand when yellow flame spat from the buckaroo's hand. The smoking gun was holstered before the card stopped spinning, and Roaming spoke softly to Texas Joe.

'Pick it up, pard. Give it to Tyson with our regards!'

The Deuce of Diamonds man did not move a muscle in his smooth dark face. He watched Texas Joe pick up the card ; took it with a nod of his head and held it up to the light. Then he nodded again and turned to Roaming Reynolds.

'You placed them where you called them,' he said quietly. 'I like that kind of work, and I'll just double that offer I made you. It would be worth it.'

'Same answer like before,' the buckaroo drawled. 'We've taken a shine to old Lafe and Manny Lassiter. They have been losing plenty of stock lately, and it don't seem like a square shake to me and Joe.'

'And you intend to do something about it,' Tyson added softly. 'Is that the way it stacks up, Roaming Reynolds?'

'Something like that,' the buckaroo agreed. 'Only it don't ever pay to go off half-cocked like a pilgrim. A gent can do better work when he knows just what to do.'

'You are a man of discernment,' the other answered heartily. 'Perhaps we can talk this thing over and come to an agreement. There is scarcely room enough here in Summit Valley for both of us, thinking the way we do right now.'

'The roads leading out ain't blocked

off yet,' Texas Joe snarled nastily.

Griff Tyson ignored him and continued to watch the face of the tall buckaroo. 'You heard what I said, Reynold?' he asked softly.

'I heard the both of you,' Reynolds answered thoughtfully, and without raising his deep voice. 'And the both of you was plumb correct.'

'Meaning that you have decided to take the back trail?' Tyson murmured softly, and smiled with his topaz eyes.

Roaming Reynolds also smiled, but his blue eyes were smouldering. 'Wrong,' he stated flatly. 'I got a job of work to do for the Lazy L, and the road is open to you if you want to take it. Me and Joe like Summit Valley, and we aim to stay awhile.'

Griff Tyson frowned and caught his breath sharply. He had not expected to meet such stubborn resistance, and then he smiled when he glanced at the smoke-grimed gun.

'Then we understand each other,' he answered with a new note in his voice.

'Like you pointed out, we both speak the same language.'

'And we can read sign with the best,' Texas Joe cut in sharply.

Tyson turned in the saddle to stare at the Button. 'I doubt that last at yore age,' he contradicted slowly, and his eyes raised inquiringly. 'You trying to tell me something you don't pack the sand to come right out with?' he demanded coldly.

Texas Joe twisted when he felt the eyes of his tall pard upon him. He was a man of direct action, and all this talk seemed unnecessary. He muttered softly when Roaming Reynolds continued to stare coldly.

'I reckon you ought to know after seeing Shorty Peters and Butch Cawdorn.'

'And I reckon you know the difference between them two and me,' Tyson murmured, but his eyes continued to study the scowling face of Texas Joe.

'Keep right on talking, feller,' he prompted.

'Talk to Roamin',' the Button grunted.

'I heard you both say you spoke the same language!'

Griff Tyson knew that he had lost the advantage but his face expressed no sign of disappointment. He shifted in the saddle to face the tall buckaroo squarely, and the two gun-fighters looked each other over. The Deuce of Diamonds owner was the first to notice the gathering gloom.

'Good head, Reynolds,' he praised softly. 'You've played poker, and the best hand don't always win the pot'

Roaming Reynolds nodded. 'That's right. You can't always tell just what the feller has in the hole … or up his sleeve.'

Griff Tyson stiffened. 'Up his sleeve?' and his voice was hard and metallic.

'You take like this morning,' Reynolds shrugged. 'Cawdorn was making talk at the girl when all the time he was lining up to give Manny Lassiter a working over.'

Griff Tyson accepted the change of subject. 'And Butch gave it to. that barn-shouldered cowhand,' he answered grimly. 'That's when you bought chips in a closed game.'

'I drew a right fair hand,' Reynolds answered softly. 'Special when them two riders of yores tried to play what they held up their sleeves.'

Griff Tyson surprised him by nodding agreement. 'That's why them two are going to ride line,' he said evenly. 'When brains were being passed around, the both of them were hiding.'

He glanced meaningly at Texas Joe, and the Button bristled instantly. 'I use my brains, big feller,' he grated, 'like yo're due to find out the next time you see them line-riders of yores!'

Griff Tyson reined with his left hand and swung the meaning. His eyes narrowed and held to the belligerent face of Texas Joe while Roaming Reynolds frowned and wondered if the Button had again talked too much. The Deuce of Diamonds man finally gave it up and shrugged his shoulders.

'My offer still stands,' he said to Roaming Reynolds.

'And the answer is the same,' the tall

buckaroo replied firmly.

Griff Tyson reined with his right hand and swung the black thoroughbred. 'I give you good day, gents.'

'*Adios*,' Texas Joe snapped waspishly.

'*Hasta la vista*,' Roaming Reynolds corrected softly.

'Till we meet again,' Griff Tyson repeated under his breath, and rode through the timber without looking back.

His face was thoughtful as he hugged the shadows and cantered toward the Deuce of Diamonds. He was conscious that something had gone wrong, and he stopped the black gelding when a man left a thicket and came to meet him — rode forward to meet Ramrod McCall with lips set in a straight line.

'Howdy, Griff,' McCall greeted. 'You see Shorty and Butch up this way?'

Griff Tyson stopped his horse. 'I didn't,' he clipped. 'My orders was to have them two ride line back in that hidden valley.'

Ramrod McCall jerked his head. 'I sent them down there, but lately them two has taken a notion to change the plays we give them,' he answered.

He stared at his boss when Tyson made no answer. The Deuce of Diamonds owner was rubbing his chin thoughtfully, trying to make sense from the hazy remarks Texas Joe had dropped.

'You meet up with somebody?' McCall asked softly, and stared at the smoke-stained gun on Tyson's leg.

Griff Tyson straightened and raised his head. 'Met Roaming Reynolds and his pard,' he admitted quietly. 'Don't make any mistake about them two, McCall. The big one is fast on the trigger, and the Button don't know the meaning of fear.'

Ramrod McCall turned his head to hide the eager light in his eyes. 'I've seen Reynolds work,' he growled. 'But there are others just as fast.'

'Being just as fast wouldn't buy a man anything,' Tyson pointed out. 'And there's only one man in these parts fast enough to escape his lead.'

'Mebbe two,' McCall corrected.

Griff Tyson whipped over his left hand and caught his foreman by the right wrist. His voice was low and gruff when he contradicted McCall.

'One man, Ramrod!'

Ramrod McCall tensed his muscles and held perfectly still. Then he turned his head slowly and locked glance with Tyson. Something warned him in the depths of those inscrutable topaz eyes, and he shrugged and turned his head before answering.

'Meaning yourself?'

'That's right. I made Reynolds an offer just now.'

'He working for us?'

Griff Tyson shook his head. 'Turned me down flat. Said him and the Button had a job of work to do for the Lazy L.'

'Too bad,' McCall muttered, and again glanced at the gun on Tyson's leg. 'I heard the shooting, and you're still alive.'

Griff Tyson smiled coldly. 'Roaming Reynolds is still alive also,' he said quietly, and related the incident, of the playing card. 'And he shot both pips out clean,' he finished thoughtfully.

Ramrod McCall leaned forward in the saddle. 'Stop and think, Griff,' he whispered tensely. 'You met them two down by Kanab creek. Just before that I had a run in with them on the other side of Hidden Valley.'

Griff Tyson swivelled in the saddle. 'That's the answer to the Button's palaver,' he growled savagely. 'Him and Reynolds must have followed sign and found the brush gate. They came through the valley shore as sin.'

'He said something about you knowing the next time you saw Shorty and Butch,' McCall reminded.

'We better back-track down there before it gets too dark.'

'The light won't hold,' Tyson muttered angrily, but he hit his horse with the spurs and rocketed down the back trail with Ramrod McCall following close.

Neither spoke as they took familiar short cuts and came to the stake-and-rider fence. McCall swung down and dropped the bars; replaced them when Tyson rode through with the two horses. Then they were racing down the long valley with just enough twilight left to see the grazing herd.

Up the steep trail at a slower pace, and Tyson grunted softly and swung down when something glittered in the short grass. Ramrod McCall reined in and studied the ground while Tyson turned the cartridge case over in his hand.

'Forty-five,' the Deuce of Diamonds owner muttered, and stooped to pick up another shell.

'A gent was roped from his kak right here to start off the play,' McCall said softly. 'Looks like the sanie gent done a lot of bleeding, and you said neither of them other two was hurt any.'

The two men straightened and locked glances. 'We got to find Butch,' and Griff Tyson rubbed the handle, of his gun. 'He made another gunplay at Reynolds after what I said!'

'Mebbe not,' McCall grunted. 'Shorty swore to dehorn that Button if it was the last thing he did,' and then he stooped suddenly and sucked in his breath. Griff Tyson smiled coldly and nodded his dark head.

'Looks to me like it was the last thing he did,' he remarked quietly. 'Now I savvy what that yearling was getting at. He would have bragged the whole yarn, only his tall pard shut him up sudden.'

Ramrod McCall was circling the ground. His grey eyes glistened when he pointed to a scraped place in the rocky trail, bent grass stems still drooping where a heavy body had passed over. Griff Tyson took up the sign from there and followed it unerringly to the cut bank.

Ramrod McCall went down in the crevice and kicked with his boots, while Griff Tyson stood above and watched with the light of hell flickering in his peculiar eyes.

'Shorty Peters,' McCall muttered, and dragged the little gunman aside. 'Butch was right under him,' he whispered a moment later.

'And I had them two under my gun,' Griff Tyson saicl slowly. 'Not more than half an hour after they rubbed Butch and Shorty out.'

'They didn't want us to know just yet,' McCall murmured thoughtfully. 'So they buried them two.'

'That's more than I would have done,' Tyson grunted callously. 'I see the whole thing now. Butch roped Reynolds from the saddle, while Shorty covered the play with a gun in his hand. Then that Texas button covered his pard from back there at the bend just inside the gate.'

'And he got Shorty first,' McCall took up the recital. 'Reynolds must have throwed off the loop to come up fighting, and Butch tied into him bare-handed. The way I see it, neither one of them two was much of a loss.'

Griff Tyson nodded. 'As far as we know, them two just disappeared,' he added. 'They couldn't do what they was told, and you better throw a little dirt on top of them.'

Ramrod McCall swore under his

breath and jerked the little gun-fighter back in position by one rusty boot. Then he kicked at the loamy dirt of the cut bank until the two bodies were again covered. Grunted angrily when he rolled heavy stones on the new earth while Griff Tyson stood above him and watched.

'Them two,' McCall said when he climbed up the bank. 'We got to get rid of 'em, Griff.'

Griff Tyson turned slowly in the gloom and fixed his foreman with an icy stare. 'That's why Shorty and Butch are where they are,' he murmured sternly. 'Neither one of them used their heads.'

Ramrod McCall studied the dark face for a moment and sighed 'I wouldn't do it, Griff,' he said quietly. 'I can see it in yore face, and we got too much to lose.'

'Did anyone ask you?'

McCall shook his head. 'Nobody did,' he admitted. 'But you was thinking about how fast Roaming Reynolds is with his tools. And you were itching for the chance to prove that you have him faded.'

Griff Tyson whipped around and flashed a hand to his gun. Ramrod McCall stiffened and stopped the hand that was reflecting the move. Held his position when he stared into the naked muzzle of the long smoke-grimed gun.

'Not me, boss,' and his voice was a soft whisper. 'I matched irons with you one time, and then I signed on as foreman. Once was enough for me.'

Griff Tyson smiled coldly and holstered his six-gun. 'Thought you had forgotten,' he muttered dryly. 'Don't do it again, Ramrod.'

The Deuce of Diamonds foreman nodded and jerked his head toward the horses. 'Getting dark,' he answered quietly. 'But we ought to take a look at the cattle before we ride back.'

'You look,' Tyson grunted, 'while I stay here and do a little figgering.'

Ramrod McCall climbed his saddle and rode down to the brush gate. The light was fading fast, but he could still make out the trampled ground where Reynolds and Texas Joe had roped the big steer. He set his lips tightly and tried to read the sign, but darkness fell like a blanket and sent him back up the trail.

Gliff Tyson was hunkered down on his boot heels tracing marks in the dust. He glanced up at McCall and came to his feet when he saw the expression on his foreman's face.

'You find something?'

'Them two roped out a steer,' McCall answered quietly. 'Hog-tied him, but it got dark before I could find out any more. What you reckon, boss?'

Griff Tyson shrugged. 'Suspicious.' he grunted. 'But we knew that from the play they pulled with old Ely Zander. They know we changed that brand to make Ely think it was the Lassiters.'

'But this stuff is under our own iron,' McCall pointed out. 'That tall buckaroo knows too much already, and he might find out more.'

'He won't talk,' Tyson answered confidently, he wants to make sure first, and by that time it will be too late.'

Ramrod McCall frowned. 'Better do

it the quickest way,' he muttered

Griff Tyson whirled angrily and raised his voice for the first time. 'Money ain't everything, McCall,' he almost shouted, and then controlled himself with an effort.

'It is, to me,' McCall grunted, but he refused to meet the blazing eyes of his boss.

'You take Reynolds,' Tyson continued more quietly. 'He could have had all the money he wanted up there with old Mormon Tucker. Did he take it?'

'He's a gun-fighter,' McCall growled. 'Roams around all over hell looking for the chance to match cutters with some fast gun-hawk!'

'That's good reading,' Tyson agreed. 'And you can see it in his face that he thinks he's the fastest. Well, he ain't!'

Ramrod McCall tried once more. 'Five years,' he began. 'Right now we have the biggest spread in the valley. We can't afford to take any chances just because. Roaming Reynolds thinks he is faster than you are with his tools!'

'Can't we?'

The Deuce of Diamonds foreman raised his head and locked glances with Tyson. Stared for a long moment while he read gun-fighter's jealousy and vanity in the cruel eyes of his chief. Then he shrugged his shoulders and dropped his eyes.

'Yo're the boss,' he muttered, and shook his head stubbornly. 'But a good rifle and a dark night …?'

Griff Tyson stepped up and gripped the smaller man by the arms. 'There's Shorty and Butch yonder,' he said pointedly. 'They disobeyed orders, and you see what they got.'

'I ain't proud,' the foreman muttered. 'And we have plenty of riders who could lay back in the brush and dot a man between the eyes at a hundred yards or better!'

Tyson tightened his grip until McCall bit his lips. Then he loosened his hands and stepped back with a mirthless smile on his dark face.

'I'll kill the man who pulls a play

like that,' he said softly. 'Pass the word around, Ramrod. I'll hold you responsible if anything like that happens.'

'It's yore funeral,' McCall grunted, and rubbed his bruised muscles.

'Wrong again,' Tyson corrected. 'When the time is right, it will be the funeral of Roaming Reynolds. After that, old Ely Zander and the Lassiters will be easy.'

'Let's be riding,' and Ramrod McCall mounted his horse. 'I'll tell the men what you said.'

Griff Tyson smiled in the darkness and snugged his gun deep in leather. Swung to the saddle and passed the grave of Shorty Peters and Butch Cawdom with a careless shrug.

'They saved me the trouble,' he muttered softly. 'I'd have done it myself to show them that there is only room up here for one boss!'

6

Old Lafe Lassiter sighed with relief when he saw Roaming Reynolds lope into the Lazy L ranch yard with Texas Joe at his side. Both horses were sweating from a long, fast run, and the old cattleman nodded his understanding. The two would talk when the time was right.

He turned to a buxom, silver-haired woman in the doorway of the rambling old house when the riders swung from saddles and came up on the porch. Texas Joe was smiling softly while he waited for an introduction.

'Roamin', I want you and Joe to meet Ma Lassiter. Don't know what we would have done without Roamin' to-day, Ma. He saved us a heap of grief.'

The tall gun-boss, was a different man when he swept off his Stetson and took the hand Ma Lassiter extended. His hard face broke into a smile to show strong white teeth, and his blue eyes were soft with happiness when the mother of Manny stood on her tip-toes and kissed him soundly.

'Couldn't help it, Roamin',' she chuckled softly. 'Manny is our only chip, and he told me what Butch Cawdom was aiming to do to him when you took a hand. You and the Button will be staying on with us for a spell of time?'

Texas Joe grinned and circled on the other side, to put an arm around Ma Lassiter. Then he bobbed his head boyishly and kissed her cheek with worship shining deep in his eyes; nodded his sandy head and swallowed noisily when he held both her toil-worn hands.

'You can count on it, Ma,' he answered soberly. 'You couldn't run us away from the Lazy L now if Griff Tyson was twins.'

The smile faded from Ma Lassiter's face at the mention of Tyson's name. Texas Joe caught his breath sharply and glared at old Lafe and Manny. Both of the big men had sobered instantly, and the lanky cowboy shuffled his feet and turned to Roaming Reynolds.

'Better tell 'em,' he muttered. 'I see both of them has got themselves dressed since we last saw 'em.'

Reynolds glanced at the guns holstered low on the right legs of the Lassiters. Then he nodded slowly, but his eyes telegraphed a warning to his young companion.

'We met the Deuce of Diamonds owner down by Kanab creek,' he began slowly. 'We didn't neither one of us see him urttil he sent his big black hoss out of the timber and straddled the trail just the other side of that old stake-and-rider fence.'

Lafe Lassiter sucked his breath in loudly. 'So you met Griff Tyson already,' he muttered.

Manny Lassiter leaned forward. 'Tyson don't do things accidental,' he said quietly. 'You mind telling us?'

'Tyson made us a proposition,' Reynolds answered slowly. 'Then he said that this country wasn't big enough for both of us when I turned him down.'

'But before that,' Texas Joe interrupted.

'Before that we was riding around to see what we could see,' the tall buckaroo answered sharply, and his voice was harsh and edgy.

Old Lafe stared at the two for a long moment. 'Both you fellers have been riding gun-sign,' he stated positively. 'Yore irons is smoked up considerable, and you tell me that you met up with Griff Tyson ...'

'Met him and talked some,' Reynolds grunted. 'Talk he didn't like any too well.'

'He don't talk unless he has something to say,' Lassiter muttered. 'And yore guns talked some for you.'

'Tyson is still hale and hearty,' Reynolds drawled carelessly to correct a wrong impression. 'Him and me shot a card to show each other what we could do along that line.'

'Cards?' And the old cattleman narrowed his eyes to stare at the buckaroo's hard face.

'Yeah,' Texas Joe interrupted eagerly.

'Tyson flipped a deuce of diamonds with his left hand and shot out part of one pip. Then he barked at me to hand it to Roamin', and I was out of the saddle and on the ground before I had time to think. You just sorter step about when he tells you to do something.'

'Tyson is fast,' Lafe Lassiter murmured. 'And usually accurate.'

'He ain't such a much,' Joe sneered. 'Roamin' took that card and flipped it high. Then he reached for his gun and rubbed out both them spots before the card turned over.'

Manny Lassiter rubbed his chin. 'You could hit a card,' he murmured, 'but most gents couldn't even see the spots, much less hit both of them thataway.'

Old Lafe Lassiter studied the hard face of the tall buckaroo and turned to Texas Joe. 'That shootin' accounts for Roamin's gun,' he said softly in his booming voice. 'What about you, Button? Was you giving an exhibition too?'

Ma Lassiter was searching the young cowboy's face with her dark-brown eyes.

129

Then she reached out and took his chin between her fingers. Turned his face slowly and shook her head when he dropped his eyes in confusion.

'You ain't tophand at lying, son,' she reproved gently. 'Now you come clean and tell Lafe what you and Roamin' has been up to. Looks like he ought to know.'

Texas Joe squirmed and glanced appealingly at the tall buckaroo. Reynolds shrugged with a frown and refused to commit himself. The lanky cowboy set his lips with a careless shrug.

'It was Shorty Peters and Butch Cawdorn,' he muttered sullenly. 'We cut their sign out in Hidden Valley where the grass grows tall. Hoot-owl country if you ask me.'

'I'm asking,' Lafe Lassiter prompted. 'You met Shorty Peters and his barn-shouldered pard!'

'Me and Roamin' had to tally for both them dry-gulching gents,' Joe blurted defiantly, 'after Butch baited another trap and roped Roamin' plumb out of the saddle.'

'Dead?' Manny Lassiter asked in a low whisper.

'Dead,' Roaming Reynolds repeated harshly. 'Which I'd have been likewise if Joe hadn't been smart enough to cover my back and spill the play. He made his fight with Shorty Peters while I was stretched out like a yearling bull!'

Ma Lassiter shuddered and stared at the lanky cowboy. Texas Joe caught her eyes on him and lowered his head. He could hold his place with men, but his southern heart bowed in the presence of any good woman.

'Butch Cawdorn,' Manny Lassiter murmured. 'You say he dabbed his loop on Reynolds?'

Texas Joe raised his head and answered with a grunt. 'Did it on a sneak,' he defended his tall pard. 'Roamin' was watching Shorty out in the open when the loop pinned his arms and spilled him to the grass. And Roamin' shot that big killer high in the shoulder to stop him,' he added resentfully.

Ma Lassiter turned her eyes on Reynolds and nodded with approval. 'I'm glad, Roamin',' she whispered.

Texas Joe made a noise with his mouth. 'That didn't stop Butch,' he said harshly. 'He went loco and charged Roamin' bare-handed, and when the' smoke cleared off some, we buried the both of them Deuce of Diamonds killers back yonder in the badlands.'

'I knew it was coming.' Manny Lassiter murmured with regret, 'knew it this morning down at the Post Office in Paradise.'

'That means yo're sorry?' Reynolds asked sharply. Manny Lassiter turned away without answering. Texas Joe narrowed his eyes to stare at the big Lazy L foreman, and Roaming Reynolds smiled and shrugged slightly. A brief expression of doubt softened his face when Ma Lassiter sighed and turned back to the house.

'We better turn in and make out our supper,' old Lafe suggested quietly. 'I want Texas Joe to ride night-herd on the second trick if it's all the same to you,

Roamin'.'

'Yo're the boss,' the tall gun-fighter murmured. 'You heard the orders, Joe.'

They walked back to the cook-shack with the old cattleman ; nodded soberly when Manny Lassiter introduced them to the three cowboys at the long table. They were tall youngsters with the marks of their calling stamped on tanned faces and rope-burned, hands; wearing heavy chaps over worn Levis for rough country brush.

Texas Joe grinned and took his place among them like an old hand, and for several minutes the silence was broken only by the clatter of forks on the dishes. After the meal, Manny Lassiter called to a tall cowboy who was on his way to the bunkhouse with Texas Joe.

'Montana, you and Joe better turn in and make out to get some sleep. Yo're to relieve Waco and Jim come midnight.'

Texas Joe grumbled and entered the bunkhouse with Montana while Manny drew Roaming Reynolds to the broad porch. Old Lafe seated himself on a step while the tall cowboy hunkered down on his heels and rolled a smoke. He inhaled deeply and waited for Manny to break the silence.

'It's war now,' the young foreman began earnestly. 'When Tyson finds out about Shorty and Butch, he won't rest none until he evens the score and adds some of his own to boot.'

'Yeah?' Reynolds grunted. 'And you, feller? How you going to take it?'

Manny Lassiter flushed in the darkness. 'You might have noticed that I got myself heeled,' he muttered. 'That tell you anything?'

Reynolds reached out and slapped the big cowboy heartily on the shoulder. 'Reckon it does, Manny,' he answered with quiet satisfaction. 'Just wanted to make sure.'

Manny Lassiter drew a deep breath. 'Six miles over to the Bar Z Bar,' he said thoughtfully. 'Ma and me has been talking some, and I got a hunch that we ought to lope over there unless yo're too tired. Ma figgers Bobbie ought to stay here until this ruckus is settled one way or another.'

'Tired?' Reynolds grunted. 'I was going to suggest that same thing myself,' he answered promptly. 'I'll have to rope me out a fresh hoss, and I'd like to clean my gun before we start.'

Manny Lassiter walked inside to a desk in the front room and pulled out a drawer. 'Cleaning tools in there,' he explained quietly. 'Fly at it while I have the boys change yore saddle. I figgered it best not to let Joe know that you and me was riding.'

Roaming Reynolds stopped and studied deeply. 'I dunno,' he muttered. 'I always kinda look for him to back me, and he'd high-tail shore as sin if he knew I was gone.'

'I'll back you,' Manny Lassiter growled huskily, and the tall gun-boss knew he was hurt because of comparison.

'Like you said, boss,' he agreed, and sat down to clean the heavy six-gun.

A few minutes later they walked their horses quietly down the lone lane and headed for the Bar Z Bar. The night was dark except for a faint light from the stars, and Manny Lassiter was plainly nervous when he turned to speak softly to Reynolds.

'Late moon, to-night, Roaming. We better mend our pace on account I got a feeling something is wrong over there at the Bar Z Bar. Special after you meeting Tyson.'

'Yeah,' the tall buckaroo answered. 'I got the same kind of feeling myself. Line on out.'

The big cowboy stung his horse with the spurs and headed for the twinkling yellow lights in the distance. He could see a faint shimmer on the water-hole at Big Springs, and checked the *cienaga* as half way between the Bar Z Bar and the Lazy L. Manny was in the lead scratching his big bay with both feet.

The lights in the house suddenly winked out when the two riders raced into the lane of scraggly pines leading to the corrals. Roaming Reynolds was still riding his spurs when he rounded a bend where the lights could again be seen.

He tried to check his speed as another horse loomed up, directly in front of him, and his left arm jerked back when a six-gun flamed viciously almost in his face. Before the surprised gunman could thumb the hammer back for another shot, Manny Lassiter slammed his big bay into the tangle and sent both horse and rider down into a kicking heap.

The Lazy L foreman jammed his boots deep in the oxbows and held the bay on its feet. The surprised gunman rolled clear and jerked his arm up to throw a shot wild. Forgotten was the heavy gun on young Lassiter's leg when the slug slapped the battered Stetson from his big head, and he spurred the bay and left the saddle in a flying leap with arms spread wide.

Roaming Reynolds checked his horse and whipped his right hand down for his gun. He held his fire when Manny sprawled out, with one thick arm knocking the gunman to his knees, and shook his head when he saw Lassiter's gun seated snugly in holster leather.

Both men came to their feet with surprising speed and the Lazy L foreman jumped forward and swung a terrific right-hand punch just as the gunman clicked back the hammer of his Colt. The gun exploded as the ambusher went down like a shot steer under that pile-driving blow.

Roaming Reynolds slid from the saddle and stared at old Lafe's son. The big waddy was swaying from side to side and mumbling softly to himself. He jerked his head up when Reynolds touched him lightly on the arm, and shook himself like a dog coming out of water while the savage killer's light faded slowly from his glowing dark eyes.

'You killed him,' Reynolds said softly. 'I heard his neck crack just before he triggered that last slug. You want to get over that habit, feller. Most times, fists ain't much good against bullets.'

Manny Lassiter was trembling violently from reaction. 'That's Red Frazier from the Deuce of Diamonds,' he muttered. 'He tried to kill me, and I only hit him one time.'

'That was plenty,' Reynolds drawled dryly, and swung up to the saddle. 'We better get on up to the house and see what happened just before you started on the warpath.'

Young Lassiter raised his head to look for his horse, and saw it standing at the corrals, up ahead. He high-heeled stiffiy beside the tall gun-fighter, when Reynolds reined his horse toward the house.

'Those lights went out sudden,' Lassiter muttered. 'Must have been a good reason.'

Reynolds nodded and swung down at the house. Then he vaulted the porch steps and jumped through, the door sideways with gun spiking out from his fist. For a moment he stood poised, after which he reached out for his knife and went down to his knees beside old Ely Zander. The old cattleman was bound ankles and wrists with rawhide thongs, and he clawed the dirty bandanna from his mouth when the thongs fell away.

'You get 'em?' he shouted shrilly. 'You tally for that Red Frazier and Ramrod McCall?'

'Take it easy, old-timer,' Reynolds answered soothingly. 'Manny broke Frazier's neck down there in the lane. Now you grab a hold of yourself and tell us about Ramrod McCall.'

Manny Lassiter limped into the room and stared at the little old warrior. 'They got Bobbie,' Zander groaned. 'Them two stepped in before me and Bobbie knew what for, and Ramrod McCall had Bobbie before I could slap for my hawg-laig. I seen Red Frazier make a swipe to buffalo me with his gun-barrel, and the next thing I knowed I was laying there hog-tied like a leppy. Then I hear gunfire down the lane, and I figgered help was coming from the Lazy L.'

'We didn't see McCall,' Reynolds said slowly.

'I'll kill him with my bare maulies,' Manny Lassiter growled savagely, and started for the open door.

Roaming leaped in and blocked the

opening. Then he pushed the burly foreman back, with contempt written on his
hard face.

'Use yore head, Manny,' he snapped
sharply. 'You can't go barging that-away
to the Deuce of Diamonds spread!'

'I'll go alone if yo're afraid to come,'
Lassiter shouted hoarsely. 'Out of my
way, Reynolds!'

'You ain't going,' the tall buckaroo said
sternly. 'You'd only get yoreself killed
without doing Bobbie a bit of good.'

Old Lafe's son glared like a madman
and once more the red killer light glowed
in his staring, dark eyes. He swung
his right fist without warning, aiming
straight at the point of the gun-fighter's
chin. Roaming Reynolds jerked his head
an inch to the side to let the blow whistle harmlessly over his shoulder and his
own fist travelled less than a foot to thud
solidly against the big foreman's jutting
jaw.

Manny Lassiter stiffened and sagged
forward with a soft grunt. Roaming
caught him and bent his knees to ease

the heavy body to the planking. When he straightened up, old Ely Zander was crouching across the barrel of his old single action Colt.

'Sky 'em, feller,' the old cattleman barked sharply. 'Yuh can't do no such a thing to the chip of my old pard. Elevate before I blast a hole through yore innards!'

'Don't be a fool, yuh o' raw-hider,' the tall buckaroo drawled softly. 'You and me is interested in saving yore gal from worse than death, and we got to quit fighting our heads to do it. Now you holster that smoke-pole and help me read the sign sensible like.'

'You fogged it fresh in here this morning,' the little cattleman argued stubbornly. 'Then you and the Button chouses off toward the Deuce of Diamonds spread by yore lonesomes. Now you pole-axes Manny right in my own house, and you can't cut a rusty like that on me. Keep 'em high!'

'Now look,' Reynolds argued softly. 'You know what would happen to him, if he barges up to Tyson or McCall with his fists waving,' and he jerked a thumb toward the floor.

Old Ely Zander followed the thumb automatically and glanced at the unconscious man. He gasped when he swung his eyes back to Reynolds and stared into the muzzle of the buckaroo's gun. He could see the hammer eared back for a shot, and he sighed when he remembered that the hammer of his own gun was still down and riding on an empty.

'Drop it!' the tall cowboy barked sternly. 'We ain't got the time to argue right now!'

'You won't shoot,' Zander muttered, and stared into the hard blue eyes. 'And I'll settle with you for what you done to Manny.'

'I'll shoot,' Reynolds answered grimly. 'A .45 slug will knock a man down wherever it hits, and I'm centring on yore left shoulder. Think it over, old-timer, and think fast.'

'Shoot,' Zander growled stubbornly. 'And I'll get you shore and sartin if you throw yore shot off!'

'Get ready to trigger,' Reynolds warned. 'Unless you want to do like you was told. And don't forget that Bobbie is yore daughter.'

The little cattleman swallowed and pouched his gun with a scowl of disappointment. Then his faded eyes twinkled with understanding when Roaming Reynolds holstered his own gun with a flip of his wrist. The tall gun-fighter turned his back squarely and leaned over Manny Lassiter.

'I knew it,' he murmured softly.

Ely Zander rubbed the handle of his gun uncertainly. He watched while Reynolds ripped the young foreman's right sleeve back to the shoulder and pointed to a clean hole high up in the bulging biceps.

'That gunnie got him one time,' he growled softly. 'Reckon you know what to do for him, Ely.'

'We can mend it,' Zander answered promptly. 'I got all the fixings.'

'You can fix it,' Reynolds muttered,

but the old cattleman let on not to have heard.

'I'm plumb regretful I went on the peck that-away, Roaming,' he murmured contritely, and clumped out to the little kitchen. When he returned he carried a small box of probes and bottles which he placed on the floor and hunkered down beside young Lassiter. 'Bullet went clean through,' he grunted, and set about washing the wound.

'Being big that-away, it won't hurt him serious,' Reynolds answered slowly. 'Meanwhile, McCall is getting a start.'

'We'll catch him up,' Zander muttered huskily. 'That's what Manny gets because he forgot about the gun on his leg.'

'Fix him up and ride back to the Lazy L with him,' Reynolds said softly, and levered to his feet. 'Me and him came over here to take you and Bobbie back until this ruckus is settled.'

'Mebbe we better do that,' and old Ely Zander poured a few drops of permanganate into clear warm water. 'We can't

145

do much, nohow, until daylight.'

'We can make a start,' Reynolds corrected.

'I'm riding gun-sign on that Deuce of Diamonds Ramrod until I pick up his trail. You take Manny back home.'

'I ain't doing no such,' the little cattleman contradicted flatly. 'You can't chouse off in the dark by yore lonesome. I'll make this jigger comfortable, after which I'm gearing my tops to side you.'

Roaming Reynolds shook his head. 'We got to think about Bobbie,' he argued quietly, 'and we can't leave Manny here and him out of his head.'

'You come here with him, and like you pointed out, Bobbie is my gal," and Ely Zander straightened to glare at the tall gun-fighter. 'You stay with him, and I'll cut out and do my own work!'

'Do you think much of Bobbie?' Reynolds asked bluntly.

'I'll kill the man who does her a hurt,' the little cattleman shouted.

Roaming Reynolds nodded without smiling. 'And you figger you can match

Ramrod McCall with a hand-gun?' he asked softly.

Zander glared for a moment and then drooped his thin shoulders. 'I'd shoot him down like a lobo,' he muttered harshly. 'I know better than to think I could match him in a straight out draw-and-shoot!'

'I can,' and Roaming Reynolds spoke quietly and without boasting. Like a man who states a plain fact. 'In a straight draw-and-shoot,' he repeated in the same drawling tones.

'Dang you, feller; you got me over a barrel,' the little cattleman moaned, 'I got a mind to tie this big jigger up so's he can't come undone. That-away I can ride along with you and lend a hand.'

'You wouldn't do that,' Reynolds muttered. 'You take care of Manny. Ramrod McCall is only one man, and mebbe so I can come up on him before he gets back to the Deuce of Diamonds.'

Ely Zander stared a long moment before coming up to offer his skinny right hand. 'I can see why you were gun-boss up there in the Strip,' he said earnestly, and the worry left his weathered face. 'You will do what has to be done, and I'll take care of Manny. Good luck, Roamin'.'

Reynolds gripped hard. 'Spoke like a man, Ely,' he praised softly, and somehow the tones of his deep voice seemed to bring confidence to the faded grey eyes. 'I'll be riding now.'

He stepped through the door and vaulted to the saddle before the little cattleman could answer. Roared down the lane to the place where Red Frazier stared up at the dark sky with sightless eyes.

'He had it coming,' the gun-fighter whispered coldly. 'There might be light enough to find some sign.'

He swung to the ground in the faint light of a yellow sickle moon that was just topping the rimrock high on the Vermillion Cliffs. Went down on hands and knees to feel his way, and gradually his eyes became accustomed to the semi-darkness.

He quartered over the loamy ground

in the Bar Z Bar lane, like a hound trying to pick up a scent. His tanned face was a craggy mask of determination that showed no emotion except for the smouldering fire in his deepset eyes. Eyes that noted every broken twig and track, and classified them with the same accuracy a scientist would use in making a laboratory test.

He passed over the tracks made when he and Manny Lassiter had ridden up the lane. Then he leaned forward to examine a third set of marks where the horse showed a broken front shoe. He traced it to the spot where Red Frazier had bounced from his horse, but suddenly sucked in a deep breath and crouched forward to follow a fourth set of thin iron hoof-marks.

'Thoroughbred,' he muttered, and straightened up to let his eyes wander down the pine-bordered lane. 'McCall rides that kind of a hoss!'

He leaped forward swiftly and stared at a brokert twig; nodded with understanding when a silver button gleamed up at him from the dust, in the light of the moon. He picked it up and slipped it in his pocket before walking back to his horse. Then he stopped to piece his findings together.

'Ramrod McCall slipped through there when he heard me and Manny coming,' he muttered. 'He had the girl on the saddle in front of him, and she tore a concha loose when he slammed through the brush!'

7

Ramrod McCall held the girl close with his left arm while he walked his horse slowly through the gun-shattered darkness. She struggled to free herself when she recognised the voice of Manny Lassiter, but the Deuce of Diamonds foreman tightened his muscles until the girl gasped with pain and leaned weakly against him.

'Good thing I gagged you,' he muttered in her ear. 'I'll kill them both if they discover us!'

Bobbie Zander closed her eyes and strained her ears to listen. She heard the confusion when Manny Lassiter crashed his horse to spill Red Frazier from the saddle. If the big cowboy tried to use his hands against the deadly gunman . . . ? She clenched her hands, tied tightly behind her back, when Ramrod McCall stopped the horse and cocked his head to listen.

'Promises,' she heard him mutter deep

in his throat. 'Nothing but gun-fighter's jealousy!'

She could almost feel the sudden anger that pulsed through his veins. A second horse was coming up fast on the other side of the pine-bordered lane, and she heard Roaming Reynolds calling sharply to Manny Lassiter. She tried to force a warning cry through the folds of cloth in her mouth, and then the horse under her began to move slowly through the night.

The sounds of struggle grew fainter and died away when McCall gigged the horse into a racking lope and headed for the foothills. She could hear his deep regular breathing just above her head, and she stiffened when he fumbled at the knots that held her bandanna gag in place. His voice was slow and toneless when he spoke.

'Won't do you any good to holler for help now, and mebbe you can breathe easier.'

Bobbie Zander wet her lips and filled her lungs with air. Her ribs ached from the strength in his arms, and she realised why it was that the Deuce of Diamonds foreman could hold his crew of hard-bitten gunmen under control. Manny Lassiter was big, but she knew that Ramrod McCall would have little difficulty in a match of physical strength.

As though he had read her thoughts, her captor grunted softly. 'It would be some different if I were in Red Frazier's boots. And I wouldn't have missed that first shot either!'

Bobbie Zander shuddered. There had been two shots, and she knew Manny Lassister's stubborn courage. A sudden fear clutched at her throbbing heart when she remembered the fight in Paradise that same morning. A fear that subsided as quickly as it had come.

'Roaming Reynolds fired that second shot,' she said confidently, and caught her breath when McCall's arm tightened convulsively.

She could hear his rapid breathing while his mind raced to picture the battle in the dark, back in the lane. And then the sickle moon topped the rimrock to light the broad valley with a faint yellow glow. Ramrod McCall loosened his arm and turned the girl until she could look into his face. A face cold and savage, with grey eyes narrowed to glinting slits.

'It was Frazier's gun,' he growled softly. 'Every six-gun has a voice of its own, and I can tell the ones I have heard speak. Right now that Lazy L ramrod is kicking hot ashes!'

The girl stared into his eyes and remained silent. His lack of emotion puzzled her and filled her with strange fear she had never experienced. McCall read the change in her pretty face and tightened his thin lips.

'They came too late,' he taunted softly. 'Five minutes sooner, when Red and me was talking to old Ely, and they would both be dead now.'

'It was cowardly,' the girl murmured, and closed her eyes to shut out his cruel face. 'I saw him hit my father with his gun.'

'Better than shooting the old mossy-horn,' McCall answered callously. 'But

Griff said to bring you back, and me, I know how to take orders as well as give them.'

Bobbie Zander felt her body turn cold. 'You are taking me to Griff Tyson?' she whispered faintly. Her captor nodded. 'Griff met that new gun-boss and his yearling pard about sun-down,' he answered grimly. 'The Button did a lot of talking, but Griff couldn't piece it out until me and him rode down into Hidden Valley.'

Bobbie Zander opened her eyes with a jerk. 'You rode there after … the fight?'

She could feel McCall squirm. 'That fight would have ended differently if you and old Ely had minded yore own business,' he muttered. 'Butch would have killed Reynolds with his hands.'

The girl stared defiantly. 'Butch Cawdorn won't try to kill another man with his hands very soon,' she snapped.

She shrank back at the savage change that swept over his face. 'That's right,' he muttered hoarsely. 'We found Butch back there in Hidden Valley.'

Bobbie Zander read the story in his dark face. 'Dead,' she whispered. 'That's why you came to the Bar Z Bar!'

'Butch was dead,' McCall husked. 'But I was coming to get you, regardless. It ought to change things considerable.'

The girl did not seem to hear him. 'Butch Cawdorn dead,' she repeated, 'I think I'm glad.'

The voice of Ramrod McCall blended with the beat of the horse's hoofs. 'They shot Butch and Shorty on a sneak,' he rasped. 'Dry-gulched them back there in the valley, but now it's our turn.'

For a time Bobbie Zander had forgotten her father back on the Bar Z Bar. McCall's words brought her back with a jerk, and she turned slightly to study his dark, scowling face. Then she shook her head slowly.

'Roaming Reynolds will read the sign back there,' she whispered. 'I'm sure of it.'

Ramrod McCall stiffened in the saddle. 'Mebbe not,' he muttered. 'Red Frazier is a mighty good shot with a hand-gun.'

Bobbie Zander continued to stare into his narrowed grey eyes. 'You mentioned about gun-fighter's jealousy,' she reminded softly. 'And you meant Griff Tyson.'

She saw the sudden change sweep over his face. Saw his mind racing swiftly in an effort to find the answer, and once more the girl felt a wave of relief that warmed her chilled body.

'I meant Griff,' he admitted slowly. 'He won't rest until he proves that he is faster than this Roaming Reynolds. I don't savvy how you knew, but Red Frazier is dead.'

The girl closed her eyes and waited until his breathing returned to normal. She could feel his heart beating strongly against the swell of her breast, but as far as Ramrod McCall was concerned, she might have been another man. When he spoke. his voice was once more low and under control.

'With Reynolds out of the way, the rest will be easy,' he stated slowly. 'And with you in our hands, the Lassiters and old Ely won't put up much of a fight.'

Bobbie Zander caught her breath and opened her eyes. 'But you forget Roaming Reynolds,' she reminded him.

'You never saw Griff handle a short-gun,' McCall said quietly. 'Alongside of him, that tall gun-boss of yores is like a creeping snail.'

His face clouded when the girl shook her head. The girl noticed the change and locked glances while the horse moved smoothly beneath them.

'You are fast,' she reminded softly. 'And your gun never cleared leather.'

For a moment she thought he was going to strike her. The angry blood rused to his thin face while his left arm tightened until she gasped for breath. Then he loosened his grip and stared until she turned her head.

'I wasn't on the ground,' he answered simply. 'It makes a big difference to me.'

Sudden courage came to Bobbie Zander. 'He will follow,' she answered positively, 'and you will be on the ground when he finds you.'

The grey eyes lighted instantly. 'That's all I ask,' he whispered, and then the light faded as quickly as it had appeared. 'Promises,' he muttered bitterly.

'What promises?' she prompted.

'The Deuce of Diamonds. He's marked that Roaming gunnie for his own iron. Swore to kill the man who tallied for Reynolds!'

Bobbie Zander turned her head and stared at a large body of water under the moonlight. The sight of Jacobs Lake brought her back to her predicament. The Deuce of Diamonds ranch was close at hand, but the time had passed so rapidly since her capture back on the Bar Z Bar. Ramrod McCall followed her staring eyes and grunted.

'The boss is waiting back there,' he told her. 'And it might help some if you do what he says.'

'I don't know what you mean.'

McCall answered quietly. 'It won't take long for you to find out. Yonder's the spread where you see those lights winking through the trees.'

The girl shuddered and remained silent. The horse slowed to a walk and passed through a long lane, stopping at a broad porch where McCall slid down and lifted her from the saddle. He guided her up the steps and pushed a door open, and the girl gasped when the single occupant of the big room came to his feet with a smile.

'Welcome to the Deuce of Diamonds, Bobbie,' he said quietly. 'I was expecting you.'

He ignored Ramrod McCall until the foreman spoke harshly. 'Red didn't make it back, Griff. Like as not he's dead.'

Griff Tyson wheeled swiftly. 'Who killed him?'

Ramrod McCall shrugged. 'We got in the house and slapped old Ely down with a gun-barrel,' he explained. 'I tied up the girl and started down the lane with Red in the lead. Just about then Manny Lassiter came roaring in, with Roaming Reynolds right behind him.'

'And you?' Tyson asked sharply.

Ramrod McCall shrugged carelessly. 'That promise you made me,' he muttered, 'if I tallied for Reynolds with my own gun.'

Griff Tyson stared at his foreman while his mind tried to picture the fight on the Bar Z Bar. 'I didn't say anything about young Lassiter,' he rasped angrily. 'I'm waiting to hear you say he's dead.'

Bobbie Zander shuddered at the savagery in his deep voice. Ramrod McCall returned the stare without winking, and once more he shrugged his square shoulders.

'Couldn't say for shore,' he answered. 'Red fired twice, and he wasn't in the habit of missing. I had my hands full with the girl, and I was obeying yore orders. There she is!'

Griff Tyson nodded his dark head and turned to study the girl. High-breasted and medium tall, with the health of sun and wind radiating from her tanned face. Chin high and shoulders back, and she faced him with a look of scorn in her brown eyes.

'You never made war on women before,' and her voice was cold and steady. 'I thought you were a man!'

Griff Tyson stared at her for a moment and then smiled. 'I had Ramrod bring you here because I am a man,' he answered evenly, but his clark eyes began to glow with desire. 'I've never wanted a woman until I saw you.'

'You beast!'

The girl ripped out the words like a lash, and the tall gunman cringed back a step. Then he straightened and bowed from the hips.

'You misunderstand me,' he answered softly. 'I am offering you the opportunity to become my wife, and Mistress of the Deuce of Diamonds.'

Bobbie Zander shrank back with the colour fading from her face. 'Marry you?' she whispered incredulously, and then she threw back her head and laughed hysterically.

Griff Tyson was beside her like a flash. His hands caught her shoulders and shook her until the laughter stopped entirely. After which he stared deep into her eyes and slowly shook his head.

'I told it too sudden,' he whispered. 'But you will have time to get accustomed to the idea.'

Bobby Zander bit her full lips to keep back the tears that followed as a reaction to her outburst of laughter. If her father and Manny Lassiter were dead? And what would happen when Roaming Reynolds followed the plain trail from the Bar Z Bar to the Deuce of Diamonds?

She raised her eyes and stared into the cruel, dark face so close to her own. She could feel Tyson's hot breath on her cheek, and she shrugged his hands away with a jerk of her strong young shoulders.

'I'll never marry you,' she muttered throatily. 'I'd rather die!'

Griff Tyson tightened his lips. 'You and several others,' he answered ominously. 'Roaming Reynolds and his pard, not to mention old Lafe Lassiter.'

'You would do such a thing to gain your ends?'

He nodded carelessly. 'That and more,' he answered. 'And don't forget that I have you here regardless of whether you marry me or not!'

The full import of his words dawned upon the girl and left her weak and shaken. Her shoulders began to droop under the burden of her responsibility, and she bit her lower lip hard to hold back the tears of hopelessness. Griff Tyson gripped her arm and led her to a low chair.

'Sit down,' he said softly, 'while I tally the score for you. It might help you to come to a decision.'

Bobbie Zander moved like a person in a daze. Seated herself without seeming to notice the thong that bit into her wrists. Griff Tyson turned to face Ramrod McCall and jerked his head toward the door.

'See you later, Ramrod. Better leave us alone for a spell of time.'

McCall grunted and turned on his heel. 'I'll be outside,' and opened the door without looking back.

Griff Tyson came back to the girl and stared at her for a long moment before he started to speak. His dark eyes rested hungrily on the beauty of her rounded young body, and the girl turned her head away while a shudder twitched her straining shoulders.

'The Deuce of Diamonds is the biggest outfit in Summit Valley,' Tyson boasted proudly. 'And it will be bigger before I get through. Yore father is an old man and Manny Lassiter was too proud to fight!' Bobbie Zander snapped back at him like an angry cat. 'Old men and women,' and her voice was harsh. 'And you sent your hired gunmen to kill Manny.' Then she leaned forward and spoke softly. 'But you have forgotten Roaming Reynolds. He is not too proud to fight!'

A sudden light of eager anticipation lighted up the dark eyes to change them to a glowing red. 'I have not forgotten,' Tyson answered swiftly, and the fingers of his right hand began to writhe and twist above the ivory handle of his gun. 'When I meet that tall gun-boss . . . !'

165

'You won't meet him like a man,' the girl taunted. 'You will have some of your killers hide back in the brush to bush-whack him. Like you tried to do this afternoon down then in Hidden Valley!'

'Stop!' Tyson ripped out the word like a pistol shot. 'I told Butch Cawdorn and Shorty Peters to lay off Reynolds, and they disobeyed my orders. I am glad they are dead!'

The girl stared at the merciless cru-elty in his thin dark face. 'You didn't kill them?' she whispered.

Griff Tyson shook his head. 'I'll give them that,' he muttered. 'That Button matched guns with Shorty Peters and right now he's whittling a notch. Reyn-olds did for Cawdorn, and it served them both right. We found them buried under a cut-bank not more than an hour after I talked to yore hired gunhands!'

The girl held her breath while she watched the play of emotions on his smooth face. Griff Tyson looked older than his thirty-five years, and she noticed the touch of grey around his temples.

He turned his head and wiped the anger from his darkly-handsome features when he saw the girl watching him.

'I was talking to those two, and didn't know they had just killed Butch and Shorty,' he muttered. 'I even had a draw-and-shoot with Reynolds,' and a thoughtful look crept into his narrowed eyes.

The girl watched in fascinated silence. She did not trust herself to ask the question that pressed against her tightly closed lips. The tall gun-fighter read the question in her eyes and nodded slowly.

'A draw-and-shoot,' he repeated. 'I gave him my card with a bullet hole through it. He handed it back with two holes. All of which means exactly nothing,' he finished slowly.

'It means much,' the girl contradicted. 'I can see it in your eyes. Roaming Reynolds is fast, and you were wondering ...'

Griff Tyson allowed his lips to twitch upward in a slow smile of confidence. 'I found out what I wanted to know,' he corrected softly. 'I knew that he was fast, but there is one who is faster.'

The girl shook her head. 'I don't believe it,' she murmured, and tightened the hands behind her back when Tyson scowled. 'And I am sure he will come' she added confidently.'

The tall gun-fighter shrugged carelessly. 'When I get the Lazy L and the Bar Z Bar, our troubles will be over. You don't seem anxious to help me do it the easy way, and Lassiter and the rest of them mean less than nothing to me.'

'You would do that to an old man?' the girl whispered. 'And you would expect a girl to love a man like you?'

He changed suddenly and caught her in his long arms. The girl started a scream which was muffled against his shoulder, and then the door opened with the face of Ramrod McCall staring from the opening. Griff Tyson loosened his arms and stepped back with a muttered curse.

'Did I send for you?' he barked, and his right hand slapped down to his holster and came out with gleaming metal.

The Deuce of Diamonds foreman held his position and shook his head. 'Yo're getting boogery, Griff,' he said softly. 'I heard the girl scream, and I thought mebbe she had pulled a trick. My mistake.'

Griff Tyson lowered his gun and pouched it with a smooth twist of his wrist. 'Don't make the same mistake again,' he warned quietly, and waited until McCall had stepped back and closed the door.

Bobbie Zander was on her feet facing him with fear in her brown eyes. 'Please,' she pleaded, 'give me time to think!'

Again she was amazed at the sudden change that swept over him. 'Sorry,' he murmured contritely, 'your beauty maddened me for a moment, and I was not myself.'

He stepped toward her with left hand reaching into a pocket. Came out with a knife and turned her to reach the thong that bound her wrists. Severed the rawhide and turned the girl slowly, but Bobbie Zander rubbed her wrists and refused to meet his eyes.

'It would save many lives,' he reminded gently. 'I do not fight to lose.'

The girl shrugged and lowered her head. 'It might be best,' she whispered brokenly, 'if it would save the lives of those I love.'

The tall man was at her side instantly. A smile of triumph spread across his face and swept away the savage cruelty of a moment before. Once more his arms tightened around her supple body, and she made no resistance when he held her close to his swelling chest.

'I love you, Bobbie,' he murmured huskily. 'You can change my whole life. People will forget when we are married, and I was sure that you would see it my way.'

Bobbie Zander closed her eyes and tried to repress the shudder of horror that rippled her muscles. His arms were tremendously strong, and she could feel the rapid pounding of his heart against her breast. Was this the boss of Summit Valley who never showed any trace of emotion?

His left hand came up slowly and played with the curls at the curve of her neck. 'I have waited for months to feel your nearness,' he murmured. 'Nothing else mattered until this morning, and that will not matter long.'

Bobbie Zander swayed and found herself powerless to escape from his arms. Her mind cleared up like fog before a strong mountain wind, but she forced herself to remain quiet.

'Until this morning?' she whispered against his shoulder.

'Until this morning,' and his voice was harsher. 'Roaming Reynolds rode into Summit Valley!'

'Oh!'

He felt the tremble that ran along her arms. 'You are interested in Reynolds,' he accused hotly. 'You have forgotten Manny Lassiter already, but the stranger dies!'

Bobbie Zander closed her eyes and tried to tear herself loose. Griff Tyson tightened his arms and his breathing became more rapid. She could feel the tingle in his hard muscles; knew he was thinking of his meeting with the tall buckaroo.

'But you said it would save trouble,' she whispered in a faint voice.

'That didn't include Roaming Reynolds,' he grated. 'There ain't room enough in Summit Valley for the both of us, no matter what happens!'

The girl stiffened and then relaxed. 'It means that much to you,' she asked quietly, 'just to find out which of you is the fastest with a six-gun?'

'It means more than that to me,' he answered grimly. 'I wouldn't be able to sleep at night if I thought he was the best. And I know I am,' he added very quietly.

Bobbie Zander had recovered from the paralysis that had momentarily numbed her muscles and mind. Manny Lassiter and Roaming Reynolds had ridden to the Bar Z Bar to lend assistance, and they had arrived too late. Her father was lying unconscious on the floor when Ramrod McCall had carried her out to his horse, and she shuddered when she recalled the brutal blow that had felled him.

Perhaps Manny was dead, and the girl felt a swift stab of pain. Roaming Reynolds was the only one she knew anything about, and the knowledge brought a swift resolve. Griff Tyson would not keep his promise even if she sacrificed herself, and again that revulsion of feeling sent a shudder through her young body.

The tall, dark gun-fighter was lost to everything except the nearness of her body. She lowered her arms slowly. Tried to repress the start of surprise when the fingers of her left hand touched the smooth ivory of his gun-handle, while Griff Tyson forgot his studied indifference and lowered his head to find her cheek.

The girl sensed the move and drew closer to him to hide her face against his broad shoulder. Her fingers were creeping down and opening wide. And then she felt his hand tilting her head back.

In a sudden desperate burst of speed,

she pushed down with all her strength and wrapped her fingers around the gun. Griff Tyson whirled like a cat to jam his leg against her arm. Then he crushed her with a grip that wedged the half-drawn gun between them, and Bobbie Zander gasped when the breath left her lungs.

She felt the steel of his muscles pressing the very life from her straining chest. Muscles that bruised her tender flesh and held her in a grip where move- ment was impossible. The yellow lights faded and became blurred. That incredulous grip tightened slowly like the folds of a gigantic snake. No let-up while she sobbed and struggled for just one breath of air, and then the room became suddenly dark.

Griff Tyson threw back his head and clenched his teeth tightly. A wild desire filled his brain. He could tighten his arms just a trifle more. Something would break, and another problem would be solved. Then he relaxed with a sigh and caught the drooping figure, as the girl sagged loosely in his arms.

'I can't do it,' he whispered hoarsely. 'I thought I wanted to kill her, but I can't fight … a woman.'

He turned swiftly when he thought he heard the door shut softly behind him. His gun hung half-drawn in the cut-away holster, and his hand made that blinding draw that had won him the respect of fast gun-fighters. The door was closed, and the room was empty.

'McCall,' he whispered softly, and nodded his dark head.

He lowered his eyes and studied the face of the girl. Held her for a long moment until her firm rounded breasts began to rise and fall with deep breathing. Then he laid her on the couch and walked across the room.

'She's mine,' he muttered. 'But she will have to be won.'

He took down a pair of latigo strings and retraced his steps, no emotion on his face when he bound ankles and wrists securely. Then he leaned over her face and stared at her lowered lashes.

'Not now,' he whispered. 'If I kissed

her ... ?'

Straightening swiftly, he blew out the lamp and opened the door. Ramrod McCall was waiting in the yard at the edge of the porch, holding two saddled horses. He turned slowly to face Tyson.

'You stay here,' Tyson snapped. 'Guard that front room with your life, and the girl will tell me if anything happens. I'll be back before sunrise!'

He jumped his black thoroughbred and roared down the lane. Ramrod McCall watched him curiously and then shrugged his square shoulders.

'His funeral,' he whispered softly, and hunkered down in the shadow of the big porch.

8

Back in the pine-bordered lane on the Bar Z Bar, Roaming Reynolds was finishing his careful study of the trampled ground. Each set of tracks was clear in his mind like the transversing lines of a map. He mounted the deep-chested mountain horse and headed for an opening in the hedge like a man who knows where he is going, and what he will find when he gets there.

The tall buckaroo smiled grimly when the rough branches whipped against his chaps going through the trees. He was positive about his findings, and he tightened his battered Stetson and spurred his horse into a swift lope. Ramrod McCall was up ahead, and this time he might be ... on the. ground.

He would have to pass the deep water-hole at Big Springs whether he headed for the Lazy L or the Deuce of Diamonds, and he could send word to old

Lafe Lassiter by one of the punchers riding night-herd. Too early for Texas Joe to be standing his trick, and he felt a secret longing to have the plucky cowboy by his side.

The yellow moon was riding high above the serrated rimrock to light the rolling valley when Roaming caught the sheen on the water at Big Springs. He checked his horse when he failed to see the Lazy L herd bedded down, and turned his head slowly in an effort to find the night-hawk skylined against the light.

'Can't be more than ten o'clock,' he muttered. 'Texas Joe and Montana was due to relieve them fellers at midnight. Something funny going on here, and I better take time to find out.'

He circled forward slowly to take advantage of the cover afforded by the lava rocks at the edge of the *cienaga*. Stopped quickly and dropped from the saddle when a low moan came from a cluster of boulders off to one side. The sound either came from a man in distress, or else it was a plant to bring him in the open.

His gun was in his hand when he crouched low and worked his way around the rubble. Sweeping the old hat from his head, he poked it above the low breastsworks and waited for a rustler's bullet. When nothing happened he placed the Stetson on top of a rock and slid to a spot six feet away before calltiously raising his head for a quick search of the open.

His blue eyes narrowed when he saw a cowboy lying stiffly in a little hollow between the rocks. He slipped over the barricade and reached for his skinning knife when he recognised a young Lazy L puncher with hands and feet bound tightly; blue bandanna tied between gaping jaws. A trickle of crimson ran down the cowboy's face, and he sat up weakly when Roaming Reynolds severed the saddle-strings and cut the neckerchief away.

'Take it easy, feller,' the tall buckaroo muttered softly. 'Looks like somebody buffaloed you between the horns with the barrel of a six-gun.'

The cowboy nodded and swallowed painfully. 'Glad you come when you did, Roamin',' he croaked, and tried to pull his swollen tongue back in his mouth. 'I was just about to choke when I heard you pounding across the valley. I'm Waco Harper like you might remember. We was dry-gulched, and like as not them rustlers killed my pard, Jim Hanley!'

His deep young voice was bitter and tinged with grief. There is something about rubbing stirrups with a saddle pard, and sharing the same blankets on round-up that brings men closer together. Roaming Reynolds nodded with understanding.

'You and Jim were riding first trick,' he prompted softly. 'Get a hold of yoreself and tell me what happened, Waco.'

'I was riding the outside circle,' Waco muttered hoarsely, and knuckled a tear from his eye. 'I was to meet Jim here like usual, and I lit down to roll me a quirly.'

Reynolds nodded. 'And you thumbed

a match,' he said quietly.

'Yeah, and the next thing I knowed a gun blasted from over yonder. A big jigger jumped out from behind that out-cropping and hit me with his gun-barrel when I made to get to my feet. I went down like a shot steer; and when I come to again, here I was tied hand and foot like a mossy-horn.'

'How long ago did this happen?' Reynolds asked gruffly.

'I don't know how late it is now, but I must have been out here a couple of hours,' the cowboy explained. 'Better get over that-away and see if you can find Jim.'

Keeping down below the rocks so as not to be skylined against the light, the tall buckaroo made his way swiftly across the gravel bed. Big Springs flowed from the heart of a cluster of giant boulders, and Reynolds swore softly and dropped to his knees when he rounded a shoulder of granite and almost stumbled across the body of the missing puncher.

Jim Hanley was down with his head

under him; a grotesque twisted body that told a plain story. Roaming Reynolds growled while his hands felt for a heartbeat, hands that came away smudged with red when he straightened up shaking his head.

'Right through the ticker,' he muttered softly and made his way back to Waco Harper.

'You find him?' the cowboy asked hoarsely. Roaming Reynolds nodded his head. 'Dead,' he answered briefly, and searched the bed-ground for Harper's horse. He spied it grazing on the far side of the water-hole, and a moment later he caught the animal and led it up to Waco.

'Climb aboard,' he said bluntly. 'Ride back to the Lazy L and tell old Lafe what happened here. Wake up Texas Joe and have him meet me in the bosky of pines over near Jacobs Lake.'

'Jacobs Lake,' the cowboy repeated incredulously. 'That's almost in the front yard of the Deuce of Diamonds spread. They'll kill you shore as hell, Roamin'!'

'I'm heading there regardless,' Reynolds answered grimly. 'Ramrod McCall took Bobbie Zander over that-away, and mebbe I will find him on the ground this time. Now you fan that hoss down the hind legs with your quirt and burn the wind.'

'The old man and Manny will be wild,' Waco answered softly. 'Like as not they will order out the whole crew.'

'Forgot to tell you,' Reynolds grunted. 'Manny got burned with a bullet, and he's on his way back to the Lazy L along with old Ely Zander. Now you get going, and tell Joe I'll be counting on him.'

Waco Harper grabbed his bridle reins and hit the saddle without further talk. Roaming Reynolds watched him roar away before mounting his own horse and checking the loads in his gun. His face was thoughtful when he studied the tracks of the rustled herd, after which he neck-reined and pointed toward the Deuce of Diamonds.

'Nine hands on that spread all told,' he tallied softly. 'Shorty Peters and Butch Cawdorn got their needings, and Red

Frazier won't be missed none to speak of. It took all of four men to handle that rustled bunch of shippers. That ought to leave Cliff Tyson and Ramrod McCall with mebbe one hand at the home ranch.'

He circled the water-hole once and frowned in the moonlight. The tracks were heading toward Hidden Valley, but there were many side trails and draws leading to brushy hiding places. His hands fumbled for the makings and then replaced tobacco and papers with a soft sigh.

'That's how they come to get Jim and Waco,' he muttered. 'I hope Waco makes it all right.'

Rattling along at a high lope in the moonlight, Waco Harper kept to cover and urged his horse with quirt and spur. He was beginning to feel dizzy when he saw the lights of the Lazy L up ahead, and old Lafe Lassiter rose to his feet on the porch when the cowboy threw his horse to a sliding stop.

'What you doing here, feller?' the old cattleman bellowed. 'Ain't time for yore relief!'

'Boss,' the cowboy began hoarsely, and half-fell to the packed ground. 'Rustlers hit us down there by the Springs. Knocked me on the head, and killed pore ol' Jim!'

Lafe Lassiter gave back a step. Then he reached for the drooping cowboy and gripped him hard by the shoulders. Shook him a time or two while he tried to collect his scattered thoughts.

'Killed Jim Hanley?' he growled under his breath. 'Pull yoreself together, cowboy!'

Ma Lassiter came out on the porch and leaned against an upright. Born to the open range, she sensed the need for silence and wisely held her tongue. Waco Harper swallowed and straightened his shoulders.

'They killed Jim first shot,' he muttered. 'Tied me up hand and foot, and when I roused 'round the herd was gone.'

Again he stopped, and once more the big cattleman shook him vigorously. 'Who untied you?' he demanded.

'Roamin' Reynolds. I heard him pounding across the valley, and I managed to make enough noise to attract his notice. He cut me loose from them latigo strings, and it was him found the body of Jim.'

'Roamin'?' and old Lafe leaned forward to peer into the dazed man's eyes. 'Was Manny with him?'

'Roamin' sent me high-tailin' back here to let you know,' Waco muttered, and braced himself when he staggered. 'Said to tell you Manny got a bullet burn back yonder on the Bar Z Bar, and old Ely was bringing him here. Roamin' wants Texas Joe to meet him in that pine bosky over at Jacobs Lake.'

'Jacobs Lake,' Ma Lassiter interrupted. 'That's close to the Deuce of Diamonds. Bobbie?' she gasped with sudden realisation.

Waco Harper nodded his head. 'Ramrod McCall got her,' he growled savagely. 'Roamin' read the sign and hit out for the Deuce of Diamonds on his own. He don't want no one but the Button chousing over that-away to cloud the sign.'

A low growl came from the shadows at the side of the porch. Texas Joe walked out stiff-legged with his right hand rubbing the grip of his old gun. Came straight up to Waco Harper and stared into the dull eyes of the staggering cowboy.

'How long since you left my pard?' he demanded hoarsely, and his voice changed on a high note. 'Get it told, feller!'

Waco Harper tried to raise his weary, battered head. 'Just time enough for me to get here from Big Springs,' he croaked painfully. 'He said for y:ou to gear yore tops and smoke yore hoss's hocks getting to Jacobs Lake.'

Texas Joe jerked away and stopped when Ma Lassiter caught him in her arms. 'Joe,' she said softly. 'Hold up a spell, young 'un.'

'I gotta go,' he almost snarled, and tried to release himself. 'My pard is making his fight out there all alone, and he's counting on me to cover his back like always!'

'I know,' the silver-haired woman answered softly. 'But he's taken time out to ride over to Big Springs. He wanted to let Pa know; and he can't do much in the dark.'

Texas Joe relaxed his muscles and nodded his head.

'Yo're right, Ma,' he murmured gently. 'I'll listen while you tell it.'

'It's Bobbie,' the woman answered with a sigh. 'You must hold yore head now, Joe. It might make a lot of difference if you go slamming over there with yore hand itching on the grip of yore gun. Hold yoreself down, Joe.'

Texas Joe nodded and kissed her cheek. 'Glad you talked me out of spooking, Ma,' he said gratefully. 'It's what Roamin' is always telling me. To stop fighting my head like a yearling bull.'

'You get along,' old Lafe cut in sternly. 'Rope out that rangy roan and give Roamin' the best you got. Me and some of the boys will be over there come daylight. Now, you fog it!'

Texas Joe roped and saddled the big roan and was gone within three minutes. They watched him speed down the shadowy lane sitting low in the saddle, and with a grim smile on his thin young face. Ma Lassiter sighed when the sound of his horse had died away.

'He has the makings of a man,' she murmured, and then raised her head to listen. 'Horses coming, Pa,' she announced quietly.

'Thought it was Joe coming back,' the old cattleman murmured. 'Look, Ma. It's old Ely bringing Manny. The boy must be hurt bad!'

'My boy!'

Ma Lassiter was down the steps like a girl and ran forward to meet the two riders. Old Ely reined in and handed the bridle of Manny Lassiter's horse to old Lafe. Lafe Lassiter swore softly and threw it on the ground, and then he was lifting his son from the high saddle.

A moan escaped the lips of the big foreman. 'My shoulder,' he muttered. 'Easy, old-timer.'

Ma Lassiter was at his side bracing him with her plump arms. 'Is it bad, Manny?' and her voice was strong and soothing.

'Naw,' the big cowboy grunted. 'Only thing is I'm a free bleeder and lost a bucket of blood. Old Ely got worse than me. They liked to've knocked his brains out with a gun-barrel.'

'I'm fit as a fiddle,' Zander growled savagely. 'I wanted to go with Reynolds, but he got me under his gun and made me promise to bring yore chip back home.'

He turned slowly and stared at Waco Harper weaving groggily toward the bunkhouse. 'More grief?' he asked quietly.'

'Tyson rustled that herd of shippers we moved over to Big Springs,' Lassiter explained bitterly.

'They killed Jim Hanley, and knocked Waco out with a gun-barrel like they did you. Roamin' rode past there to send me word and found Waco tied up like a yearling.'

Deep growls came from the little

man's corded throat. 'Roaming Reynolds,' he spat. 'Seems to me like that big saddle tramp is everywhere at one time. Makes us look like a crowd of pilgrims who don't know our way about!'

'I killed a man,' Manny Lassiter interrupted, and his deep voice held a note of regret.

Ma Lassiter gripped his big hand and bit her lip. 'You, Manny?' she asked, and her voice expressed doubt.

Manny Lassiter nodded his big head. 'Red Frazier,' he muttered. 'It was him shot me through the shoulder.'

'Manny hit him with his fist,' Ely Zander explained with open contempt. 'He forgot all about the gun riding in his holster, but he done a right good job regardless.'

'Forgot yore gun and killed a man?' old Lafe repeated slowly. 'It don't make good sense, son!'

Ely Zander cackled derisively. 'Hit him with his fist once, and broke that killer's neck,' he explained dryly. 'And then he wanted to high-tail over to the Deuce of

Diamonds and tie into Ramrod McCall with his maulies!'

'I'll kill him with my naked, bare hands,' the young giant growled fiercely, 'for what he did to Bobbie!'

'You won't,' old Lafe contradicted flatly. 'I hate to admit it, but a better man than you or any of us has gone to take that salty Ramrod his needings. Yeah; I mean Roamin' Reynolds!'

'I got a score to settle with that brash gun-fighter,' Manny growled. 'He hit me with his fist and knocked me cold!'

'Roamin' did that to you?' old Lafe asked slowly.

Old Ely Zander chuckled again. 'Manny swung out from his hip and tried to put Roamin' away first,' he explained. 'That tall buckaroo just turned his head enough to miss the punch, and then he rocked one over that didn't go more than a foot. Manny fell face forward, and Reynolds caught him and eased him to the floor. We dressed his shoulder while he was still sleeping.'

'He done just right,' Lafe Lassiter

growled. 'You know better than to use yore fists against gun-smoke, Manny!'

'I ain't a gun-fighter,' the big foreman muttered, 'but I'll get even with Reynolds for what he done.'

Ma Lassiter came in front and faced her son squarely. 'You won't,' and her voice was sharp. 'Right now he is facing death to save the girl you love.'

'And the man don't live who can make a play at him and make it stick,' Ely Zander seconded. 'I threw down on him when he hit you, and he matched his draw against my drop. Only I didn't have the hammer eared back to go,' he explained ruefully.

'I'll get him,' Manny grunted. 'I ought to be over there right now,' and he started for his horse.

Ma Lassiter had him by the arm and swung him toward the steps. 'You are going to bed,' she said sternly. 'You and Waco Harper both. You leave the fighting to fighting men!'

'You turn me loose,' the young foreman snarled angrily, and held up his right fist. 'That there done killed one man to-night, and it can do the same again.'

Lafe Lassiter glanced at the big, skinned knuckles and grunted to express his disgust. 'What you reckon Roamin' will be doing all that time?' he asked softly, 'or Ramrod McCall, if you happened to cut his sign, and him riding gun?'

'Not only that, but you tried once,' Zander pointed out softly. 'You never even saw what hit you, Manny. That tall jigger saved yore life when he rocked you to sleep. You never saw speed until you see him come uncorked!'

Manny Lassiter stiffened and shook himself. His head seemed to clear suddenly, and he turned to Waco Harper as though he had just noticed the Lazy L rider.

'Looks like we're taking the worst of it, all the way around,' and now his voice was clear. 'I'll do like you said, Ma. C'mon, Waco.'

Ma Lassiter smiled and took an arm of

each man. Led them up the broad steps and into the house while Ely Zander and old Lafe stared at each other.

'You feel all right, Ely?' Lassiter asked anxiously.

The little man bristled indignantly. 'I'm a real cow hand,' he snapped. 'The kind you can't kill unless you cut off his head and hide it from him. You and me going to stand here and bite our finger-nails?'

'Just wanted to know,' old Lafe answered grimly. Like as not Roaming and Joe are going to need some help. Better turn that animal in and rope you out a fresh hoss.'

Ely Zander nodded and high-heeled to the holding corral. 'Lafe,' he said softly, and his old voice was broken. 'You reckon they'll hurt my gal?'

Lafe Lassiter stopped his throwing arm and drooped his wide shoulders. 'She's the prettiest filly in these parts,' he muttered, 'and Griff Tyson knows he has us both beat if he can hold Bobbie.'

Ely Zander half-drew his gun. 'I'll

kill him the minute I get him under my sights,' he threatened. 'Should have done it when we found out that he had changed yore brand to throw the blame on me. Gentle Annies, that's what we've been,' he accused bitterly.

Old Lafe stepped close and touched the little man's arm. 'Can't you see it, pard?' he asked slowly.

Zander raised his head and stared angrily. 'I can see that we've been a pair of old fools,' he rapped.

'Roaming Reynolds,' Lassiter continued. 'He don't let on to be anything but a gun-fighter. We thought we were better than him. Sorter looked down on him like Manny done tonight. And all the time tat all buckaroo was doing what had to be done. Fightmg the devil with his own tools!'

'I can see it now,' Zander agreed. 'But in a way he was responsible for them taking Bobbie. If him and the Button hadn't killed Shorty Peters and Butch Cawdorn ...?'

'Tyson would have had two more

fighting men,'

Lassiter added dryly. 'That there's the point, you old raw-rider. You and me has been getting old, and it's about time we was priming our cutters and making some smoke of our own!'

'Which same I aims to do *pronto*,' and Zander made a dexterous cast and roped out a barrel-chested grulla.

Old Lafe Lassiter roped out his own horse and saddled in silence. Then he rode to the bunkhouse and growled at the sleepy riders, sitting on the edges of their bunks cleaning their guns.

'You jiggers lost a pard to-night,' he informed them gruffly. 'What you aim to do about it?'

The tall Montana came to his feet and spoke for the crowd while they growled approval. 'We aim to square up for Jim Hanley, boss, and on top of that we aim to fight for the iron that pays us our wages and grub. Spell it out, ol' Lafe!'

'That's what I wanted to find out,' Lassiter grunted. 'Get out there and saddle yore broncs for a fast ride. Griff

Tyson wanted war, and he's going to get it. Ramrod McCall went over to the Bar Z Bar to-night and made off with Bobbie Zander. Reckon you know what Bobbie means to Ma and me, and Manny,' he added softly.

He waited in the darkness while boots were stomped on and cartridge shells dumped into pockets; nodded with satisfaction when fighting growls came from the bunkhouse. Then he rode to the house when he saw Ma Lassiter come out on the porch.

'Yeah, Ma,' he called softly in his wind-roughened voice. 'You put them jiggers to bed?'

'I put them there, but I'm afraid they won't stay put,' the silver-haired woman answered. 'I wanted to speak to you about Bobbie.'

'Go on and say it,' he studied her face.

'Manny thinks the same thing,' she whispered.

'You saw it, too, Lafe. She thinks a heap of Roamin'.'

The big cattleman growled deep in his

throat. 'You can't chip in on that kind of a layout,' he said slowly, and then his faded eyes brightened. 'Roaming Reynolds is a fighting man,' he continued, 'he always will be.'

'And every girl likes a man who can take care of her,' Ma Lassiter whispered. 'Manny didn't do it.'

'He will from now on out,' the old cattleman declared positively. 'He kinda woke up after what you told him before you cut him out of the herd and bedded him down.'

'I'm afraid,' the woman murmured, 'Roamin' could have her for the asking. I'm afraid he might ask after to-night.'

'Now looky, Ma,' old Lafe said earnestly. 'You take a gun-fighter. They get the tang of powdersmoke in their blood, and nothing else seems to matter much. They just can't help themselves when they hear about another top-hand gun-hawk cutting in on their territory.'

'Lafe,' she said suddenly. 'I believe you are right. And Griff Tyson is also a gun-fighter.'

'He won't be for long,' the old cattle-man growled. 'Not after he steps back for a show-down with Roamin'!'

'Can't you stop it?' Ma Lassiter asked hopefully. '... I love that boy, Lafe.'

Lafe Lassiter pulled at his white cow-horns and rumbled deep in his throat. 'Putting it that-away, I reckon you might say I do, too,' he admitted. 'But nothing on earth will keep them two from lock-ing horns.'

'I'll tell Manny,' and Ma Lassiter moved up the steps. 'I know it will make him feel better.'

'Wait up a spell,' Lafe Lassiter called sharply. 'I don't like the idea of our chip finding what he wants at the expense of some gent who risks his life to save us, when we can't save ourselves. Leave well enough alone, Ma. Them young 'uns will work it all out without no help from us.'

'I believe you are right, Lafe,' and the woman nodded thoughtfully. 'Do take care of yourself.'

'It's about time I was learning,' the old cattleman growled softly. 'I don't feel any too proud as it is.'

Ely Zander rode out from the shadows with three Lazy L cowboys close behind. All carried Winchesters under saddle-fenders, and the Bar Z Bar owner called gruffly:

'You all talked out, Lafe?'

Lafe Lassiter waved a gnarled hand at his wife and rode to meet them. 'Got it all,' he barked. 'From now on we let our guns do most of the talking. Tyson wanted war, and he's going to get it until his outfit, or ours, quits doing what they've been doing!'

'It's my idea to cut down by Big Springs and pick up trail where they rustled the herd,' Zander suggested.

Lafe Lassiter raised his head to stare. 'And Bobbie?' he asked softly.

'An army would only get her killed,' and Zander's voice was a muffled whisper. 'I've been thinking while you was talking to Ma. Most of the Deuce of Diamonds crew is with that rustled herd, and we both know that Roaming Reynolds don't need any help.'

'If he does, he has it,' Lassiter agreed earnestly. 'Texas Joe rode out to meet Roamin' just before you came in with Manny. Hit them horses with the rowels, you rannies!'

9

To those who knew Summit Valley, Jacobs Lake meant the Deuce of Diamonds. Roaming Reynolds broke his horse out of the fast lope that had carried him across the rolling mountain meadows from the Lazy L. Stopped to blow the animal while he watched the moonlit waters of the big lake and tried to form a plan.

He nodded with satisfaction when the pointed crests of stubbly pines showed against the sky, for the trees would provide some shelter against detection. Not that he lacked confidence, but the tall young gun-fighter had learned the ways of outlaws from bitter experience.

A good hand with a rifle could remain hidden in one of the many brush-covered draws. One gentle press of the trigger finger would decide the margin of victory. Griff Tyson had the men who would gladly press that trigger, and

Reynolds was not so sure about the riders of the Lazy L.

The tall gun-boss knew that the issue would be determined in a more personal way. Griff Tyson was proud of his prowess, just as he, Roaming Reynolds was confident of his own ability. Years of practice had brought to them both a sure co-ordination of mind and muscles, and with it the rancour of jealousy that became a living part of every master of the six-gun.

Now the sweating horse was again breathing evenly, and Reynolds headed into the timber and held his mount to a walk. He could see the dim outlines of the ranch buildings in the distance, and he loosened the gun in his holster against any possibility of hang. A man wouldn't get a second chance to correct a mistake against either Ramrod McCall or Griff Tyson.

A long lane of pines led up to the Deuce of Diamonds, and Reynolds kept close to cover while he walked his horse between the trees. He was half-way through the shadowy passage when thudding hoofs pounded toward him from the house. Reining into the brush, he leaned over to hold the nose of his horse against a warning nicker while his narrowed eyes strained through the gloom.

The thudding hoofs came closer. Roaming Reynolds drew his gun swiftly when the rider came into view, sucked his breath in sharply when he recognised the square shoulders of Ramrod McCall. Twice he raised the heavy gun in his right hand, and both times he lowered the weapon with a little shrug of impatience.

'Might bring down the lightning,' he muttered softly. 'And with the girl up there ...?'

The slim-legged black thoroughbred flashed past his hiding place without breaking pace. The tall gun- fighter holstered his gun and stared at the broad back of Ramrod McCall until the sound of hoof-beats died to a whisper, while a devil of desire pulsed through his veins to make the tips of his fingers tingle.

'Didn't dare take a chance,' he growled softly. 'Griff Tyson comes first, and he ought to be up at the house.'

A moment later he rode up the long lane and swung down to tie his horse well back in the trees. Cutting a saddle-string, he made a loop over the smooth muzzle to prevent a warning nicker. McCall had worked the same plan on the Bar Z Bar, and two could play that game. His shoulders were stooped when he stalked up the rest of the lane in the deeper shadows of the pines.

He stopped again where the trees ended, and he studied the broad yard until the locations of the vanous buildings were clear in his mind. He made out the tack shed close to the long bunkhouse, and shifted his eyes to the main ranch house. A light was burning low in the front room, and the tall buckaroo stiffened slightly when he saw a cowboy hunkered down in the shadow of the porch. Only the glow of a burning cigarette had warned him of the guard.

For a moment he studied the sentry,

and then he removed his spurs to prevent the jingle-bobs from betraying his presence. After which he began to creep through the brush while he circled the rambling old house.

Occasionally a horse would snort back in the holding corral to break the chilly stillness. The tall creeping figure reached the back of the house and inched his way along the weathered siding until he came to a jutting corner of the front porch. There he paused again and put both feet down lest straining muscles would creak to betray him.

Just around the corner he detected the sounds of deep, heavy breathing. The silent guard could not be more than twenty feet away, and Reynolds drew a slow deep breath and started forward. Placing the thin soles of his hand-made boots carefully with each advancing step.

Ten feet away he could see the crouching guard under the shadow of the porch rail. A gun-shot now might spoil his plans, and then a twig cracked under his slowly shifting boot. The sentry levered up, with hand slapping down for his holster. Reynolds was caught off balance, but he righted himself and went for his gun just as a flash of orange stabbed at him from the murky gloom.

He felt the tug of the bullet against his calfskin vest while his own thumb was dogging back the hammer. The flash of his gun outlined his body briefly before the sentry could fire again, and the tall buckaroo cleared the space between them in one long jump.

The Deuce of Diamonds cowboy dropped soggily to the ground with the smoking gun spilling from nerveless fingers. Reynolds grunted and held his hand while he crouched below the level of the porch. Then he jumped across the twitching boy and hit the planking on his heels. Skidded through the door and shifted to a sidewall with his gun making little jabbing motions while his slitted eyes searched the room.

Nothing moved in the yellow glow of the low-burning lamp. Bobbie Zander was lying on a low couch, tied hand and foot. The tall buckaroo held his position and watched a door leading off to a back room. Waited tensely for Cliff Tyson to come through, and finally shrugged with disappointment when the silence became oppressive.

Perhaps the Deuce of Diamonds had slipped out through the kitchen to circle the house. Reynolds strained his ears for a foot-fall and faced the front door, leaning forward. Minutes passed with no sound to break the silence. After which the tall gun-fighter expelled his breath noisily and turned to stare at the girl.

His left hand reached for his knife as he crossed the room jerkily, fumbled with the blade and severed the thongs with two quick slashes. A moment later Bobbie Zander was on her feet, reaching toward him.

'I knew you'd come,' she whispered huskily, and threw her arms around him while a shudder rippled over her lithe body. 'I was sure you would find the trail!'

The tall cowboy shifted his feet uncomfortably and holstered his gun. The nearness of her soft body was a new experience that dulled the sharpness of his mind, and lessened his sense of hearing. He could feel her heart beating wildly against his chest, and he patted her shoulders gently.

'Don't take on now,' he whispered. 'You got to keep up yore nerve.'

The girl shuddered and clung to him tightly. Roaming Reynolds filled his big chest with a deep breath until the clinging arms began to slip. Then he slowly disengaged himself and held the girl at arm's length.

'Better tell me about it,' he murmured gruffly, and left her to blow out the light. A soft silvery glow filled the room, but the gun-fighter shrugged and came back to the girl.

'Father?' the girl whispered, and searched his craggy face with fear in her brown eyes. 'He was down on the floor, bleeding bad, when Ramrod McCall carried me out!'

'Old Ely is safe and raring to trigger a gun,' Reynolds answered grimly. 'And Manny Lassiter done killed a man to-night trying to save you.'

The girl drew away and stared at him. 'Manny killed for me?' she whispered.

He nodded. 'I'll tell a man he did. He killed Red Frazier with one blow of his fist. Frazier shot Manny up some, but nothing serious. Met that Deuce of Diamonds killer right there in the Bar Z Bar lane not far from the house.'

'I heard the shooting,' the girl answered, and tried to cover the sob in her throaty voice. 'I thought Manny was … dead!'

'The big feller takes a heap of killing,' Reynolds muttered. 'Where was you to hear Frazier's gun?'

'On the other side of the hedge, among the trees,' the girl explained. 'Ramrod McCall had me in front of him with my hands tied and a gag in my mouth. I heard the horses go down, and for a moment I thought McCall was going to leave me and kill both you and Manny.'

Roaming Reynolds stiffened. 'McCall,' he whispered. 'You know where he went?'

'Griff Tyson left him here to guard me,' the girl answered. 'I heard the shot outside just before you came in and my heart stopped beating there for a time. I thought he had shot you from the dark.'

Reynolds shrugged. 'He lit out on that black hoss of his just as I started up the lane,' he muttered. 'Left a cowboy to guard the house and the feller saw me when a twig snapped under my boot. He got first shot,' and again the tall gunfighter shrugged.

'Dead?' the girl whispered.

'I'd tell a man!'

The girl stared at him through the silvery light of the moon, and when she again spoke her voice was a low whisper. 'Manny, he didn't come with you?'

Roaming Reynolds shook his head. 'He was all for coming over here to fight McCall and Tyson with his fists. I argued him out of it, and sent him back to the Lazy L with old Ely. You say Griff Tyson was here?'

The girl came closer and gripped his hands. 'He said I would have to marry him, or he would kill Lafe Lassiter and my father,' and her voice trembled. 'And you,' she added.

Roaming Reynolds snorted. Again he felt the exhilarating tingle of anticipation surge through his veins. He did not seem to notice the girl's grip on his hands, and she knew he was wrapped up in his own thoughts.

'Griff Tyson will get his chance,' he murmured softly, and then his deep voice changed suddenly. 'You say he wanted to marry you?'

Bobbie Zander felt comforted at the note of jealousy. 'He said he was going to get both the Bar Z Bar and the Lazy L. Promised not to kill Lafe Lassiter and my father if I would be his wife.'

'And you,' the tall cowboy grunted, 'what did you do?'

'He held me in his arms,' and the girl shuddered. 'My fingers touched his gun, and he nearly killed me when I tried to pull it from his holster.'

'He did that to you? He raised his hand against a woman?'

Bobbie Zander shook her head. 'Not his hand,' she explained with her head low. 'He just tightened his arms until my ribs felt like they were breaking. I couldn't get my breath, and then I lost consciousness. When I came to again, I was lying there on the couch all tied up like you found me.'

'Griff Tyson,' and the gun-fighter's voice was gruff. 'You know where he went?'

'It was about cattle,' the girl answered slowly. 'It had something to do with those cattle you and Texas Joe found back there in Hidden Valley.'

'Me and Joe found something else back there' Reynolds said carelessly.

The girl gripped his hand. 'I know,' she murmured and tried to repress the shudder that shook her body. 'Ramrod McCall and Griff Tyson found the same thing.'

Roaming Reynolds raised his head

and stared at her through the half-light. 'Meaning to say they found Butch Cawdorn and Shorty Peters?' he asked thinly.

The girl nodded. 'Tyson was going to kill the both of them for not obeying orders,' she whispered. 'He told them he was saving you for his own gun. And he made Ramrod McCall promise not to …'

'Not to lay back in the dark and shoot me on a sneak,' Reynolds finished for her. 'I'd admire to meet that Deuce of Diamonds right now.'

'I haven't thanked you,' the girl answered earnestly. 'You have done so much for all of us.'

Roaming Reynolds shrugged. 'Done what I was getting paid for doing,' he muttered. 'I hired on as a gun-fighter!'

The girl shrank away from him. She could see the craggy outline of his fighting jaw. The smouldering fires of battle deep in his blue eyes. Her voice was low and hopeless when she spoke, with her head turned away.

'The Lazy L is ruined now. Ramrod McCall bragged about it while he was bringing me here. Now he has gone to help the men who rustled that herd of shippers!'

Roaming Reynolds came to his feet with a jerk. Reached down and raised the girl and started for the door.

'C'mon,' he growled. 'We got to make tracks before they get back here.'

The girl staggered and fell to the floor. 'My ankles are stiff and swollen,' she murmured. 'I can't walk, Roamin'.'

He picked her up in his arms and carried her out on the porch. She shuddered and hid her face in the hollow of his shoulder when she saw the dead cowboy on the ground. Reynolds smiled grimly and picked his way to the side of the building where a saddled horse was tied to the rail.

The girl clung to him and refused to loosen her arms. He could feel the velvety smoothness of her cheek against his chin, and he closed his eyes as a wave of weakness swept over him. A deep growling rumbled up in his throat when he tried again to release himself.

'Reckon you can sit a saddle, Miss Bobbie,' he grunted, and lifted her across the scarred hull. 'I got to meet a pard of mine down yonder at Jacobs Lake. Did Ramrod hurt you any?'

Bobbie Zander loosened her arms and snugged her boots down in the stirrups. 'None to speak of,' she answered huskily. 'He was terribly strong, but Griff Tyson is like a bar of steel,' and she shuddered as she picked up the bridle reins. 'My chest still hurts where he crushed me against him.'

'I'll remember that,' Reynolds muttered harshly. 'And I'll remember about Ramrod McCall when I meet up with him. Walk yore hoss down the lane to where I left my jughead.'

The girl stopped him. 'I'm afraid, Roaming. Griff Tyson made the same threat last month. Said he always got what he wanted, and that he wanted to marry me!'

The tall cowboy faced her in the

moonlight with right hand rubbing the grip of his gun. She stared at the look on his face, and Reynolds turned to her with little ridges of muscle framing his stern mouth.

'Don't you worry yore pretty head none about Griff Tyson,' he said slowly. 'He spoke the truth when he mentioned that there wasn't room enough here in Summit Valley for both him and me!'

'Then you are going to stay here in Summit Valley?' the girl whispered happily. 'Are you, Roamin'?'

'For a spell of time,' he answered carelessly, and refused to meet her brown eyes. 'Now we better be high-tailing to meet Texas Joe and old Lafe Lassiter.'

'And Manny?'

'Manny and me rode over to the Bar Z Bar to get you,' he answered. 'Ma Lassiter fi.ggered you ought to stay with her until this ruckus is settled. We know you will be safe there.'

'I'll stay there,' the girl promised.

'Manny will be mighty glad to hear that,' Reynolds assured her, and frowned when the girl dropped her hand from his shoulder and turned her head away. 'You can nurse him,' he added lamely.

'I guess so,' the girl sighed. 'But I was hoping ...'

'You was hoping he was with me when I rode in here to the Deuce of Diamonds,' Reynolds finished for her. 'He took a slug through the shoulder, but he ought to be up and about in a few days. I know it will help a lot to have you there.'

'We better hurry,' the girl answered, and her voice suddenly sounded tired. 'Ramrod McCall or Giff Tyson might come back to find out what the shootmg was about.'

He stiffened and faced the shadowy lane. 'Might help things if they did,' he answered grimly, and walked away to get his horse.

The girl followed without speaking, and the tall buckaroo disappeared in the heavier brush. She waited until he rode back through the lane; followed him to the valley where the reflection of the moon shimmered on the big water far below.

'You want to wear a gun all the time after this,' he broke the silence, 'and stay close to the Lazy L until Manny gets his feet under him again.'

'I can take care of myself,' the girl muttered resentfully.

He turned slowly and stared at her. 'Did you do it to-night?' he asked quietly ...

The girl bit her lip. 'I'd like to meet Grff Tyson again, when I have my gun,' she answered in a low, grim voice. 'Things would be different after what he did to me!'

'He did what any man like him would do,' Reynolds pointed out. 'You was fixing to kill him with his own gun. You had it half out of the holster when he felt it slipping. Instead of stepping away to free the gun, he crowded close and you got hurt some in the scuffle.'

'You can say that to me?' she whispered incredulously.

He shrugged his big shoulders. 'Didn't

it happen just that-away?' he countered.

The girl sighed and turned her head. 'It happened just that way,' she admitted honestly. 'But he put his hands on me, and I could kill him!'

'So could I,' and she turned at the savagery in his deep voice. 'Manny Lassiter is a pard of mine.'

'Oh!'

He turned his head and stared at the disappointment in her throaty exclamation. The girl was biting her lips to keep back the tears, trying to hide from him the ache that numbed her body.

'We got to think about Manny,' Reynolds continued gently. 'It was him suggested that we go over to the Bar Z Bar to get you and old Ely, yore Pa. He came mighty close to getting himself killed, Bobbie.' His eyes were watching the shimmering waters in the distance. Talking against the time when Texas Joe would ride out to meet him, talking to keep up the girl's spirits. A Texas yell echoed from the pine-fringed border of Jacobs Lake when the two topped a rise and dipped down into a sloping hollow where Deuce of Diamonds cattle were bedded down.

The girl raised her head and came closer to Reynolds when a slim rider left the shadows and raced forward to meet them. Roaming Reynolds was smiling when he snugged the gun back in the scabbard.

'That's Texas Joe,' he grunted. 'I sent word for him to meet me here.'

The lanky cowboy came up fast and slid his horse to a stop a few feet away. His grey eyes lighted up when he recognised the girl, and then he gigged his roan close and gripped her hands.

'Roamin' got there in time,' he almost shouted, and his face expressed disappointment. 'I was hoping to make a hand against that outfit.'

'You will, Joe,' Reynolds promised soberly. 'Ramrod McCall and Griff Tyson are still both on the loose.'

Texas Joe remembered himself and released the girl's hands. 'I was so dang glad to see you,' he murmured. 'Did they hurt you any, ol' pard?'

'I could hug you, Joe,' the girl answered warmly. 'They didn't hurt me any to speak of. Did you see Dad?'

Texas Joe shook his sandy head. 'I roped out that snake-eye and lit a shuck like Roamin' said,' he answered hoarsely. 'Waco Harper rode in with the word that Jim Hanley had been killed. Wouldn't surprise me none if the boss comes fogging it down here with the boys.'

The girl turned to Reynolds accusingly. 'You didn't tell me about Jim Hanley.'

'I didn't have time,' he explained. 'The Deuce of Diamonds made a raid on Big Springs while Manny and me were on our way to yore place. I didn't know it until I stopped there to send word back to Joe.'

'Can't you see?' the girl pleaded. 'We can't fight them that way. They will kill all our men!'

'Not all of them,' Reynolds corrected soberly. 'Only those who try to fight with their fists. You might try to talk some sense into Manny's head while he's down in bed.'

The girl drooped with weariness, and her voice was low and toneless when she answered. 'I'll try, Roaming.'

Roaming Reynolds was keening his ear to listen to some sound far down the valley. He did not seem to hear her, and they watched him for a long moment. 'Hosses coming up,' he clipped. 'Get back there among the trees in case it's that Deuce of Diamonds crowd!'

The three horses moved into the shadows of the trees and waited while the pounding hoofs came closer. It was Texas Joe who first identified the riders.

'That's old Lafe,' he said positively. 'I heard him say he was coming when Manny and old Ely hit the spread.'

'And Dad is with them,' the girl answered. 'Dad! Oh, Dad!'

Old Lafe Lassiter and Ely Zander turned their horses, racing toward the three riders coming from the trees. Three Lazy L cowboys brought up the rear with Winchesters across saddles, and the little cattleman dropped from the saddle and hurried to his daughter.

'Bobbie,' he muttered hoarsely. 'Yo're safe, gal.'

'Thanks to Roaming Reynolds,' the girl answered, and kissed the little man on the cheek while her arms held him tightly.

'Manny Lassiter,' old Ely muttered. 'He was shot up some, Bobbie. I took him to the Lazy L like Roaming said.' Then he stepped back and studied her face. 'You see Griff Tyson?'

The girl shuddered and hid her face against his shoulder. 'I saw him,' she answered in muffled tones. 'He wants to marry me. Said he would . . .'

'Said he would let you and Lafe keep on living,' Roaming Reynolds finished harshly. 'What you gents got to say about that?'

'It's war,' old Lafe answered for the first time. 'I'd lose every head of stock on the Lazy L before I'd knuckle to a killer like him. What did you tell him, gal?'

Bobbie Zander glanced at Roaming

Reynolds and sighed. 'If it would stop all this killing,' she murmured.

'It wouldn't,' the tall gun-fighter rapped out hoarsely. 'And you know it the same as me!'

The girl nodded her head. 'That's what Griff Tyson said. He is living for the time when he will meet you for a show-down.'

Roaming Reynolds smiled grimly. 'Knew it,' he grunted. 'That's the only thing that really mattered to both me and him!'

Texas Joe sidled close to his tall pard. 'Spoke like a man, Roamin',' he praised. 'And you can count on me to back you up all the way.'

Ely Zander stared and then turned to study the face of his daughter. For the first time he noticed her utter weariness, and he growled in his throat and patted her hand.

'Ramrod McCall,' he asked. 'He dead?'

The girl shook her head. 'He went to help the men who rustled the Lazy L herd,' she answered slowly.

'He dogged it,' Reynolds accused harshly. 'I'll settle with him, but right now we got other work to do!'

10

The faint light of approaching dawn was lighting the highest peaks of the Vermillion Cliffs. Summit Valley was still in darkness except for the hazy light of a paling moon. Ely Zander was hunkered down beside his daughter, and old Lassiter stared at the tall buckaroo and tried to read what was going on in his mind.

'I left Manny and Waco Harper at the house with Ma,' he explained to Reynolds. 'What's this other work we go to do right now?'

'Figgered mebbe Texas Joe had told you,' the gun-boss answered softly. 'Him and me run across a blind valley back in the brakes where Kanab creek cuts a bend. Better than a thousand head of Deuce of Diamonds critters held back there. Most of them long threes and fours,' he added pointedly.

Old Lafe showed his disappointment. 'Thought you was going to say they was

Lazy L critters,' he muttered.

'That's just what they are,' Reynolds clipped. 'Griff Tyson had a good reason for picking the brand he did, and he had a better one for buying that foundation stock from you three years ago. Hunker down here where you can see while I show you something interesting.'

He swung down from the saddle and took a thick tally pencil from a vest pocket. Smoothed the damp ground with his hand and moved aside until the fading light fell between them. Then he started to draw a few lines while old Lafe and Ely Zander sat on their heels and watched him sulkily.

Bobbie Zander leaned back against a tree while the Lazy L cowboys sat their saddles and faced different directions to guard against a surprise attack. The tall buckaroo gripped his stubby pencil and drew a brand.

'Here's the Lazy L,' he explained softly. 'Now you gents watch me close while I do a little sleight of hand work.'

'I've had that brand for more than

twenty years,' Lassiter complained irritably. 'Reckon I ought to know it when I see it.'

Roaming Reynolds continued to draw without making answer. His pencil scratched sideways to enclose the Lazy L. Then he added a curve at the top and bottom of the Letter L and leaned back to watch the face of old Lafe Lassiter. The cattleman stared for a long minute, and his voice was a husky whisper when he spoke.

'It ain't a Lazy L no more. He's vented it to make a Deuce of Diamonds slick as a whistle!'

'That's right,' Ely Zander snapped. 'Now I reckon you know what happened to yore calf tally the past two years or more!'

'I been looking at that Deuce of Diamonds brand for three years and never figgered it out,' and Lafe Lassiter rubbed his stubbled chin. 'You say Tyson is holding them critters somewhere close around here?'

'Right back in a blind valley not more

than ten miles from here,' Texas Joe interrupted eagerly. 'That's where Roaming and me met Shorty Peters and Butch Cawdorn. Ramrod McCall sent them out there to guard the bottle-neck, and we found out all we wanted to know.'

'What we waiting for?' Lafe Lassiter growled, and climbed erect to hitch the gun-belt on his thick hips. 'There's seven of us here not counting Bobbie, and she can make a hand with the best when it comes to working stock.'

'Yeah, working stock,' Texas Joe muttered softly. 'From the way you all made medicine, it didn't sound to me like we was going to do that kind of work.'

Lafe Lassiter turned slowly and stared at the tall buckaroo. 'Just a minute,' Reynolds said quietly. 'Griff Tyson is on his way to Paradise to talk price with the cattle buyers. Looks like you might let him make a deal, and then sell at the same figger when we get yore herd back.'

Old Lafe growled deep in his throat. 'They won't take 'em now,' he rumbled. 'Account of them critters being burned with the Deuce of Diamonds iron.'

'That's what I'm getting at,' Reynolds drawled softly. 'Did you ever hold a green hide up to the light and look through the brand?'

Lafe Lassiter caught his breath and nodded slowly. Recognition crept up in his eyes when he nodded his head. Ely Zander slapped his lean thigh and muttered his understanding.

'You can always make out the new burns,' he agreed.

'Roamin', I ain't never going to let you go,' Lafe Lassiter shouted excitedly. 'We never thought about it, but you can always tell a vented brand that-away and no mistake!'

'All we have to do is furnish proof to the U.S. Inspector,' Reynolds added with a grim smile. 'Not only that, but the rest of yore shippers from Big Springs was shoved back into that valley tonight after the rustlers killed Jim Hanley.'

Texas Joe mounted his horse and turned to the three Lazy L cowboys. 'You jiggers follow me and Roamin',' he said grimly. 'We know the way into the bottle-neck, and now I reckon you know what to do when we come up on those rustlers.'

He sided up to Roaming Reynolds and raked with his spurs when the latter nodded and jumped his horse into a lope. Old Ely Zander and Lafe Lassiter followed with the three Lazy L cowboys bringing up the rear. Roaming leaned across to shout at his pard.

'How's Manny?'

Texas Joe reined down to answer. 'Able to sit up, and he was asking about Bobbie,' Joe said slowly. 'He was sore as hell at you for hitting him the way you done before you left the Bar Z Bar.'

'You did that after Manny was shot?' and Roaming Reynolds turned to find Bobbie Zander riding close to his left side with anger in her dark eyes. He had forgotten about the girl while talking to Lafe Lassiter, and his jaw tightened as he studied her face.

'Had it to do, ma'am,' he answered jerkily. 'He was all for tracking down

Ramrod McCall with his bare hands. He made a pass at me when I objected, so I let him have what he got for his own good … and yores.'

'Wimmin is all that-away, Roamin',' Texas Joe interrupted carelessly. 'Like as not Manny will thank you for what you did when he gets over his mad. He wouldn't have had a chance against McCall, and he knows it as well as we do.'

'I didn't know,' the girl faltered, and came closer. 'Can you forgive me, Roaming?'

The tall buckaroo shrugged. 'Forget about it,' he growled. 'Now you better drop back and ride with yore Dad. We're coming close to Kanab creek; and McCall might have a lookout staked close to give him warning.'

'I won't do it,' the girl snapped, and loosened the gun in her holster. 'I can handle a six-gun as well as you can!'

'You can likewise stop hot lead the same way,' Texas Joe sneered coldly. 'You better do what Roamin' said.'

Reynolds reined down his horse and held up a hand for silence. 'No more wind-jamming now,' he remarked quietly. 'We'll cross the sand bar one at a time so as not to make too much target.'

He wheeled his horse and started down the sloping bank with Texas Joe crowding his heels to cut off Bobbie Zander. The girl fell in behind, and Reynolds walked his horse through the ford and waited. until the rest of the party had made the crossing. Then he motioned for Texas Joe and whispered instructions to the little group.

'There's a drift fence up yonder, men. Tyson has a gate swinging behind it, and Texas Joe will dab his twine like before and swing the gate wide. The rest of us rides through slow and easy to make our fight,' and his eyes narrowed while he studied each grim face. 'Have yore slickers handy so we can booger the herd, and keep the critters running!'

The black of night was giving way before a pale moon when the tall buckaroo counted heads. Eight guns all told, counting the girl. Seven fighting men eager to even the score against them, and Reynolds smiled grimly and turned to the old cattlemen. Lafe Lassiter was trembling with excitement when he nodded his big head.

'They'll high-tail for the opening when powder begins to burn,' he whispered hoarsely. 'I never figgered I'd have to stampede my own critters, but this is one time when it's going to be a pleasure.'

Roaming Reynolds took the lead and rode along the shadows at a walk and stopped by the drif t fence. His young pard made a deft cast and sat his horse down to pull the heavy gate back. The Lazy L cowboys stared in surprise when the bottle-neck gleamed in the fading moonlight.

'Sun-up ain't far away,' Ely Zander muttered softly. 'The last one some of them rustlers will ever see!'

Reynolds shrugged and rode through the narrow pass to lead the way. They could hear the cattle bellowing restlessly up in the valley, and the sounds drowned the clap of the horses hoofs on the lava rock.

'Let's stop for a look-see,' the tall cowboy whispered, and swung down to the ground. The rest of the party sat their saddles, and when he returned several minutes later, his face was grim and purposeful.

'They're up at the far end,' he informed them. 'Get yore guns ready, and ride like hell when we hit the valley, and don't throw yore shots off on my account!'

The men from the Lazy L levered shells into the chambers of their rifles. Roaming Reynolds and Texas Joe lifted their horses into a gallop and hit the valley floor with the Button shrilling the old Texas yell. Keeping close to the right-hand edge of the canyon wall, they raced toward the herd with slickers flapping in the wind.

The restless cattle came to their feet and faced the yelling riders with eyes rolling. Horns started knocking together to add to the din, and then the herd was away at a dead run toward the bottle-neck. Roaming Reynolds swore softly under his breath and veered sharply to cut off a fleeing rider.

Five night-herders left the running cattle and spurred for the shelter of the rocks. Old Ely Zander slid his horse to a stop and stepped down from the saddle. After which he flattened out in the grass and snugged his old Winchester to his shoulder with a soft grunt. He emptied two saddles with as many shots, and grinned when old Lafe Lassiter bellied down beside him and accounted for another raider.

'Squaring up for Jim Hanley,' the Lazy L owner growled, and squinted against the black powder smoke. 'I wonder who that jigger was that Roamin' took out after?'

Ely Zander looked for fresh targets before answering. 'Whoever it is, he won't get far,' he grunted. 'Them two gun-hands is cutting down his lead up yonder.'

Texas Joe and Reynolds were riding

furiously toward the stake-and-rider fence that blocked the regular entrance to the valley. The three Lazy L cowboys were behind the running herd, waving their slickers and firing their six-guns to stampede the panicky steers through the bottle-neck. Every man had his work to do and was doing it.

Texas Joe stung his horse with the hooks and raced at an angle to cut off a Deuce of Diamonds rider. A medium-sized man with broad shoulders, sitting a tall black horse that was running easily and swiftly.

'It's him, and he can't make it,' the lanky cowboy muttered against his teeth. 'And I didn't make no promises!'

Two swift shots blasted out when the fleeing rider turned in his saddle and fired point blank. Texas Joe hurtled over the smooth neck when his sorrel pitched headlong in full stride and turned end over end. Horse and rider thudded solidly and flattened out on the short grass as the rider held his black to the same smooth pace.

Roaming Reynolds was coming up fast. An angry roar burst from his tight lips when he recognised the fleeing cow-boy as Ramrod McCall, too far away for six-gun range. He groaned when the gun blasted to send Texas Joe looping through the air.

His left hand tightened to check the tall roan when he swept past the still fig-ure, and then he changed his mind and spurred with both feet. The half-grown Button was the only intimate friend he. had made in his years of roaming, and his lean jaws cracked with the effort he was making to control the blinding anger that swept over him like an engulf-ing wave.

'Not yet, pard,' he whispered hoarsely, and cut his roan sharply with the rowels.

Ramrod McCall threw a glance over his shoulder and sucked in his breath. Roaming Reynolds was close behind and gaining on him, and he spurred the black unmercifully through the murky half-light. Both horses were going at top speed when the snaky stake-and-rider fence loomed suddenly ahead.

'He can't make it, and I can,' McCall rumbled in his throat. 'Other work to do right now!'

The Deuce of Diamonds foreman jammed his boots firmly in the oxbows and sent the long-legged gelding straight as an arrow for the split-cedar barrier. His right hand came up to lift the thoroughbred into a leaping jump that cleared the fence with inches to spare.

Roaming Reynolds flipped his hand and sent a shot between two jumps of his racing roan. Ramrod McCall felt the high-peaked hat jerk from his head just before the black came down lightly without a stumble, and stretched out into a smooth flowing gait. A sneering smile curled his full lips when he felt the tug of lead against his tall Stetson.

Roaming Reynolds knew that only a trained jumper could take the hurdle, and he was fighting his roan down to avoid smashing into the fence. He finally succeeded, and allowed his horse to blow while he stared after the fleeing rider with gun hanging loosely in his right hand.

The seething anger had now passed away to leave him once more steady and cool. Texas Joe was lying back there in the upper valley, and he neck-reined his roan and loped toward the huddle. Blue eyes snapped open when he saw another man, and he stopped the jumping gun when he recognised the wide shoulders of old Lafe Lassiter.

The Lazy L owner was kneeling beside Texas Joe when the tall bucka-roo stepped down from the saddle and anchored his horse by dropping the split reins to the ground. Hard blue eyes that were now tender and misty when he cra-dled the tousled head of his young pard against his shoulder and reached down to find a heart-beat. Then a smile spread fleetingly across his craggy face while his left arm dropped down to hug Texas Joe affectionately.

'He's just knocked out,' he told old Lafe, and his deep voice hummed with happiness. 'Open up them blinkers and speak to yore ole pard, young feller!'

He waited for the answer that did not come. Fear tugged at his heart when he raised his head and stared into the face of old Lafe Lassiter. The cattleman leaned forward and pointed with a gnarled finger.

'He's doing it,' the old cattleman whispered huskily. Texas Joe sighed deeply and winked his eyes. Then he slowly opened them and stared into the face above him. Snarled with disgust when he saw where he was, and Reynolds propped him to a sitting position.

'Ramrod McCall,' he grunted slowly. 'You git him, Roamin'? You tally for the white-livered son?'

Roaming Reynolds shook his head slowly. 'Only knocked his hat off,' he admitted bitterly. 'He put that black hunter of his at that stake-and-rider fence, cleared it like a bird in flight and lit a shuck through the timber.'

'Dogged it,' Texas Joe sneered. 'He was afraid to stop and face show-down!'

'He wasn't afraid,' Reynolds corrected

quickly. 'He knew the time wasn't right, and McCall is Ramrod of the Deuce of Diamonds. Figgered he had other work to do first.'

'He dogged it,' Joe insisted stubbornly. 'You can't tell me no different when there was just you and him to settle his argument.'

'You ain't using yore head, Joe,' Reynolds reminded softly. 'Like McCall said one time, he wants to meet me when he has both feet on the ground.'

Texas Joe stared for a moment. 'What we keeping him waiting for?' he almost shouted. 'Like as not right now he's lining out for the Deuce of Diamonds, figgering to get Bobbie Zander so's he can take her to a new hideout. We better be riding, Roamin'!'

'You forgetting that Bobbie is down here with us?' Reynolds asked softly, but his right hand stole down to his gun and rubbed the worn handle.

'Naw yuh don't,' Texas Joe snarled. 'You can't cloud the sign on an old hand like me. Ramrod McCall will have both feet on the ground by the time we get to the Deuce of Diamonds!'

Roaming Reynolds sighed and turned his head away. 'You better stay with old Lafe and the boys and help him get the herd bedded down,' he suggested. 'Them cattle has done shoused off across the creek, and I'll see you at the Lazy L.'

'Like hell,' the lanky cowboy exploded blasphemously. 'That jigger shot my hoss and set me on foot. I owe him one for that, and I don't trust him none regardless!'

'But you ain't clear-headed right now,' Reynolds pointed out, and Joe knew that further argument was useless.

'You might need me to cover yore back,' he answered hopefully.

'I'll see you at the Lazy L,' Reynolds repeated firmly. 'You savvy?'

'Yeah, boss,' the lanky cowboy growled hoarsely. 'We'll be seeing you at the Lazy L.'

'Boss?' and Roaming Reynolds vised down on the cowboy's arm while he studied the old cattleman's face.

Lafe Lassiter winked gravely and nodded his head.

'Joe is right, Roamin'. You and him. He is yore saddle-pard like you said yore own self, and next you he rates tophand with that old Colt of his.'

Texas Joe smiled proudly and straightened up. 'That there makes good sense,' he remarked with quiet satisfaction. 'So we will be seeing you at the spread about breakfast time.'

Roaming Reynolds set his lips and studied the two faces thoughtfully. Shrugged when old Lafe Lassiter slapped Texas Joe on the shoulder.

'I'm figgering on you to cover Roamin's back, like always,' he said gravely. 'He just might get in a tight over there. Like he did the time when Butch Cawdorn roped him out of his hull.'

'I know when I'm beat, Lafe,' and Roaming Reynolds made the admission grudgingly. 'I see you caught up one of them Deuce of Diamonds hosses.'

'Feller what rode him into here won't be needing him no more,' Lassiter replied dryly. 'He's yores, Joe.'

Roaming Reynolds caught up his reins and swung to the saddle with Texas Joe copying every move. Lafe Lassiter stepped back and waved a gnarled hand.

'He's fast on the ground,' he warned softly. Roaming Reynolds jerked his head and started across the valley. Both he and Texas Joe reloaded their smoke-grimed guns while the horses racked through the dimly fading moonlight. Silence for a while until guns were once more snugged down in holster leather.

Not a steer remained in the hide-away when they clattered through the pass and twisted down through the narrow bottle-neck. Texas Joe pointed at the drift fence trampled to splinters by the stampeding herd.

'She ain't a blind valley no more, Roamin',' he remarked thoughtfully. 'Shore would make a swell layout for a feller what was thinking about getting married and starting a spread of his own.'

'Yeah, but Manny Lassiter will be the big Augur of the Lazy L one of these days,' the tall buckaroo answered carelessly. 'Like as not he will use this valley for winter feeding. Good grass and water, and plenty of shelter.'

Texas Joe heaved a deep sigh of relief. 'Reckon he will, but you had me some worried there for a while, pard. I seen the way that little filly was eyeing you, and I was wondering if mebbe you was getting tired of roaming around the way we been doing.'

The tall buckaroo turned slowly in the saddle and glared at the Button. 'Looks like that bump didn't knock no sense in that hammerhead of yores,' he growled irritably. 'You know dang well I didn't make up none to Bobbie Zander. She's promised to Manny Lassiter like you and me both knows.'

'Women changes their minds mighty easy sometimes,' Joe muttered doubtfully. 'Course, I don't rightly know what you said to her when you found her all tied up.'

Roaming Reynolds rode closer and shot out a big hand to grip Joe by the shoulder. 'I told her about Manny being hurt,' and his voice was frigid. 'Likewise I told her that I wasn't nothing but a gun-fighter, and never would be. Now you take a hitch in that loose jaw of yores if you want to stay pards with me!'

'Shake, feller,' Texas Joe answered gravely, and extended a grimy paw. 'Like you remarked back yonder there in the Strip, there's lots of places we ain't seen yet. You shore took a load off my mind.'

Roaming Reynolds shook soberly and heeled his roan down the bank into the creek. Far ahead they could hear faint yells that told them the Lazy L cowboys were milling the herd. Texas Joe cocked his head forward and reached out a hand to check his pard's horse.

'Somebody up ahead,' he whispered.

Roaming Reynolds listened and pushed into the trees. 'It's Bobbie and old Ely,' he muttered. 'Hold the nose of yore hoss, cause I don't want to see them two right now.'

They stopped in the dense shadows and waited until the two riders came along the creek to their hiding place. The girl was talking softly with a note of weariness in her deep throaty voice.

'He was wonderful, Daddy. I nearly died of fright when I thought of Griff Tyson coming back.'

'Roamin' Reynolds is an up and comin' young feller,' Ely Zander growled slowly. 'But he's a gun-fighter, Bobbie. The kind that don't never stay put long in any one place.'

'He might,' the girl answered softly, and stopped her horse just beyond the hidden pair. 'I've never felt the same about any other man. When he looks at me …?'

Old Ely Zander snorted. 'Yo're forgetting Manny Lassiter,' he reminded her almost savagely. 'And him laying back there wounded on the Lazy L.'

'Manny wouldn't be here at all if it wasn't for Roaming,' the girl answered stubbornly. 'He's big and strong, but we can't fight rustlers and outlaws with our fists!'

'Reckon yo're right,' the little cattleman agreed soberly. 'Me and old Lafe tallied for three of these rustlers, and I saw Roaming and Joe cutting out after another one.'

'It was Ramrod McCall.' The girl spoke with a shudder. 'He got away,' she added in a whisper.

Old Ely chuckled grimly. 'He won't get far with them two pards after him,' he prophesied. 'I'd bet every steer on the Bar Z Bar on that.'

The girl shook her head. 'McCall was riding that black hunter,' she pointed out. 'Let's move up ahead and meet them. I saw Lafe Lassiter riding up toward the other end.'

Roaming Reynolds was silent when the two rode along the creek and entered the pass. Texas Joe turned his horse to face the tall pard. Spoke his thoughts with a note of worry in his changing voice.

'You heard her, Roamin'. She don't think near so much of Manny Lassiter since you rode into Summit Valley."

'Now looky, Joe,' and the tall buckaroo spoke angrily. 'She loves Manny, and he got a lot of bad breaks. Right now she ought to be back there nursing him, and you and me has other work to do!'

Texas Joe drew a deep breath. 'You and me,' he repeated slowly. 'Meaning Ramrod McCall and Griff Tyson!'

'That's right. About Ramrod McCall, Joe. That's between him and me, and I want you to set yore hoss easy and stay out of the ruckus. I'm riding over there to the Deuce of Diamonds spread to take him showdown like you know.'

'Both of us,' Joe answered grimly.

'Just me,' Reynolds corrected. 'For what he did to the girl ... and for making a try at you. You savvy my wawa?'

'I heard what you said,' Texas Joe grunted. 'But if that Ramrod pulls a gun-sneak, I aim to blow a hole through his back big enough to throw a dog through. I ain't noways gun-proud that-away about drawing evens with a jigger that don't know the code his own self!'

'McCall knows the code,' Reynolds answered sharply. 'All he asks is to have both feet on the ground, and I'm telling you plain he ain't the kind to pull a sneak. Now tighten up yore cinchas and let's ride!'

11

The two riders passed grazing bunches of Deuce of Diamonds cattle when they left the edge of the badlands and struck south toward Jacobs Lake. They held to a steady pace without pushing the horses, and the miles fell behind them in the waning moonlight.

Roaming Reynolds turned in the saddle and stared at the rimrock high up on the distant Vermilion cliffs. Checked his horse and swung down when the moon dropped down behind Mount Logan.

'Better rest the hosses a spell,' he grunted, and hunkered down to build a spill quirly. Flicked the match with his thumb-nail and inhaled deeply in the velvety darkness. He could barely see Texas Joe six feet away, and the younger cowboy fired his own smoke and sucked noisily.

'Not long until false dawn,' he remarked carelessly. 'You aim to take it to him come sun-up?'

'Yeah,' and the tall buckaroo lapsed back into moody silence.

'He's reckoned pretty rapid with his iron,' Texas Joe muttered as though he were talking to himself. 'Up here in Summit Valley they say he's top next to Griff Tyson.'

'Yeah,' Reynolds grunted again. 'There always has to be a gun-boss, regardless.'

'It ain't Ramrod McCall,' Texas Joe snapped.

'It might be the Deuce of Diamonds,' the buckaroo answered carelessly. 'I've seen a lot of fast ones, and Tyson had most of them beat.'

'I'll string along with you nohow,' Texas Joe grunted. 'And I might get some practice if any of them rustling hands made a get-away.'

'Fair enough,' Reynolds monotoned, and the lanky cowboy knew he was thinking of the coming test.

'Yonder comes daylight,' Texas Joe announced softly, and pointed to a streamer of light high in the East.

Roaming Reynolds ground his smoke out under a high heel and stretched to his lean six feet. Hitched up his gun-belt and loosened the heavy .45, tightened his cinchas in the faint light and nodded his head.

'Let's ride,' he said briefly. 'I hate to keep a game gent waiting too long.'

The hazy light grew stronger and held for a few moments. Then darkness fell again, and Texas Joe grumbled under his breath.

'That false dawn always fools me. Feels like there's two nights in one day, or two days in one night. Better hitch a spell and wait for daybreak. We're getting close.'

'Yeah,' and Roaming Reynolds reined to a stop. 'It won't be long till sun-up.'

Twenty minutes later they were walking their horses across the short mile of rolling prairie curving into the lane of scrubby pines. Up the lane they went, to where the body of the guard was visible near the porch. Texas Joe stared for a long moment and spoke in his deep bass voice.

'Steers and men is all the same. Once they gets their heads under them, they can't get up. Looky up yonder, pard!'

Roaming Reynolds was already staring at a lean figure on the broad porch of the Deuce of Diamonds ranch house. Without removing his gaze, he heeled his horse forward and held the roan to a slow walk. He crossed the deserted yard and swung down from the saddle with left hand dropping the split reins for a ground hitch. Then he spread his long legs and hooked his thumbs in his gunbelt.

'Knew you'd be waiting,' he said to Ramrod McCall. 'And I see you got both feet on the ground.'

Ramrod McCall did not smile. The old lines in his hard face belied the youthfulness of his well-knit body, and his bare head was streaked with grey to give him a certain dignity. His hard grey eyes were like mountain granite; his long-fingered brown hands steady as steel.

'Knew you'd come, Roamin',' he said

slowly, and moistened his lips with the tip of his tongue. 'I figgered you'd ride up the lane come sunrise.'

The tall buckaroo nodded gravely. 'I'm glad I only nicked yore hat back yonder,' and he stared at the uncovered grey head, 'for a minute I thought you had rubbed out the Button.'

Ramrod McCall shrugged. 'I put 'em where I call 'em,' he grunted. 'I was aiming at his hoss.'

Texas Joe sat his saddle ten paces away. 'You hit that sorrel plumb centre,' he snarled. 'Which makes me out to ride away from here on that black thorough-bred you dogged it on, seeing as how you won't be needing him no more.'

McCall stared without smiling and nodded his head. 'He's yores if I don't need him no more, Button,' he agreed soberly, and turned back to Reynolds. 'You came here and got the girl?' he asked quietly.

Roaming Reynolds jerked his head. 'That's right. Me and Manny Lassiter hit the Bar Z Bar just about the time you left the house.'

Light dawned in the cold grey eyes of Ramrod McCall. 'So that's how come Red Frazier to get a broken neck,' he murmured. 'But Red got to that big puncher with a slug just the same.'

'You ought to know,' Reynolds grunted. 'You was on the other side of the hedge all the time.'

'Had my hands full,' McCall answered dryly. 'Young Lassiter take it hard?'

'Scratched Manny in the muscle is all,' Reynolds drawled. 'Teach him to stop fighting his head, and not to fight with his fists against guns.'

'Yeah, it might,' McCall agreed. 'He ain't so much of a fighter either way.'

'You might ask Red Frazier when you meet up with him,' Texas Joe interrupted sneeringly. 'Manny only hit that rustler one time.'

Ramrod McCall ignored the lanky cowboy and locked glances with Roaming Reynolds. 'You mind telling me why you took old Ely's girl?' Reynolds asked softly.

The Deuce of Diamonds foreman shrugged. 'Griff Tyson wanted her,' he grunted. 'I don't take 'any interest in women myself.'

'Every gent to his tastes,' Reynolds agreed. 'Looks like the Lazy L is back in business again. All on account of yore men not rubbing out sign, down there by that hidden gate.'

'And they paid for their carelessness,' McCall answered without emotion. 'But the Lazy L won't stay in business very long.'

'You can't tell,' Reynolds came back at him. 'Old Lafe aims to sell that herd we recovered to them same cattle buyers yore boss has been dickering with down in Paradise.'

'I'll tell Griff when I see him,' McCall promised soberly. 'He figgered on matching sixes with you himself, but this is one time when I come first.'

'Yeah, and yore boss is next,' Texas Joe sneered nastily. 'Looks to me like you gents would be about all talked out!'

'You ain't lived long enough to know,' McCall answered evenly. 'And it don't seem like you will live to learn any better. What's the rush?'

Roaming Reynolds stopped Joe with a wave of his hand. 'In a way the Button is right,' he said slowly. 'You talked considerable about wanting both yore feet on the ground!'

'I'm letting yore pard ride away to tell old Lafe Lassiter what happened,' Ramrod McCall murmured carelessly. 'Providing he don't make a pass for his gun.'

'I'll make my pass now,' and Texas Joe leaned over his saddle-horn.

'Joe!'

Roaming Reynolds spat the word like a bullet. Texas Joe twisted his shoulders and growled with disgust. Then he leaned back against the cantle and refused to meet the eyes of his pard. Ramrod McCall watched the little play soberly.

'You ready?'

'Well, it's just about sun-up,' the tall

gun-fighter answered, and pointed to the rimrock in the East. 'Yo're still up there on the porch, and you mentioned something about wanting both feet on the ... *ground!*'

Ramrod McCall gave back a step with a flush sweeping over his face. Then he stepped down to the ground and carefully measured the distance between himself and Reynolds, while the tall buckaroo waited and nodded approvingly when McCall stopped at the usual ten paces.

'Ready,' McCall said quietly.

Both men went into a crouch with shoulders tilting forward. Texas Joe reached for the makings and poured a smoke. He yawned carelessly and started to roll the paper. Swore under his breath when the wrapper split between his trembling fingers. An anxious light burned deep in his pale blue eyes, but neither of the men on the ground paid him any attention.

McCall was poised like a hawk getting ready to strike; Roaming Reynolds was watching those long-fingered brown hands, and the only expression to betray his calmness was in the smouldering blue of his narrowed eyes. His left hand hung loosely in the belt above his moulded holster. Not a movement between the two while the sun ranged up above the serrated peaks full-born.

'Right there between you,' Texas Joe whispered silkily, so that his voice would not set off tautened muscles. 'Looks to me like a centipede hunting his grub.'

Ramrod McCall frowned and lowered his eyes carefully. A six-inch centipede was poised before a moth-hawk that had been caught by the rising sun. Neither insect moved so much as a feeler, and Texas Joe grinned when he saw Roaming Reynolds watching. 'Let that centipede give the sign,' Joe suggested, but somehow his voice was dry and rasping. Every minute the fight was postponed was another minute his tall pard would live.

'Suits me,' McCall answered softly, and barely moved his lips. 'Well?'

Roaming Reynolds started to nod and

stopped the movement when his hat cast a shadow out on the ground toward the insects. 'Like you said,' he murmured.

Once again the two crouched low with eyes fastened on the glistening centipede. Every joint in that long slim body was poised for swift and deadly action. The giant moth hung suspended with great wings resting in the dust, and then the beady black eyes raised slightly and saw the killer.

Texas Joe hardly dared to breathe while he stared with open mouth. The moth seemed to gather its muscles, and even at the distance, the silent watchers could see the centipede set all its feet without seeming to move. Now the moth was staring with little eyes contracted. Trying to furnish strength for muscles paralysed with fright.

Ramrod McCall expelled his breath jerkily and refilled his chest slowly. Roaming Reynolds heard the soft sound and copied the action. And then ... the moth uncurled a long coiling feeler instinctively.

The lightning struck like sudden thunder riding out of a clear sky. One twisting, sinewy move hurled the centipede forward with mandibles behind the hind legs sinking into the plump body of its victim.

Like a flashing reflection, the Deuce of Diamonds Ramrod made his strike like a hawk in full flight. Still as the mountain air one second; galvanized into deadly action the very next. His hand slapped down with fingers cuddling the grip of his gun, and the polished metal leaped up hissingly against the oiled leather of his scabbard.

Roaming Reynolds dropped his hand at the very first twitch of shoulder muscles. His thumb locked over the hammer while his wrist was swivelling sideways on the up-pull. Pale flame licked hungrily from the tilting muzzle before the blasting roar snuffed out the gun-light.

A second roar echoed his shot when Ramrod McCall triggered a slug through the bottom of his holster. The Deuce of Diamonds foreman staggered back and tried to drag his smoking Peacemaker clear, but death overtook him to send him toppling like a lightning-struck pine in a mountain thunderstorm. He pitched forward with hand locked to the handle of his gun, and Roaming Reynolds lowered the hammer of his own gun and pouched the weapon with a soft sigh.

Just a few feet from the dead man's head a silent struggle was still ensuing. The giant moth was flopping its great wings wildly. Several times it lifted the glistening centipede from the ground. Roaming Reynolds was staring in silent satisfaction and Texas Joe was leaning forward with perspiration dripping from his chin.

The centipede rippled its jointed body and caught a hold with every foot biting deep. Then the tail snapped over and down with the poisoned pincers clamping to release a stream of death. The big wings folded gently, and the centipede wriggled away and disappeared under the porch.

Texas Joe grunted and raised his head.

Roaming Reynolds met his glance and turned to stare at the body of Ramrod McCall.

'His feet is still on the ground,' Texas Joe said softly, and swung down from the saddle. 'I like to shook myself apart there for a minute, worrying about that black gelding.'

Roaming Reynolds did not smile. 'You figgered he might shade me, eh?' he asked bluntly.

'He was calm and steady as a rock,' the lanky cowboy admitted. 'There wouldn't be much fun chousing over the hills by myself, pard.'

'And then you saw that centipede,' Reynolds grunted. 'You threw him off some when you interrupted. He was all ready to go.'

'He got all ready now, didn't he?' Joe answered. 'A feller can do better work when he has a sign.'

'A gent can't do his best fighting when he's wrong,' came the answer. 'Ramrod knew he was wrong when we caught him out there in Hidden Valley, and likewise when he admitted to stealing the girl.'

'He knew it was deadline,' Texas Joe agreed. 'Otherwise he wouldn't have gone against his boss the way he done.'

'You mean Griff Tyson?'

Texas Joe nodded. 'You heard him yore own self. Said Tyson had you marked for his gun, but this was one time Tyson could take seconds.'

'That's right,' Reynolds grunted. 'But he was one game gent if you was to ask me.'

'And right now he's deader than four o'clock,' Joe muttered, and loosened his latigo to pull the saddle from his sweating horse.

'Wait a spell,' Reynolds objected. 'What you aiming to do?'

'Gear up a new hoss,' Texas Joe answered gruffly. 'You heard what McCall said before he stepped down off the porch.'

'Yeah,' Reynolds agreed tonelessly. 'And we got to take care of the corp. He was dead game right up to the time his ticker stopped pumping. Trying to give his muscles the old go-ahead.'

Texas Joe faced around quickly. 'You mean bury the gent?' he almost shouted, and waited for his pard's answer.

'Head and heels,' Roaming Reynolds answered soberly. 'We can carry him inside and cover him up on that couch where I found Bobbie Zander. A couple of those Deuce of Diamonds hands got away, and 'they will be sloping back here to pack up their plunder. Grab his boots, feller.'

Texas Joe sighed with relief and picked up the polished bench-made boots. He walked slowly up the steps behind the tall buckaroo, walked out again and jerked his head at the dead cowboy who had been left to guard Bobbie Zander.

'Him?' he asked sharply. 'With the sun getting high and all?'

Reynolds nodded and helped to carry the cowboy up the steps and inside the room. His eyes lighted briefly when he saw a playing card lying on a scarred desk, and he high-heeled over and picked it up.

'That's the card you and Tyson were practising with,' Texas Joe whispered in a solemn voice. 'We better be making tracks, Roamin'.'

'The dead can't hurt you none,' Reynolds answered carelessly. 'But I want to get a message to Tyson. This ought to turn the trick.'

Texas Joe stared when he walked over to the couch with the card in his hand. The tall cowboy nodded thoughtfully and placed the Deuce of Diamonds with both pips shot out on the dead foreman's chest, covered the staring eyes with a blanket and walked stiffly from the room.

'What you mean by that, Roamin'?' the lanky cowboy whispered. 'About a message?'

'Took two shots to rub that Deuce of Diamonds card,' the tall cowboy explained coldly. 'It should take the same number to close up this outfit.'

'Now looky, pard,' Texas Joe argued seriously. 'You just beat Ramrod McCall by the wink of an eye, and he was supposed to be slow alongside his boss.'

Roaming Reynolds raised his head slowly and looked the cowboy squarely in the eyes. 'That's twice to-day you been some doubtful, Joe,' he said slowly. 'Up to now, have you knowed me to shoot second?'

Texas Joe shifted uncomfortably. 'There always has to be a first time,' he muttered. 'Seems to me like you crowd yore luck at times.'

'Did anybody ask you?'

The lanky cowboy raised his head quickly at the sharpness of the big gun-fighter's tone. 'They didn't,' he answered slowly, and his voice was muffled. 'But things have happened so fast since we hit Paradise that it seems we been here a month.'

'About me being slow,' Reynolds continued relentlessly. 'Mebbe you'd rather throw in with some faster gent. That it?'

Texas Joe leaned forward with his grimy right hand shadowing the grip of his gun. 'Take it back,' he snarled savagely, 'or I'll match you my own self.'

271

Roaming Reynolds twitched his shoulder and filled his hand with a speed that left Texas Joe gasping. His own hand was glued to the handle of his gun, and the weapon was still snugged deep in holster leather.

'Says who?' Reynolds asked softly.

The lanky cowboy set his jaw and started forward. 'Shoot,' he snarled. 'But I'll match my draw against yore drop if you don't unsay them words!'

Roaming Reynolds glared for a moment and slowly holstered the long-barrelled Colt. 'Taking 'em back, pard,' he said slowly. 'The way I put it made out as though I thought you wanted to join up with Tyson. Saying I'm sorry.'

Texas Joe gulped and turned his head away. 'Damn yuh, Roamin',' he creaked brokenly. 'That's for why I stick around and foller you all over hell. Just to cover the back of a square-shooting gent who gives a Button a show for his taw. Touch skin, you long-legged rannihan,' and he stuck out his hand and thwacked palms.

Roaming Reynolds swallowed noisily and slapped Texas Joe on the back. 'Rather have you at my side than an army,' he said soberly. 'Now we better be getting.'

Texas Joe nodded and walked over to the black thoroughbred. Pulled the latigo and dumped Ramrod McCall's carved saddle on the ground. Bolted his own scarred henskin in place and mounted expertly.

'Where to?' he asked tersely.

'Back to the Lazy L for breakfast,' Roaming Reynolds grunted softly. 'People die every day, but them that live has got to keep right on eating. I'm hungry.'

'You and me both' Joe seconded, and then searched the tanned face of his companion. 'About that talk we heard last night,' he muttered.

Reynolds turned sharply. 'Meaning Bobbie and her Pa?'

Joe nodded. 'I felt like a chicken thief there in the dark,' he confessed. 'Don't know how I'm going to look at her and not give myself away.'

'Listen, Joe,' the tall buckaroo said sternly. 'You so much as breathe a word about what you heard and I'll fan yore saddle-sides with my chaps. On top of that I'll up and leave you cold!'

'Aw gee, Roamin',' the cowboy muttered. 'You wouldn't do that if I made a slip.'

'You just slip and see,' Reynolds warned, and then he became more earnest. 'Don't you see what it would do to her?' he asked. 'She wouldn't ever look either of us in the face again.'

'That shore would be too bad,' Joe grunted. 'Seeing as you ain't interested in women folks.'

'You trying to hooray me?'

'You said so yore own self,' Joe growled. 'You put them earmarks on the critter yoreself.'

'I mean to say I ain't the kind to go around falling in love,' the tall buckaroo answered with dignity. 'Aside from that I like decent women, and you know it.'

'Shore, Roamin',' the lanky cowboy answered with a grin. 'And I'll tell a man they like you.'

'Now you take Ma Lassiter,' Reynolds attempted to explain. 'You kinda feel good all over when she kisses you.'

'Well, kinda,' Joe admitted with a grin. 'But I feel just as good and more of it when some filly like Bobbie does the same thing. Course you and me is different that-away. I don't pretend to hate none of them.'

Roaming Reynolds glared and caught up his whangs. Vaulted to the saddle and lined out for the lane leading to Jacobs Lake. Rode in silence until Texas Joe caught up with him down by the water. The lanky cowboy called in a low tense voice.

'Roamin'. Take a look behind you.'

Roaming Reynolds whirled in his saddle and then sent his horse to the cover of the trees by the water's edge. Texas Joe followed his example, and they watched two riders circling the lake from the west side. 'It's Tyson,' Joe whispered. 'But I don't know that other gent.'

'Lawman,' Reynolds grunted. 'Badge

on the left side of his vest.'

Texas Joe scratched his lean jaw. 'Tie that one,' he murmured. 'Griff Tyson riding with the law.'

'Wait a minute,' and Reynolds leaned forward with a new light in his blue eyes. 'I know that jigger, and he's straight as a die.'

'Yeah? What's his handle?'

'Joe Bailey, United States Inspector!'

Texas Joe whistled. 'Let's ride out and give him Howdy,' he suggested. 'Might save us a lot of grief.'

Roaming Reynolds shook his head. 'Bailey would get killed if he tried to arrest Tyson,' he explained. 'They ain't no use in him taking chances.'

'The three of us could throw down on Tyson,' Texas Joe suggested.

Roaming Reynolds tore his eyes away from the distant pair and stared coldly at his young pard. 'You heard what I told McCall,' he murmured softly, but his blue eyes were gleaming with a glowing fire. 'And I promised Tyson a chance.'

'Gun-dog,' Joe sneered. 'You couldn't

get no rest if you thought the Deuce of Diamonds had you faded with yore tools!'

Roaming Reynolds continued to stare, and then nodded slowly. 'Right,' he agreed. 'I couldn't take no rest if he had me beat.'

Texas Joe shrugged and dropped his eyes. 'I'm going out there,' he announced firmly. 'I'll tell the Inspector.'

Reynolds was on him like a cat with both hands locked in the upper muscles of the cowboy's arms. 'Just make a peep,' he warned harshly. 'And I'll do you a meanness you won't ever forget!'

Texas Joe gasped and bit his lips. Then his grey eyes saw the expression on the tall gun-fighter's bleak face, cold anger and a ruthless determination to carry out his threat at whatever cost. Slowly the tousled head nodded with under-standing.

'I got it coming, Roamin',' he admit-ted honestly. 'Me trying to tell you what to do.'

Roaming Reynolds loosened his grip

while the harsh look left his face. 'Glad you savvy, pard,' he almost whispered. 'It's something I can't do anything about.'

'Them two,' Texas Joe muttered, and pointed at Tyson and the Inspector. 'They're going over them Deuce of Diamonds critters.'

'Fair enough,' Reynolds grunted, and then his face lighted up. 'Don't you get the play, Joe?'

Texas Joe shook his head. 'Can't say I do,' he admitted.

'Tyson don't know about the stampede,' Reynolds explained. 'He is showing his own stuff to Bailey, and he figgers to run in that rustled stuff with the brand vented. Reckon I better have a talk with Bailey myself.'

12

Riding up the east trail that led over from the Lazy L, Roaming Reynolds and Texas Joe came out of a fringe of timber skirting the big water. Griff Tyson glanced up sharply and studied the tanned face of the tall buckaroo intently. Satisfied at what he found, he leaned against his horse and waited for Reynolds to state his errand.

The Deuce of Diamonds owner was immaculate in black broadcloth trousers tucked down in polished calfskin boots. Broad-shouldered and slender, with a calmness and poise that evoked a secret admiration in the racing mind of Reynolds. The tall buckaroo nodded at Tyson and swung down from the saddle to face the Federal Inspector.

'Howdy, Joe,' he greeted the stocky officer. 'Long time no see.'

'Roamin' Reynolds!'

Inspector Bailey came forward with

hand outstretched and a warm light of welcome in his grey eyes. The two men gripped hands and appraised each other silently for a moment. Startled surprise showed momentarily in the eyes of Griff Tyson. Surprise that faded as quickly when he saw Texas Joe watching him.

'Last time I see you was up on the Mascalero range,' the Inspector told Reynolds. 'Looks like you are still roaming.'

Reynolds nodded. 'You remember Texas Joe, Inspector,' and he jerked his head at his companion. 'Me and him are making a couple of hands for old Lafe Lassiter on the Lazy L. Lafe wanted to see you about some shippers he aims to round up for market.'

Joe Bailey glanced at the speaker and swung his eyes briefly to the face of Griff Tyson. 'Didn't know old Lafe had any amount of shipping steers,' he said slowly. 'But he's a square shooter, and I'll be glad to pass on his stuff. You ever meet Griff Tyson, owner of the Deuce of Diamonds?'

'Met him yesterday,' Reynolds answered. 'Howdy, Tyson. Yo're out early this morning.'

'I could say the same for you,' and Tyson smiled to show strong white teeth. 'The Inspector and I got up early to finish our business, and we haven't finished it yet.'

Roaming Reynolds nodded his understanding. 'Didn't figger to cut in on you, Tyson,' he said softly. 'I can see Joe Bailey later.'

'You mentioned Lafe Lassiter getting ready to ship prime beef,' and Tyson watched the face of the tall buckaroo. 'I've been riding every day, and I didn't know he had any to speak of.'

'Grass-finished stuff,' Reynolds explained. 'Three's and four's another feller has been looking after for him.'

He watched the changing expressions flit across the dark eyes while Tyson tried to solve the problem. Noted the hang of the ivory-handled six-gun thonged low on the long right leg, while Inspector Bailey made notes in his tally book concerning the grazing cattle branded with the Deuce of Diamonds.

'Ramrod McCall ought to be close,' Tyson said suddenly, and his eyes flicked over the smoke-grimed gun in Reynolds' holster. 'You seen him lately?'

'Saw him not more than an hour ago,' the tall gun-fighter answered without hesitation. 'He was riding over this way like he was in a hurry.'

Griff Tyson set his lips tightly and did not answer. Roaming Reynolds turned his head quickly. The Deuce of Diamonds owner was staring at the black thoroughbred under Texas Joe, and the lanky cowboy grinned lazily and hooked a leg over his worn saddlehorn.

'Talk straight, Button,' and Tyson leaned toward Texas Joe. 'How come you to be straddling Ramrod McCall's private hoss?'

'He gave it to me,' the cowboy answered easily. 'On account of him making a mistake and shooting my hoss in the dark.'

Griff Tyson stood poised and deadly with his right hand hooked above the grip of his gun. Joe Bailey saw the danger and walked carelessly in front of Tyson. 'The Deuce of Diamonds owner stopped his slapping hand and shrugged with resignation.

'I hope you are telling the truth, Button,' he said thinly. 'Ramrod set a heap of store by that black.'

'Yeah, he did,' Texas Joe answered. 'But he gave him to me, and I can prove it by Roamin'.'

Roaming Reynolds nodded confirmation and Inspector Bailey broke the tension by asking a question.

'These other cattle, Tyson. Where are you holding them?'

Griff Tyson glanced at Reynolds and drew a deep breath. 'Over near Big Springs,' he answered. 'Three and four-year-old white-faced steers burnt with my Diamond Deuce.'

Joe Bailey stepped back and rubbed his chin. Wise to the ways of the range, he sensed the feeling of enmity between the two tall gun-fighters. No trace of suspicion was in his voice when he spoke quietly to the tall buckaroo.

'I'll see you and old Lafe later, Roamin'. And if you see Ely Zander and his pretty daughter, give 'em my regards.'

Reynolds nodded. 'Saw the both of them late last night,' he said softly. 'They are staying at the Lazy L until after shipping time.'

He saw the startled light that leaped to the dark eyes of Griff Tyson. The latter started to speak and changed his mind, and once more the Deuce of Diamonds owner turned to stare at the horse under Texas Joe. Inspector Bailey chuckled softly.

'That's a great gal,' he told Reynolds. 'Last time I was up this-away, Manny Lassiter was sweet on her.'

'He still is,' Texas Joe remarked carelessly. 'Last night Manny killed a feller for talking out of turn to Bobbie Zander. Hit this jigger one time with his fist, and broke his neck.'

'That don't sound like any hand from Summit Valley,' Bailey answered slowly. 'You know who it was?'

284

'Old Ely said it was a rustler by the name of Red Frazier,' Texas Joe muttered. 'I never saw him before.'

Griff Tyson spoke harshly. 'Mind yore words, Button. Red Frazier was one of my riding hands!'

Joe shrugged carelessly. 'Didn't seem to make no never minds to Manny,' he answered. 'C'mon, Roamin'. I'm so hungry I could eat the hoofs and horns of a mossy-horn.'

'Just a minute, Reynolds,' Tyson said harshly. 'I'd like to know more about Red Frazier.'

Roaming Reynolds faced him coldly. 'I turned down an offer to work for you, Tyson,' he said icily, but his blue eyes narrowed. 'I'm working for the Lazy L, and right now I got business with them.'

The tall Deuce of Diamonds owner returned the stare and then shrugged his broad shoulders. 'I'll ask Ramrod,' he murmured.

'Good idea,' and Reynolds swung up to the saddle. 'See you later, Inspector.'

He waved his hand and sent his horse

across the valley toward the Lazy L with Texas Joe rubbing stirrups beside him. Inspector Joe Bailey watched them out of sight and turned back to Griff Tyson.

'I'd like to know,' he drawled slowly. 'You and Roamin' have words before you fell out?'

Tyson smiled with a gentle shrug. 'None to speak of,' he answered carelessly. 'Only I wanted him on the Deuce of Diamonds payroll, but Manny Lassiter saw him first.'

'He's fast with a six-gun,' the Inspector remarked musingly. 'And he has a habit of selling his guns to some gent who needs help bad. Something funny up here, Tyson.'

'He's a gun-fighter,' Tyson answered softly. 'I'm not slow with a cutter myself.'

'So-o-o!'

Inspector Bailey leaned back against the shoulder of his horse and studied the dark face intently. Shoved his tally book back in his hip pocket and picked up his reins.

'Better leave him alone,' he suggested.

'That's a friendly tip, Tyson.'

'Did I ask you?'

The Inspector held his foot in the stirrup. 'No,' he admitted slowly. 'Guess I'll be riding back to Paradise. I'll pass on yore stuff when you drive them through the chutes.'

'Better stop up at the house and have breakfast,' and Griff Tyson changed the expression on his face to a friendly smile. 'I want you to meet Ramrod McCall.'

Joe Bailey shook his head. 'Business back in town,' he grunted, 'which is why I rode out here so early with you. Be seeing you, Tyson.'

Cliff Tyson watched him ride away with a scowl on his dark face. He had spent the night in Paradise, and there were several problems that needed answers. Ramrod McCall would be waiting to make his reports, and then Tyson stopped abruptly and stared at the trail Roaming Reynolds had taken.

'Said he had seen Bobbie Zander,' he muttered. 'If Ramrod turned her loose …?'

He mounted his horse and rode furiously for the lane leading to the Deuce of Diamonds ranch house. Roared into the yard and flung down in front of the big porch. Stared at the closed door for a moment before mounting the stairs. Then he was in the room with gun half-drawn.

'Ramrod!'

His sharp voice echoed hollowly back at him. His dark eyes darted to the low couch and fastened on the cut thongs that had held the girl a prisoner. Eyes that widened and changed colour when he saw the outlines of a man under the heavy wool blanket.

'You, McCall,' he shouted hoarsely. 'On yore feet, feller!'

No answer from the couch while Tyson balanced easily and waited. Then he moved cat-like across the planking and twitched the blanket loose. Stepped back with a startled exclamation when the staring eyes of Ramrod McCall seemed to look into his own.

'Dead!'

Griff Tyson spoke in a whisper and dropped the gun back in leather. For a long moment he studied the face and hands before leaning forward. A playing card rested on the dead man's chest. A Deuce of Diamonds with both pips shot neatly out.

'The same card,' he whispered. 'And Reynolds said he had seen Ramrod not more than an hour ago!' Silence for a long time while the tall man stood motionless and pieced out the tragedy. Roaming Reynolds had rescued the girl, had shot it out with McCall, and then Tyson frowned.

'I left Ramrod to guard her,' he muttered. 'And Reynolds said he had seen Ramrod not more than an hour ago.'

Shuffling boots turned him toward the open door like a stallion on the fight. A bedraggled figure swayed on the sill, swathed in bandages that gleamed redly in the early sun. The eyes of the wounded man were dull with pain, and he steadied himself against the door frame.

'You, Deming,' Tyson almost shouted.

289

'Who done this to Ramrod?'

The answer came slowly and indistinct. 'That jigger they call Roamin' Reynolds. Him and the kid rode over here at sun-up. Ramrod was waiting, and they pulled a draw-and-shoot!'

Griff Tyson jerked erect when he saw another covered bundle on the floor against the back wall. 'Him?' he asked quietly.

'Buck Tudor,' the wounded man grunted. 'Ramrod left him here to guard the girl while he rode out to lend us a hand with the herd. Reynolds came over to get the gal. He got her,' he added simply.

Griff Tyson stared at the bandaged head and set his white teeth. 'That herd,' he barked sharply. 'The boys holding it like I said?'

Deming shook his head slowly. 'They ain't,' he answered stolidly. 'Me and Ben Tyler got away, and I'm shot up bad. Ben lit a shuck for the line after the rest of the boys was killed.'

'Who killed them?'

Deming shrugged. 'Reckon old Lafe Lassiter and Ely Zander did the most of it,' he answered wearily. 'Reynolds and the Button was there, and they come near to getting Ramrod down in the valley. Would have done it, only Ramrod killed the Button's hoss and jumped his black over that stake-and-rider fence to make a get-away.'

Griff Tyson relaxed then and leaned against the wall. Now he had some of the answers. He knew why old Lafe Lassiter had grass-finished steers to sell. Then his dark eyes came back to the face of his dead foreman.

'You say Ramrod shot it out with Reynolds?' he asked quietly.

Deming nodded painfully. 'Ramrod said he wanted both feet on the ground. Said that this was one time he came first. I never even saw Reynolds move his hand, but there he lays,' and he closed his eyes to shut out the sight.

Griff Tyson sucked his breath in quickly. 'Said he was first this time, eh?' he whispered. 'Served him right, Deming. How come you didn't lope with Ben Tyler?'

The wounded man shrugged. 'Can't sit a hoss,' he mumbled. 'Just managed to make it here, and it looks like we was whipped.'

Griff Tyson leaped across the room and fastened his hands on the drooping shoulders. 'Whipped, eh?' he said quietly, and then remembered the condition of the cowboy. 'Sorry, Deming,' he murmured. 'Where you hurt?'

'Slug in the right arm, and one through the left leg,' the cowboy mumbled. 'And I got creased just above my left ear.'

Griff Tyson stepped to the couch and covered the staring face of Ramrod McCall. Then he led Deming to a chair and lowered him to the seat. After which he disappeared into the back room and stirred up the coals in the big stove. Carried a small box in his hand when he returned to the front room.

'I was going to be a doctor one time,' he remarked carelessly. 'It's going to hurt some, but those slugs must come out!'

Deming Taylor groaned and nodded slowly. 'Figgered Ramrod would do it,' he muttered. 'But he was too busy.'

'And now he's dead,' Tyson answered grimly, and set out his probes.

For the next half-hour he worked skilfully to extract the bullets while the wounded man gritted his teeth and took the punishment without complaint. Griff Tyson forgot everything except the task at hand. His long fingers moved with exact precision, and when the wounds were neatly bandaged, he washed his hands and rolled down the sleeves of his white linen shirt.

No sign of tremble in his hands; no concern in his handsome dark face. Walking over to a cupboard, he took down a flask and poured half a tumbler of whisky which he handed to the wounded man.

'Drink this, Deming,' and his voice was gentle. 'You stuck with me when the rest all dogged it, and I'll do the best I can by you.'

Deming Taylor drained the glass and

straightened his shoulders. 'Boss,' he said slowly.

'Yes, Deming.'

The wounded man shifted uncomfortably. 'This here gun-boss Lassiter brought in.'

'What about him?' Tyson asked softly, but his dark eyes were glowing.

'Never saw a gent so fast in my life. Him and Ramrod stood out there when the sun was coming up. Heard 'em talking about a centipede getting ready to eat a big butterfly.'

Griff Tyson cocked his head. 'Keep on talking,' he murmured.

'Them bugs was right between Reynolds and Ramrod,' Deming continued. 'Seems like they used it for a signal. When the centipede grabbed the butterfly …?'

Griff Tyson's quick mind grasped the picture instantly. 'Seen it many's the time,' he answered with a nod. 'And Ramrod?'

'Ramrod was fast next to you,' Deming answered slowly. 'He slapped down for his iron like a streak of light, but his gun never cleared leather.'

'Reynolds?' Tyson asked softly. 'What'd he do?'

'He just rocked the hammer, boss,' Deming answered simply. 'I never saw his hand move. I heard his gun roar one time, and Ramrod shot through the bottom of the boot without finishing his draw. Then he went down like a pole-axed steer.'

Griff Tyson narrowed his eyes. 'Why are you telling me this?' he inquired softly.

'I saw it in yore face, Griff,' Deming answered slowly. 'I could see that you was figgering on taking it to Roaming Reynolds.'

The Deuce of Diamonds owner nodded one time. 'One way or the other,' he murmured. 'Like I told Reynolds, there is room for only one gun-boss here in Summit Valley.'

Deming Taylor shuddered and turned his head. 'Him and the Button carried them two in here,' he said slowly. 'I was hiding out in the bunkhouse. Remembered what you said about marking that big buckaroo for yore own cutter, and on top of that I was gun-naked.'

'Thanks, Deming,' Tyson murmured. 'Texas Joe was straddling Ramrod's hoss when I last saw him. Said Ramrod gave it to him.'

'That's right. Ramrod said the kid could have the jumper if he lost to Reynolds. He lost!'

'Yeah, he lost,' Tyson agreed. 'But I won't!'

'Looky, boss,' the wounded man persisted. 'Why don't you get them the law way now? They can't prove anything about those vented brands.'

Griff Tyson stood in the centre of the room with a smile on his dark face. 'That,' he shrugged lightly. 'A man can always get cattle or money if he wants them bad enough. But Roaming Reynolds is supposed to be the fastest gun-fighter in the State.'

'What about it?' Deming growled.

'You wouldn't understand,' Tyson

sighed. 'It's something that gets into yore blood. Gun-fighters are born that-away, and they can't help themselves when they hear about another fast gent. That's why Roaming Reynolds rode in here to Summit Valley.'

Deming shuddered and looked away. 'Ramrod said the same thing,' he muttered. 'And what if you lose?'

Griff Tyson shrugged. 'What difference would it make to me if I lost?' he asked slowly, and then a scowl crossed his face. 'I don't aim to lose,' he barked. 'Now I must ride to Paradise and make arrangements for them two.'

He moved swiftly to the door when the sound of wheels clattered in the lane. A black covered wagon drawn by two black horses rattled into the yard. A little bird-like man jumped down from the driver's seat and laid his black Stetson on the porch. Not more than five-feet-three, with mutton-chop whiskers and a scraggly goatee.

'Give you good mornin', Mister Tyson,' he began in a deep bass voice. 'Inspector

Joe Bailey said there was some business for me out here.'

Griff Tyson stared at the little man for a long moment. 'Bad news shore travels fast,' he said at last. 'You'll find the bodies inside, buzzard.'

'The name is Thomas Kirby,' the undertaker corrected with quiet dignity. 'I assume that you will underwrite the expense of burial?'

'Send me the bill,' Tyson grunted. 'Put 'em away right.'

The little man showed the resentment he felt at the nickname when he answered. 'My terms are cash at the graveside,' he announced slowly. 'Five hundred will cover both cases!'

Griff Tyson flushed with anger and then restrained himself. 'Something go wrong with my credit?' he asked softly.

The undertaker nodded his head emphatically. 'You and him are about of a size,' he murmured judicially. 'My terms are still cash at the graveside.'

'Me and who?'

'Roaming Reynolds. Like you mentioned, bad news travels fast.'

Griff Tyson reached into a vest pocket and produced a flat package of bills. Counted out five and handed them to Thomas Kirby. Then he raised his head and stared at the bobbing goatee.

'There's yore money, you damned buzzard,' he said clearly, but without raising his voice. 'So you think Reynolds and I are about the same size?'

'Not an inch between the two of you,' Kirby answered. 'You called me *buzzard* again,' and once more he frowned. 'Perhaps you would like to make a deposit with me in the event that the hand is quicker than the eye?'

'Meaning what?'

'Meaning that I can't collect from a dead man,' the undertaker answered bluntly. 'Unless you would like for the buzzards to take care of yore mortal remains.'

Griff Tyson stiffened and then his face broke into a smile. 'Serves me right, Kirby,' he admitted. 'You win. I'll put up another five hundred, and you can use it either way the cards of Fate fall on the table of Life.'

'Or Death,' Kirby corrected, and walked behind his black wagon to open the doors. 'Any help hereabouts?' he asked in his solemn bass voice.

Griff Tyson shrugged. 'Do it the best way you can,' he murmured. 'I never did like to handle a corpse.'

'Someone will have to handle you one day,' the undertaker told him gravely. 'Perhaps you will do it as a gesture of respect for the departed.'

Griff Tyson shrugged again. 'I haven't any respect for the departed,' he answered coldly. 'You will find what you come after in the front room.'

He started to walk away, and Thomas Kirby closed the door of his wagon and climbed into the driver's seat. Tyson slapped for his gun and covered the little man.

'Light down out of there,' he ordered sharply. 'You have yore money, and you do yore work!' The little undertaker stared into the muzzle without blinking while he slowly shook his head. 'Rock hammer,' he whispered calmly. 'But I can't touch the bodies unless I can do it decently and with proper respect. You can shoot if you care to, but there are ethics in every profession!'

Griff Tyson stared and then lowered the heavy gun in his right hand. 'That's right,' he agreed softly, and removed the Stetson from his head, laid it carefully on the porch and motioned to the little man to precede him.

Thomas Kirby removed his own hat and laid it on the seat. Grave dignity on his seamed face when he alighted and bowed from the hips. Then he walked solemnly up the steps and into the room with Tyson following.

'We will take due care to keep the bodies of the deceased covered at all times,' Kirby murmured. 'It is the last thing we can do for those who have gone before us.'

He moved over to the couch and tucked the blanket carefully around the still figure. Then he reached under the arms and raised his head to look at Tyson until the tall man picked up the polished boots. With a strength surprising in such a slight body, the undertaker carried his part of the burden without effort. Placed the body in his wagon, and repeated the procedure with the dead cowboy. Then he turned to Griff Tyson and bowed again.

'Thank you, Mister Tyson,' he said gravely. 'The funerals will be to-morrow at ten.'

Griff Tyson did not answer. Stood and stared until the black wagon had disappeared down the lane of pines. Then he turned back to the house and climbed the steps to the front room. Deming Taylor watched him in moody silence.

'It's a message,' Tyson said, and picked up the card Roaming Reynolds had left on Ramrod McCall's chest.

Deming Taylor started. 'Don't get you,' he muttered.

Griff Tyson answered without turning his head, like a man speaking his thoughts aloud. 'Reynolds and I showed each other what we could do the first time we met,' he murmured softly. 'I kept the card as a reminder.'

'Reynolds shot that card?' Deming prompted.

'I shot out one pip,' Tyson answered thoughtfully. 'Reynolds flipped the card and shot out both pips.'

'I wouldn't meet him, Griff,' Taylor muttered. 'If he shot out both pips …?'

'Meaning what?' and the voice of Tyson was edgy.

'There was two of you,' the wounded cowboy continued doggedly. 'Both of you was more than fast, and Ramrod McCall stopped doing what he was doing!'

'And you figger I might be the other pip in the card; that it?' Tyson purred silkily, but his dark eyes were glowing with an inner anger.

'Yo're the Deuce of Diamonds,' Taylor pointed out. 'That tall jigger ain't afraid of nothing on earth.'

Griff Tyson faced around slowly. 'Meaning I am?' he asked softly.

Deming swallowed noisily. 'But you

seen what he did this morning,' he answered. 'Rode away from here after carrying Ramrod inside. Then he rides right up to you and makes his talk without batting an eye. Even told you that he had seen Ramrod, and that he could tell you some of the answers!'

Griff Tyson nodded grimly. 'That's right,' he conceded, and tucked the card in a pocket of his vest. 'Ramrod told me all I wanted to know!'

13

It seemed like a homecoming to Roaming Reynolds and Texas Joe when they rode into the Lazy L yard and dropped down at the broad porch in front of the rambling old ranch house. Ma Lassiter and Bobbie Zander came out of the kitchen, and Texas Joe slid forward to plant a resounding kiss on the older woman's cheek. Ma smiled happily and hugged the lanky young cowboy, and then walked up to Roaming Reynolds and put her arms around him.

'Bobbie told me, Roamin',' she whispered close to his ear. 'About you riding to the Deuce of Diamonds to rescue her. Just wanted to thank you for both me and Manny.'

The tall buckaroo shifted uneasily and patted her shoulders with his big hands. 'Any feller would have done the same, Ma,' he growled. 'Neither McCall nor Tyson was there, so it didn't take much doing.'

'Buck Tudor was a good hand with a six-gun,' Lafe Lassiter answered seriously. 'Sorry you had to do what you did, but Buck was running with the wrong crowd.'

'He won't run no more,' Texas Joe interrupted. 'Nor some other fellers I could name.'

Old Ely Zander glanced at Lafe Lassiter and nodded knowingly. 'Meaning you caught up with that fence-jumper?' he asked softly.

Roaming Reynolds frowned down at his boots, but Texas Joe chuckled grimly. 'Looks like yo're a mind reader, Ely,' he answered importantly. 'The feller you mentioned was waiting back there on the porch. He was a dead game sport, but he over-played his hand.'

Ma Lassiter and Bobbie Zander both raised their heads and stared at Roaming Reynolds. The girl sighed softly and looked away when he caught the reproach in her eyes, and the tall gunfighter shrugged his shoulders slightly while his lips set in a straight line.

'Ramrod McCall,' Lafe Lassiter said slowly. 'You killed him, Roamin'?'

Reynolds nodded shortly. 'He had both feet on the ground, Lafe. That's all he asked.'

'Looks like that was enough,' Zander grunted. 'He nick you any before he went down final?'

Texas Joe answered for his tall companion. 'Ramrod never cleared leather, and his shot went through the bottom of his scabbard. He gave me that black hunter he was riding just before he rattled his hocks up the one-way trail.'

Lafe Lassiter refused to be diverted. 'He was fast, Roamin',' he said slowly. 'And if he didn't clear leather, I reckon the rest of us can set our minds at ease.'

Bobbie Zander caught her breath sharply. 'No,' she cried, and the word came instinctively. 'You mustn't, Roamin'!'

The tall buckaroo looked at her curiously, and made no attempt at evasion. 'Reckon I got it to do when the time is right,' he said quietly. 'I passed him my word, and I ain't never broke it up to now.'

Ma Lassiter tightened her hand on his arm. 'Breakfast is waiting,' she interrupted. 'You and Joe must be hungry enough to eat yore weight in flannel cakes.'

'Lead me to 'em,' Texas Joe shouted. 'Right now my backbone is reaching across to tell my stummick howdy, they're so close. Grub pile, Roamin'!'

Reynolds sighed with relief and followed Ma Lassiter into the kitchen. Texas Joe made a run for the table and heaped hot cakes on his plate, while Lafe Lassiter and Ely Zander talked in the front room, and Bobbie Zander stared through the open door.

Ma Lassiter waited until the two cowboys were down to their last cup of coffee. Then she took a seat near Reynolds, knowing that they would bolt as soon as they had finished eating.

'Roamin',' she began softly. 'Manny wants to talk to you.'

The tall buckaroo frowned and turned to study her face. 'He on the prod?' he asked gruffly.

Ma Lassiter smiled. 'Not any more,' she answered 'He had all night to think things over, and like as not he wants to thank you. I wanted to ask you just to be patient until he finds the words he wants to say.'

Shuffling feet sounded in the little hall, and Manny Lassiter came into the kitchen and made straight for Roaming Reynolds. Laid one big hand on his shoulder before the tall buckaroo could turn.

'Saying I'm thankful for what you did to me back on the Bar Z Bar, Roamin',' and his deep voice was sincere. 'I never was hit so hard and so fast in all my life, and nothing ever done me so much good.'

The corners of Reynold's mouth curled in a smile. 'Glad you feel that way about it, Manny,' he answered softly. 'Figgered mebbe you would get up yore hackles, and I don't hanker for what you

309

gave Red Frazier.'

A brief frown crossed the big Lazy L foreman's face. 'Sorry I had it to do,' he muttered. 'But he asked for it.'

'And he got it,' Texas Joe cut in. 'Me and Roamin' saw him down in the lane where you left him.'

'Bobbie told me about last night,' Manny said slowly, and his fingers kneaded the muscles in Reynold's shoulder. 'I'd have tried to kill Tyson with my hands, and you know what would have happened!'

'I know,' Reynolds agreed, and turned to glance down at the big cowboy's holster. 'See you got yoreself the difference,' he remarked approvingly.

'Not that it means much where Tyson is concerned,' young Lassiter growled. 'That's what I wanted to say, Roamin'. I'm asking you not to take it to him.'

Roaming Reynolds stiffened. 'Yo're talking out of turn, feller,' he growled. 'You got yore work to do and I got mine. Reckon I know best how to do my part,' and he stared levelly.

'We can get the law now,' young Lassiter persisted, and frowned when his father and Ely Zander came into the room.

'Tell 'em about the Inspector,' Texas Joe interrupted eagerly. 'He said he wanted to see ol' Lafe.'

'Huh? What Inspector?' the old cattleman asked quickly.

Roaming Reynolds was glad to change the subject when he faced the two older men. 'United States Inspector Joe Bailey,' he began slowly. 'We met him looking over Deuce of Diamonds stuff with Griff Tyson.'

'Dag-nab a feller like you, Roamin',' Lassiter shouted with exasperation. 'Why didn't you say so when you lit down?'

'Didn't get no chance to talk,' Reynolds grinned. 'Nohow, me and Joe rode out and made medicine with Bailey.'

'And some with Tyson,' Texas Joe interrupted slyly.

Now the two women came into the kitchen to listen. Reynolds scowled at his young companion and searched for words to begin. Then he squared his shoulders and talked in clipped sentences before Joe could make matters worse.

'Joe Bailey is a Federal man like you know. Rode in to inspect brands. Tyson figgers to ship better than a thousand long three's and four's. He won't.'

'Thanks to you and Joe,' Lafe Lassiter muttered dryly. 'About Bailey?'

'Said to tell you he would be glad to pass on yore stuff,' the tall buckaroo continued. 'Said he didn't know you had that much stuff ready, but I told him a feller had been finishing the stock for you.'

'And then Griff Tyson took the play,' Texas Joe edged in. 'Said he had been riding the whole valley and he knew you didn't have no such a herd.'

'Did you get that bunch rounded up?' Reynolds asked the old cattleman.

Lassiter nodded with a slow smile. 'Milled the bunch and got them bedded down close to Big Springs,' he answered. 'The boys is riding circle down there right now.'

'Better keep them there until you see Bailey 'Reynolds advised.'

'Griff Tyson,' old Ely Zander interrupted. 'I'd like to know how he took it.'

'He didn't know about Ramrod McCall,' Reynolds answered thoughtfully. 'Seems like he spent the night in Pardise, and he rode out early this morning with Joe Bailey.'

'He spooked when he saw me sitting McCall's hoss,' Texas Joe chuckled. 'Even then he didn't tumble to what had happened.'

Lafe Lassiter glanced nervously through the open window where he could see the long lane. 'Tyson will be over here as soon as he finds his Ramrod 'he muttered, and his deep voice expressed worry. 'And you ain't had no sleep, Roamin'.'

Roaming Reynolds shrugged lightly. 'I can make up my sleep any time,' he answered carelessly. 'Just wanted to say that our work is almost finished here boss.'

'Not by a dang sight,' Lassiter contradicted quickly. You and Joe has a job here the rest of yore lives!'

'I'm needing a Ramrod on the Bar Z Bar,' Ely Zander interrupted hurriedly. 'You can write yore own ticket, Roamin'. What you say?'

Roaming Reynolds carefully avoided looking at Bobbie Zander. 'You see, Ely,' he drawled slowly, 'me and Joe is afflicted with the itching heel. We can't stay put long in one place after we finishes up a job of work. Reckon we won't never be any different.'

Manny Lassiter shifted his big boots and sucked in a deep breath. 'There's a job right here for you as Ramrod,' he began slowly. 'Yo're a better man than I am, and I know it.'

He turned abruptly on his heel and left the room, and Ma Lassiter came forward to take the tall buckaroo by the hand. Roaming Reynolds avoided her eyes while he watched the broad back of Manny Lassiter.

'We could all be happy, Roamin','

Ma Lassiter said softly. 'I couldn't think any more of you if you were my own chip.'

'That's ... that's fine, Ma,' he murmured softly, but she knew his thoughts were far away. 'Just happened to remember that I didn't take care of my hoss.'

He left the room abruptly and slipped through the back door. Manny Lassiter was nowhere in sight, and Reynolds caught up his bridle reins and led his horse to the big barn. Rubbed the tall roan down with dry hay and measured a feeding of grai, and he turned quickly when a light hand touched his arm.

'Was looking for you feller,' he began, and stopped when he saw his mistake. Bobbie Zander caught his two hands and stared deep into his wide blue eyes.

'Won't you stay, Roamin'?' she pleaded. 'Won't you consider the offer Dad made you to rod the Bar Z Bar?'

'I thought you was Manny,' he grunted. 'Wanted to have a quiet talk with him.'

'He said all he had to say,' the girl pouted. 'That's why I came out to the barn. Manny as good as told you that anything you did was all right with him. Didn't you understand?'

He searched her face silently for a long moment. 'Reckon I understand too well,' he murmured. 'Manny is cowfolks from hocks to horns, and he'd die before he would let on what was in his heart. The way I see it, little pard, you ain't trying to understand yore own self.'

The girl twisted her strong fingers and dropped her eyes. 'I feel that I owe more than my life to you, Roamin',' she whispered, and he caught a subdued sob in her throaty voice. 'All night I just sat there, thinking,' and her shoulder suddenly shuddered.

'I know,' the tall buckaroo muttered gently. 'A man's life ain't worth much compared to those kind of things, Bobbie gal. That's why Manny said what he did. He would have died of a busted heart if . . . things had happened to you.'

'Something happened to me, way down inside,' the girl whispered. 'I couldn't help saying what I did. Can't help it now,' and she threw her arms around his neck before he could step back.

Roaming Reynolds coloured up and glanced around the big barn. 'You mustn't let down now,' he said lamely.

The girl began to sob as her arms tightened. 'Please hold me, Roamin',' she pleaded. 'I hurt all over where Griff Tyson crushed me. I feel things crawling, and it stops when I touch you.'

The tall buckaroo's face was gentle when he held the sobbing girl in his arms, careful lest he bruise her soft flesh, and a troubled expression crept into his eyes when the nearness of her brought a panic of uneasiness to him. And then he waited awkwardly until her sobs became less and stopped entirely.

'Any honest gent would die for a good woman, Bobbie,' he said softly. 'You can get men twelve to the dozen any day in the week, but folks like Ma Lassiter and yoreself come in little bunches.'

'Ma loves you too,' the girl whispered in a little voice. 'We don't want you ever to leave us.'

Her words brought him back to the present, and he gently released himself from her arms and stepped back. 'Like I told you last night,' and his voice was gruff. 'I won't ever be any different, Bobbie. I'm telling you honest, and you ought to be thinking about a better man. Manny Lassiter is yore own kind of folks. Me; I'll always be different.'

'Oh,' and the girl stared at him with the tears shining in her brown eyes. 'I feel so ashamed of myself!'

'No,' he contradicted softly. 'You went through too much the last day or two, and it like to got you down. Just because I happened to come along at the right times to help some, it kinda upset you. All of us feels the same way when things happen so fast like they have been doing.'

The girl stared down at his big boots

and held tightly to his hands. 'The Lazy L and the Bar Z Bar were both ruined when you came,' she murmured. 'Now we have more than we had before, and you won't stay and share them with us. But those things ...' and she broke off suddenly.

'I understand, Bobbie,' he told her quietly. 'But now you are home safe, and you will soon forget what happened on the Deuce of Diamonds.'

'I won't ever forget,' the girl cried. 'If you could have seen the look on Griff Tyson's face when he said he was going to marry me. Like a lobo that can see in the dark!'

She shuddered at the change that swept over his tanned face. The blue eyes narrowed and glowed with a savage fire that robbed his craggy features of every vestige of softness. Little ridges of muscle framed his mouth; jutted out on his lean jaw like shoulders of rocky granite. And his voice was edgy and harsh when he spoke without seeming to see her.

'That's one of the reasons why I aim to take it to him. He ain't fit to live among decent folks!'

'Don't,' she pleaded. 'You frighten me when you look like that!'

'Don't you see,' and he refused to meet her eyes. 'I can't change myself, and it would always be the same. Nothing ever makes a gun-fighter change … after he has … killed!'

'Nothing?' and her voice was a faint whisper.

'Nothing!'

For a long time she studied his face while he stared through the double doors. 'But there won't be any more gun-fighters here in Summit Valley,' she said suddenly.

'There is one now,' and his words cracked like pistol shots.

He turned his head to look at her when he heard her gasp.

'I thought I could persuade you …' she began, and Reynolds seized the chance she offered.

'And now you know it can't be done,'

he finished for her. 'It's part of cow-country code, just like Manny Lassiter's love for you. You and him are the same kind of folks, and a better man never wore out boot leather.'

The girl nodded and turned slowly toward the door. Roaming Reynolds stood still and watched her go. Pulled a sack of makings from a vest pocket and rolled a smoke very slowly. Then he walked out through the back door and flicked a match with his thumbnail.

He was smoking meditatively when boots scraped from the side of the barn. He glanced up when Manny Lassiter came from the horse corral, and for a minute he studied the face of the Lazy L foreman. Could Manny have heard what the girl had said?

'Wish you'd think it over, Roamin',' the big cowboy began earnestly. 'It ain't like Dad and me was giving you something. You gave us all we have, and more than that.'

'I did the work you hired me to do,' Reynolds answered stiffly, still conscious of his talk with Bobbie Zander. 'And I still have some unfinished business in town,' he added coldly.

'I was talking to Dad,' young Lassiter answered eagerly. 'With the Inspector here, we can prove that Tyson vented our brand, and Joe Bailey is the Federal law. I'll go in and sign the complaints myself!'

Roaming Reynolds raised his head and eyed Lassiter sternly. 'You'd do that to me?' he asked softly. 'After knowing me the way you do, and hearing what I told Tyson?'

Manny Lassiter twisted uneasily and dropped his eyes before that level gaze. 'But we think too much of you, pard,' he muttered hoarsely. 'You can take anything I have, and I'd still feel the same.'

'Stick to the point,' Reynolds barked savagely. 'We were talking about my promise to Griff Tyson. They call him the Deuce of Diamonds, and there's two spots on that card.'

'You mean …?'

'I mean there is still one spot left on the card,' the tall buckaroo growled softly. 'I took on a job of work, and it won't be finished until that other spot is rubbed out!'

'He'd get twenty years in prison,' Lassiter argued. Roaming Reynolds shot out his left hand and vised down on Lassiter's good shoulder. 'You'd do that to a man?' he asked savagely. 'You'd take a man who has spent all his days out under the sun, and you'd put him behind stone walls until he was wore out and broke down?'

'It would be better than dying,' Lassiter growled.

'It would like hell,' Reynolds barked. 'I'd rather be dead from now on than to spend a year in a cell. So would any other cowhand that has rolled his soogans on the ground under the stars!'

Manny Lassiter stared and shook his head. 'Reckon I don't savvy, Roamin',' he admitted honestly. 'You mind spelling it out?'

'It gets in yore blood,' and Reynolds spoke low and tense. 'You can feel a gun jumping in yore hand; powder-smoke wreathing up around yore eyes. You feel light as a feather, and you just can't stop.'

'You mean gun-fighters,' Lassiter whispered. 'Keep on talking.'

'Nothing else matters,' the tall buckaroo muttered harshly. 'Not a day goes past that you don't practise to keep the feel of yore iron, and you know there don't a man live that can beat you with yore tools. Nothing else gives a gent the freedom he gets from keeping in shape!'

'Freedom,' Lassiter murmured, and nodded with a new light in his eyes. 'I think I know now.'

'You take a man like that,' Reynolds continued, and he might have been talking to himself. 'Put him in prison away from the sun and the open country. Hell, feller. Killing him would be an act of mercy!'

Manny Lassiter kicked the ground with sudden anger. 'I'd have no mercy with Griff Tyson after what he did to Bobbie,' he boomed hoarsely. 'He held her in his arms until he nearly broke her ribs. Said he'd kill her and all the rest of us, if he couldn't have her for himself.'

Roaming Reynolds was smiling coldly. 'You'd get it in yore blood like the rest of us,' he almost sneered. 'After you killed yore first man … with a gun!'

Manny Lassiter dropped his hand instinctively and rubbed the handle of his colt. 'Reckon I would, Roamin',' he admitted, and then his wide shoulders drooped. 'But I can't match Griff Tyson.'

'I can match him,' Reynolds said softly. 'Well?'

Manny Lassiter raised his brown eyes and extended his hand. 'Thanks for drawing the picture, pard,' he murmured. 'You can match him, and I won't sign the complaint. It must be hell behind the stone walls,' and he shuddered at the thought.

'That squares everything up between you and me,' and Roaming Reynolds allowed one of the rare smiles to ripple across his face.

'Hidden Valley,' Lassiter said suddenly. 'It would make a first-class spread if a feller wanted to settle down and give his mind over to raising cattle.'

'Reckon it would,' Reynolds agreed without interest. 'If a feller wanted to settle down and stay put. Now you take me and Joe, for instance. We don't stay long enough in one place to fat up our lean spots.'

He locked glances with the big cowboy without winking. Each understood the other, and gradually the tension left Manny Lassiter. Again he gripped hard and nodded his curly head.

'That's the code of cow-country, pard,' he said softly. 'I've learned a lot about it since you and Joe rode in.'

The tall buckaroo stiffened while his blue eyes narrowed to search Lassiter's face. For a moment he was tempted to speak, but he locked his teeth and held back the words.

Cow-country code? Those were the words he had used to Bobbie Zander. Now he understood that feeling of being watched. Manny Lassiter had heard him talking to the girl, and the big cowboy had slipped to tip his hand. And after hearing what he had heard, Manny Lassiter had offered to step aside. Had still wanted to be pards with him.

Roaming Reynolds thought swiftly and decided to remain silent. Action and excitement do strange things, and the tall buckaroo shrugged lightly. Turned to point at the black thoroughbred in the horse corral.

'Texas Joe is going to be mighty proud of that hoss,' he chuckled. 'Right now he's figgering on tophand gear as soon as we get to a good saddle-maker.'

'He's earned the best,' Lassiter agreed, and Roaming Reynolds knew that the big man was unaware of his slip. Both turned when old Lafe Lassiter and Ely Zander came across the yard and through the barn.

'What'd he say?' Lassiter asked eagerly.

Manny Lassiter shook his head. 'No luck,' he answered sadly. 'But about that complaint, Dad. We won't sign it.'

'What's the reason we won't?'

'Roamin' made a promise to Griff Tyson,' Manny explained. 'He ain't never broke his word up to now, and we owe him something special when he outs and asks for it.'

'Put a name to it, son,' the old cattleman barked. 'And count it done beforehand.'

'It's the Deuce of Diamonds,' Reynolds said gravely. 'He claimed there wasn't room here in Summit Valley for two gun-bosses. I took that job over when I hired on the Lazy L.'

'You mean show-down?' and old Lafe leaned forward and held his breath.

'That's just what I mean,' and Roaming Reynolds tightened his jaw.

The old cattleman sighed with disappointment. 'We figgered there was a better way,' he mumbled. 'But I said it, and it still goes. Luck to you, Roamin'.'

'I don't hold with it,' Ely Zander cackled suddenly. 'The best you can get out of it would be a draw, and that long-coupled gun-hawk ought to have his wings clipped. You can't win nothing with a draw!'

'I can win my own self-respect,' Reynolds answered softly. 'Which I wouldn't ever have again if you gents put Tyson behind the bars. On top of that, neither me nor Joe would appear against him!'

Old Lafe Lassiter stepped forward and held out his hand. 'You can have anything you ask for, Roamin',' he said gruffly. 'I was young and salty myself one time. Figgered nothing could ever change me, but I lost all that when I met up with Ma. Might be you won't be any different one of these days.'

'Just what I was telling him,' Manny Lassiter interrupted.

'About that herd we stampeded last night,' and Roaming Reynolds changed the subject abruptly. 'I'd say it was a good time to start them critters moving toward the shipping pens. Joe Bailey don't aim to stay over in Paradise very long.'

'I'm riding in to see Bailey,' the old cattleman answered, and his voice showed the relief he felt. 'You Manny; better tell the boys to get that herd started for the siding.'

'Looky yonder,' and Reynolds pointed to the house. 'If that don't make a picture.'

All eyes turned toward the porch where Texas Joe was standing with his arm around Ma Lassiter, an impudent grin on his thin face when he shouted at Lafe Lassiter.

'What's he say, Lafe?'

Roaming Reynolds turned to stare at the old cattleman. Lafe Lassiter grinned ruefully and shook his head.

'He said … *No*, Button,' he called back. 'And I don't know but what it takes a load offen my mind, coming in here the way you do, and making love to my wife.'

Texas Joe tightened his arm and kissed Ma Lassiter loudly on the cheek. 'Always wanted me a gal like Ma,' he chuckled, and then the smile faded from his face when a rider came up through the lane and headed for the men down by the barn.

'That's Thomas Kirby,' he heard Ma whisper. 'Sometimes they call him the buzzard,' and she shuddered slightly.

'He's the undertaker,' she whispered, and Texas Joe left the porch with a leap and headed for the barn.

14

The little undertaker swung down from his horse and addressed himself to Roaming Reynolds. He seemed strangely out of place in his black broadcloth, but if he felt the difference, his solemn face gave no sign.

'Thought you would want to know, Reynolds,' he stated bluntly. 'The funeral of the late Ramrod McCall takes place at ten this morning!'

The tall buckaroo was startled, but only his eyes betrayed the fact. 'Interesting,' he murmured, and studied the little man's face. 'You come out here to collect for the job?'

Thomas Kirby shook his head slowly. 'Griff Tyson paid in advance,' he answered in his deep bass voice. 'In fact, he paid for both cases, and something extra.'

Lafe Lassiter shoved forward to face the little man. 'You use damn pore taste at times, buz … that is, Kirby,' he said angrily. 'What in tarnation does Roamin' care about all that?'

The undertaker did not remove his eyes from the tall gun-fighter. 'My business is to bury the dead,' he answered without emotion. 'But even I have some feelings at times. I thought, perhaps, Reynolds could be persuaded to leave the valley before it is too late.'

Silence fell over the little group until Reynolds spoke softly. 'Too late?'

'That's right. Griff Tyson paid me another five hundred in advance, and you and him are of a size.'

'Like you pointed out, yore business is to bury the dead,' the tall buckaroo answered carelessly. 'And Tyson paid you for his funeral. What more you want?'

'He paid me for a funeral, but it might be yours,' Kirby answered soberly. 'I know Tyson!'

'Mebbe, you don't know me,' Reynolds retorted sharply 'Up to now, I ain't been buried.'

'There always has to be a first time …

and a last,' the little undertaker answered. 'But you gentlemen misunderstand me. You, Reynolds, you did what had to be done, and I appreciate it. You are young to die.'

Ely Zander moved around the group and faced Kirby with flashing eyes. 'You runty buzzard,' he rasped angrily, 'riding in here in yore funeral clothes with a speech like that!'

'I was addressing myself to Mister Reynolds,' the little man answered with quiet dignity. 'And I would advise you against repeating the mistake you just made. The name is Kirby!'

'I don't give a hootenhell what it is,' the little cattleman shouted. 'Now you hit saddle and get long gone out of here before I come uncorked and do you a meanness!'

'Just a minute, Zander,' and Roaming Reynolds pushed between the two little men to face Kirby. 'All right, Thomas Kirby,' he said quietly. 'Spell out the rest of it.'

'Spoke with some degree of understanding,' the little undertaker growled. 'Griff Tyson is in Paradise. Trying to close a deal for a herd of steers. Joe Bailey won't pass inspection until he sees the cattle, and I thought you might want to know.'

Reynolds glanced at Lafe Lassiter. 'Our stuff is on the way now,' the old cattleman answered quickly. 'Ought to be there right after the burying.'

'I know,' and Thomas Kirby set his mutton chops to wagging. 'That's what Tyson is figgering on.'

'Looky here, feller,' Zander interrupted harshly. 'Yore rightful business is burying the dead. How come you to know so much about the cattle trade?'

'A man learns to listen,' Kirby answered. 'Both you and Tyson are trying to sell the same cattle. I found some papers in the pocket of McCall's vest. Turned them over to Tyson, of course, as required by law, and now you know.'

'Thanks,' Lafe Lassiter murmured dryly. 'Aside from that, what else you got on yore chest?'

'Roaming Reynolds,' and the little man looked the tall buckaroo squarely in the eye. 'Tyson means to kill him, and Griff Tyson has never been beaten.'

The tall gun-fighter smiled coldly and nodded his head. 'Him and me being of a size, you got nothing to worry about,' he said quietly. 'Thanks just the same.'

'I might,' and Kirby rubbed his chin. 'If the contest should be a draw?'

'Then you get twice as much work,' Reynolds grunted. 'Did Griff Tyson tell you to invite me to the funeral?'

'How'd you know?'

The little man leaned forward with a startled look in his pale eyes. Roaming Reynolds curled his lips and stared back.

'Just read the sign,' he answered softly. 'Tell him I'll be there.'

Thomas Kirby set his thin lips and mounted his horse. 'I'll tell him,' he murmured, and spurred with both heels. They watched his long coat flapping until he disappeared down the lane, and Texas Joe stepped up to his tall pard.

'You going to that planting?' he demanded. Reynolds nodded one time. 'You heard me,' he muttered. 'Tyson invited me to attend, so you better gear up yore hoss.'

He walked toward the house when Ma Lassiter beckoned, and old Lafe and Ely Zander began to talk in low tones. Texas Joe caught the black gelding and muttered under his breath, while Reynolds stopped in front of Ma Lassiter with a question in his eyes.

'Don't go, son,' she pleaded softly. 'It don't seem right.'

'There's some things that just work themselves out, Ma,' he answered thoughtfully. 'You can't force them any, but sometimes it saves a lot of trouble to take what comes.'

'You didn't,' she reminded softly. 'And I think more of you for it, Roamin'. Manny is our only chip, and I thought for a while …?'

'You didn't,' he contradicted quietly, and smiled at her. 'You knew all the time, and so did I.'

She nodded slowly. 'Reckon I did, son,' she admitted. 'But I was hoping that you and Joe would stay on with us. We need the both of you.'

'Looky, honey,' he said seriously, and took her hand. 'You and me both knows that Tyson would start all over again if he got a chance. Right now he don't believe that he is beat, and he won't ever admit it until Kirby does the work he gets paid to do!'

'Roamin'! You mean …?'

'Show-down,' he answered harshly. 'I just can't help it, Ma!'

She sighed deeply and kissed him on the forehead. 'I know, son. Like Manny and old Lafe, I'm cattle folks from hocks to horns. Good luck to you, Roamin', and …'

'Yeah,' he prompted softly.

'Speed to yore gun-hand,' she whispered, and turned to run inside the house.

For a moment he stared uncertainly, and then a throaty voice called from the front room. 'Roamin'? Could I see you for just a little minute?'

He frowned and jerked his square shoulders. Then he climbed the steps and pushed into the room. Bobbie Zander wiped a tear from her eye and held out her hand.

'You won't come back,' she said positively. 'I wanted to say good-bye. And I wanted to wish you the same as Ma.'

'Thanks,' he murmured, but his voice was strained.

The girl held his hands and pulled herself toward him; raised up on her toes and kissed him full on the lips.

'That's for remembrance,' she whispered. 'I was hoping … Hidden Valley … Good-bye, Roamin'!'

'Bye, Bobbie,' he muttered. 'Me and Joe will be riding by one of these days to give you and Manny howdy.'

'Shore you will,' and Manny Lassiter came into the room and put his good arm around the girl. 'I started the herd to Paradise, and Ely and Lafe are waiting to ride in with you and Joe.'

'Guess we better be starting,' Reynolds muttered. 'Sorry we can't stay no longer, but we'll be seeing you.'

He shook hands hurriedly and walked out to mount his tall roan. Texas Joe winked at Lafe Lassiter and vaulted to the saddle on the black thoroughbred. The two old cattlemen climbed their saddles and followed down the long lane, and Manny Lassiter held the sobbing girl against his big chest until the sounds of hoofs had died away.

'Yonder goes a man,' Lassiter said softly. 'I'll try to make it all up to you, Bobbie.'

Roaming Reynolds refused to talk until they sighted the trail herd about a mile from town. 'We'll pen the critters,' he said to Lassiter. 'Lacks all of an hour till ten o'clock.'

'The boys can handle the herd,' Lafe Lassiter replied, and his grey eyes were twinkling with repressed excitement. 'I just saw an old friend of mine down at the Stockmen's hotel.'

Roaming Reynolds jerked around in the saddle and studied the two old cattlemen. 'Mind telling a hand?' he asked quietly.

'Jim Telford, the cattle buyer,' Lassiter answered. 'Him and his son buy for one of the big outfits down Kansas City way. Both know cattle, and they do their own cutting.'

'And he was having considerable conversation with another gent,' Ely Zander added. 'Gent by the name of Tyson.'

Roaming Reynolds nodded. 'You and him,' he said briefly. 'Me and Joe will stick with the boys.'

Lafe Lassiter shook his head. 'We want you to meet them Telfords,' he answered quietly, but Reynolds could detect the undertone of anticipation. 'Let Joe stay with the boys, but you come along with us.'

Texas Joe scowled and stared at the herd moving toward the collection of postoak corrals. 'Like the boss says, Joe,' Reynolds told him. 'You can find me at the burying grounds at ten.'

He wheeled his horse and rode away with the two old cattlemen while Texas

Joe stared uncertainly. Lifting the heavy gun one time in his holster, just in case of a riding crimp, the lanky young cowboy muttered to himself and rode after the drag. Lafe Lassiter headed straight for the little frame hotel where he swung down and threw his reins over the tie rail.

Roaming Reynolds sat his saddle when a tall rawboned man came out of the hotel and boomed a greeting at Lafe and Lassiter. The two shook hands while the cattle buyer spoke to Zander and allowed his shrewd grey eyes to wander over Roaming Reynolds. The old cattleman saw the glance and made the introductions.

'Want you to meet Roaming Reynolds, Jim. Roamin', meet up with Jim Telford from down Comanche way.'

'Howdy,' Telford grunted without offering to shake hands. 'Heard a heap about you, Reynolds.'

'Yo're like to hear more,' Lafe Lassiter said grimly when Reynolds made no answer. 'Things got to looking bad, Jim. So bad that I hired Roamin' and his pard to ride gun for the Lazy L.'

'Yore business,' the cattle buyer grunted. 'I figgered on talking buy to you, but not after I got one look at that herd you just walked in.'

'You'll talk,' Lassiter answered confidently. 'And like as not you'll buy.'

'Not me,' Telford answered positively. 'That bunch of beef was burned with Griff Tyson's iron, and him the fastest gunhand in these parts!'

'I doubt that last,' Roaming Reynolds interrupted coldly, and he stared levelly when Telford shot a quick glance at his craggy face.

'So-o-o,' the cattle buyer murmured. 'Better tell me, Lafe,' he almost whispered.

'The United States Inspector is here in Paradise,' Lassiter stated slowly. 'You buy subject to his inspection, of course.'

'That's right,' Telford agreed. 'But even Joe Bailey won't pass that herd under yore Bill of Sale.'

'He'll pass it,' Lassiter assured the cattle buyer. 'That herd was rustled, Jim. Hid out on good grass after the brand had been vented. We got the proof!'

Jim Telford rubbed his chin. 'Now look, Lafe,' he countered softly. 'I'm a buyer, not a fighter or judge. I'll buy at a dollar a head above the market, and I don't care who I buy from. I'll talk to you after you have settled yore argument with Griff Tyson!'

'Remember what you said,' and Roaming Reynolds spoke clearly, 'and you might as well get ready to do business with Lafe.'

'Pretty shore of yoreself, stranger,' Telford answered sharply. 'But my offer stands like I put it.'

Reynolds shrugged and turned to Lassiter. 'You better stay with Telford,' he said quietly. 'He can start cutting any time in case he has a press of business on. Like he said, he will buy either way, according to Jim Bailey.'

'Where you going?' Lassiter demanded.

'Burying ground. Ramrod McCall was a game gent, and like as not he would do the same for me.'

'Me and Ely will just shag along in case of,' Lassiter muttered.

Roaming Reynolds shook his head. 'Better not,' he advised. 'Tyson won't start anything up there. Fact is, I don't think he will even be there.'

'I want the straights of this tangle,' the cattle buyer interrupted. 'Reynolds won't need any help from what I've heard, and sometimes a gent works best alone.'

Roaming Reynolds looked at the gaunt buyer with a new respect in his blue eyes. 'Thanks, Telford,' he murmured. 'Every head of that stuff belongs to Lassiter, and you and him better go over the tally and cut for culls. Be seeing you before you get yore work done.'

'And I'll be seeing you after you finish yore's,' Ely Zander said suddenly as he offered his hand. 'Luck to you, Roamin'.'

Reynolds shook gravely and gigged his horse down the dusty street. He was through talking, and the task ahead of him was distasteful. One he had never done before in all his days of roaming.

But he had passed his word, and he shrugged slightly and lined his horse for the burying ground on top of the hill.

He pulled a heavy silver watch from his chaps pocket and glanced at the time. Ten minutes to ten. Up ahead a black wagon drawn by two black horses was climbing the grade, with Thomas Kirby on the driver's seat, and not a single horseman in sight. Reynolds studied the wagon and shook his head, after which he touched the roan with a spur and arrived at a big open grave just as the wagon stopped.

The little undertaker alighted and opened the door in the back. Roaming Reynolds swung down and removed his tall Stetson. Ground-hitched his horse with trailing reins, and found the eyes of Thomas Kirby on him when he turned.

The undertaker drew a long breath and jerked his head toward the two caskets. 'You will help me?'

Roaming Reynolds nodded and walked forward. A moment later they carried the first casket to the grave and rested it on a pair of stout bars. A gun cracked spitefully just as the tall buckaroo leaned over with his burden, and the moment saved his life. Before he could straighten up, two more shots blasted the stillness of the graveyard, and Thomas Kirby straightened slowly with anger blazing in his little eyes.

'He did not even respect the dead!'

Roaming Reynolds was leaning toward a tall headstone with right hand poised above his gun. Smoke curled from behind the monument, and then a deep boyish voice called across the grave-dotted hill.

'It's me, Roamin'. Hold yore hand!'

Texas Joe stuck his tousled head around the big stone and followed it slowly Both Reynolds and the undertaker stared at him with open disapproval etched on their faces. The lanky cowboy grinned and pouched his old gun after jacking out the two spent shells and reloading fresh.

'I had it to do, Roamin',' he began nervously. 'I cut away from the herd down yonder when I got me a hunch.'

'That other shot,' Reynolds said sternly. 'Griff Tyson?'

Texas Joe shook his head. 'You know better than that,' he muttered. 'Gent by the name of Ben Tyler. You remember two of that rustler band got away?

'Tyler was working for Tyson,' Kirby interrupted. 'What about him?'

'Don't seem to be much law up this-away,' Texas Joe answered slowly. 'I came on out here just in case of. Saw that jigger sneaking around looking for a hiding place. Recognised him as one of the hands that was riding with Ramrod McCall the first time we met the deceased.'

Roaming Reynolds spoke softly. 'Which deceased?' he asked.

'Both of them, yuh might say,' Joe answered carelessly. 'Tyler ought to be about through kicking, back yonder. I ain't learned to throw off my shots!'

'In the midst of life, we are in death,' the little undertaker murmured, and walked back to the head of the grave. Pointed to a pair of straps and waited for

Reynolds to take his place.

Texas Joe stared for a moment and thought to remove his battered Stetson. The grave was deep and wide, and both caskets were lowered to the bottom before anyone spoke again. Then Thomas Kirby fished a worn book from the pocket of his black coat and read a brief service. After which he closed the book and turned to Reynolds.

'My men will fill the grave,' he murmured, and turned his eyes on Texas Joe. 'Will you show me?'

The lanky cowboy slapped on his hat and cuffed it low over his eyes. Highheeled across the rocky ground without speaking. Stopped near a huge marker and pointed behind the jutting shadow. Thomas Kirby leaned over and nodded.

'It's Ben Tyler,' he identified the dead man. 'Griff Tyson will want to know.'

'Better tell him,' Reynolds murmured, and turned to his younger pard. 'Saying thanks,' he murmured, and there was no excitement in his deep, quiet voice.

'You can thank old Ely Zander,' Joe

confessed with a grin. 'It was him saw Ben Tyler watching us make the drive just as we hit town. He dropped back and gave me the high sign to come on up for a look-see.'

Roaming Reynolds turned to the undertaker. 'Better roll back to town, Kirby,' he suggested. 'Me and Joe will be along *poco tiempo.*'

Thomas Kirby set his jaw and climbed the driver's seat. Rolled down the hill in a cloud of dust with his mutton-chops wagging angrily, and he set his brake when he saw a tall figure waiting in front of his place of business. Wrapped the lines around the whip-stock and climbed down with shoulders squared back.

'Do you respect the dead, Griff Tyson?' he asked solemnly.

The Deuce of Diamonds owner stared for a long moment. Then: 'Sometimes, but I don't attend funerals.'

'You will, one day,' Kirby snapped. 'I needed help up there, and I got it!'

'Yes?'

'You heard me. Roaming Reynolds

rode out to pay his respects, and to lend a hand. Said he knew you wouldn't be there!'

Sudden anger clouded the big man's dark eyes. Anger that was quickly controlled when Tyson shrugged his shoulders.

'I might do the same for Reynolds,' he answered softly. 'There always has to be a first time.'

Thomas Kirby shook his head positively. 'I don't think so, but let it pass. Somebody tried to kill Reynolds while he was helping me lift the casket of Ramrod McCall!'

Griff Tyson jerked forward with eyes open wide. Eyes that changed colour when they caught the light, and his stern mouth was a thin gash of colour in a face that had suddenly paled.

'He thought it was me?'

Kirby shook his head. 'No; Reynolds said he was sure you would not be there. The dry-gulcher was Ben Tyler!'

'Tyler! I thought he had lit out for the border!'

'He did,' the undertaker answered dryly. 'Seems like old Ely Zander got a look at Tyler when they drove in the beef herd. So he played a hunch and sent young Texas Joe up ahead. The Button said he never learned to throw off his shots, and he rocked hammer twice!'

'I won't forget,' Tyson breathed softly, and the colour returned to his face. 'Reynolds will know that Tyler was acting on his own, and without my knowledge.'

'That's what he said,' Kirby agreed. 'Said he figgered you would want to know.'

'Tyler? You bring him in?'

Thomas Kirby shook his head. 'You know my terms on those kind of cases,' he muttered. 'Cash at the graveside, and we left him where he bled out.'

Griff Tyson leaned forward and tapped the little man on the chest. 'I'm going to kill you, buzzard,' he said bluntly, 'after you have finished the work you were paid to do,' and he reached into a vest pocket and drew out several bills. Handed them to the undertaker who took the money and shrugged his shoulders. 'Thanks,' he muttered grimly. 'But you won't kill anybody after I have finished the job of work I was paid to do. And I will do my best to make you look natural.'

No fear in his pale little eyes while he stared at the tall gun-fighter and held his ground. Griff Tyson shrugged and turned to face the lower end of town; hitched up his gun-belt and settled his hat firmly.

'One of us is wrong,' and his voice was calm and quiet. 'In the meantime, you better go back after Tyler. And when you haul him up there again, take some help along to put him away.'

'Help is cheap when a man knows he will need it,'

Kirby grunted, and pocketed the money. 'Saying good-bye to you for the last time … but one,' and he climbed back into his black wagon.

He frowned when he saw Griff Tyson smiling with amusement and he brought down his whip and sent the horses into their collars with a jump. 'Yo're the buzzard,' he shouted in his deep bass voice, and wagged his Van Dyke when he saw the smile turn to a frown of hatred.

Roaming Reynolds and Texas Joe were leaning against their saddles when he clattered into the graveyard. Both cowboys were smoking, and the tall buckaroo looked up and waited for Kirby to speak.

'He was waiting down there,' the undertaker growled. 'So I collected for this other case and delivered yore message. He said to tell you he never attended funerals, but he might make an exception in your case.'

Roaming Reynolds dropped his cigarette to the ground and rubbed it out with a high heel. 'You better bring some help along when you bring Tyler up here,' he said softly.

'Just what Griff Tyson told me,' Kirby rumbled, 'Will you gents help me put that bush-whacker in the wagon?'

Texas Joe scowled. 'Me and Roamin' ought to be deputy marshals,' he sneered. 'Them fellers has to bury their dead when they kill an outlaw, and lately we ain't been any different.'

Thomas Kirby smiled and went about his work. When the door of the black wagon was closed, he turned to the lanky cowboy with a twinkle in his eyes.

'Tyson said to thank you for what you done,' he told Texas Joe. 'Right now he is free to leave town, but he won't stir a boot until he takes his pleasure.'

'I told you he didn't know,' and Texas Joe glanced at Reynolds. 'I don't like that big jigger, but he packs more cold nerve than any man I ever run my eyes across.'

'He will need it,' the undertaker muttered, and he studied the craggy face of Roaming Reynolds. 'Watch him,' he cautioned slowly. 'Griff Tyson never fights to lose!'

'Where could a man find him about now?'

Reynolds asked quietly.' After he leaves yore place of business?'

'You know where the shipping pens are,' Kirby answered. 'Might sound funny, but the saloon across from there is called the ONE SPOT. Like as not he will be waiting there. He always has.'

Roaming Reynolds lifted his eyes. 'Meaning what?' he inquired softly.

'Meaning that so far I've had four cases from the ONE SPOT,' the undertaker answered grimly. 'And Griff Tyson paid all the bills. I'll give him that much.'

Roaming Reynolds tightened his cinchas and turned slowly. 'Asking you to wait a spell until me and Joe get going,' he requested. 'It might be bad luck to follow you again.'

Thomas Kirby did not smile when he nodded his grey head. 'Was going to suggest the same thing myself,' he answered solemnly, 'and Reynolds?'

Roaming Reynolds knew what was coming. 'Yeah?'

'I'm hoping my next case won't be yoreself, but if it is ... I'll do my best work.'

'Shore you will,' and there was a twinkle in the deep blue eyes. '*Adios*, Kirby,' and the tall buckaroo forked his saddle. Somehow the idea of shaking hands was repulsive, and he sent his roan down the

356

hill with Texas Joe at his side.

'Roamin',' and a worried note crept into the deep voice of Texas Joe. 'You got the feeling this morning?'

The tall gun-fighter smiled confidently. 'Right down to my finger tips,' he assured his pard, and then the smile faded from his face. 'There's just Tyson and me left,' he continued harshly. 'Him and me both know the code … and so do you!'

'Damn him!' Joe muttered savagely, and his voice trembled. 'I'm taking seconds in case you run up against something you can't cut down!'

15

Roaming Reynolds felt the eyes of men studying him when he walked his horse through the deep dust arid headed for the long adobe saloon. Texas Joe stared back until eyes dropped before the challenge in his thin face. And then the tall buckaroo spoke softly.

'Shuck it, Joe. You won't never make a poker player showing everything you feel that-away.'

Texas Joe grunted and twisted his shoulders. 'I either like a gent, or else I hate him to beat hell,' he snapped. 'These rannies been taking slack from Tyson and his hands all these years, and not one of them with the sand to do something about it!'

'Four of them made a try,' Reynolds reminded dryly. 'And most every one of them fellers is wishing us luck without saying so. Remember what I told you a while back about staying out.'

The lanky cowboy growled in his throat and kicked his horse closer. 'This here code, Roamin',' he began slowly. 'I don't hold with it, like you know.'

'Every gent to his own ideas,' Reynolds answered, but his eyes stared coldly. 'I hold with the code, and you heard what I said.'

'Yeah, I heard yuh,' Joe admitted. 'But one of the days yo're going to run up against a gent who will pull a fast sneak. After which me and my black hoss will be riding the trails alone!'

Roaming Reynolds was staring at the little hotel and did not seem to hear. 'Old Lafe is making medicine with the cattle buyers,' he murmured softly. 'Just as well they don't see us pass.'

'Yonder's the One Spot,' Joe grunted. 'We tying up there?'

Reynolds nodded and neck-reined to the rail. Swung down and passed his fingers automatically against his gun handle before shouldering through the swinging doors. With Texas Joe stepping in like a cat to slide against the side wall while his grey eyes ran over the crowd.

'Not here,' he murmured softly, and sneered when several drinkers along the bar looked hastily away. 'Reckon he dogged it, Roamin'!'

The tall buckaroo shook his head slightly. 'You know better,' he grunted. 'Down to the shipping corrals. He ought to be there.'

Not a word as the two passed through the batwing and paused outside. Texas Joe let out his spurs and stomped importantly to set the jingle-bobs chiming. Walked stiff-legged through the deep dust alongside Reynolds when they started for the shipping pens.

The Lazy L cowboys were busy passing cattle through the pens and making their final tallies. The office of the freight agent stood apart, near a platform, and the tall buckaroo spoke softly.

'You take one side; me the other. And you might bring up the horses.'

'Dogged it, I tell you,' Joe muttered, and started back up the street.

Roaming Reynolds watched him while

he filled his big chest with the bracing air. Then he started around the long building at a slow walk. Unhurriedly and without excitement, except for the tingle that ran down his right arm to his finger tips.

Texas Joe pulled the slip-knots and mounted his black. Rode back at a trot and slid down with both bridle reins in his left hand. Two men were talking quietly along the further wall, and the taller of the two glanced up and brushed his gun with the finger tips of his right hand.

'You bring Roaming Reynolds with you?' he called softly.

Texas Joe swore under his breath and turned slowly. Then he faced Griff Tyson with no attempt to conceal his feelings.

'You mean the gun-boss of Summit Valley?' he asked insolently.

Tyson smiled and shook his head. 'No,' he answered softly. 'You are *looking* at the boss of Summit Valley. After finding this card I figgered he would back up his palaver,' and he made a little movement with his left hand.

Texas Joe lowered his eyes and stared at the card. The Deuce of Diamonds with both pips shot out. And then he frowned again when he realised that he had taken his eyes away from the tall gunfighter's right hand. Men had died because of such carelessness.

'That's right good figgering,' he answered hoarsely. 'Roamin' put it where he thought it would do the most good.'

Fleeting anger swept over the dark, handsome face and was gone as quickly. 'I found it,' Tyson murmured. 'And I likewise heard what you did this morning. Saved me the trouble of killing Ben Tyler myself.'

'Don't mention it,' Texas Joe growled. 'I needed a little practice, and I sorter figgered you didn't want that kind of help.'

Griff Tyson nodded. 'You got the makings of a man, Joe,' he praised. 'If yore pard has run out on you, there's a job on the Deuce of Diamonds.'

Texas Joe leaned forward in a crouch. 'Talking with yore mouth,' he sneered. 'Roamin' ain't never dogged it up to now, and he's kinda set in his ways!'

Griff Tyson smiled and shook his head. 'You can't always tell,' he answered sof tly. 'After what he said that day back in the valley, I looked forward to the time when him and me would settle our argument.'

'You ain't got long to wait,' Texas Joe answered dryly. 'Just swing yore head around and see if yore eyesight is as good as yore line of gab!'

The Deuce of Diamonds owner spun around and stared at Roaming Reynolds near the corner of the office. Both were tall men, and Griff Tyson's voice was low and steady while a faint smile crinkled the corners of his mouth.

'You are a man of caution, Reynolds. The Deuce of Diamonds has never been guilty of a gun-sneak.'

'Interesting if true,' Reynolds murmured softly. 'But I heard you say that you were the gun-boss of Summit Valley. I signed on for that job my own self. Looked for you in the One Spot,' and he shook his head slightly. 'Couldn't find you, so I came down here to the pens.'

'Sorry I missed you,' Tyson murmured. 'And what you heard was true.'

'See you found the card,' Reynolds answered.

Tyson nodded his well-shaped head. 'I found it, and I'm sorry I was absent when you called. You didn't mention it later when I met you and the Button.'

Roaming Reynolds shrugged. 'I figgered you would get all the information you wanted when you found yore foreman.'

'I found two dead men in my front room,' Tyson grated harshly. 'You killed Ramrod McCall 'and carried him into the house. Then you put a Deuce of Diamonds on his chest where you knew I couldn't miss it!'

'Keno,' the tall buckaroo agreed softly. 'I met yore Ramrod for show-down just as the sun came up over the Vermilions. Like you know, he shot second.'

'And he had both feet on the ground,' Texas Joe cut in loudly. 'He dogged it last night when we caught him in Hidden Valley!'

'Knew you found the valley,' Tyson answered, and his eyes did not leave the face of Roaming Reynolds.

'We found it before we met you up in the pines,' Texas Joe sneered. 'Butch Cawdorn and Shorty Peters tried to pull a sneak play, and you could have found them if you had looked close.'

'I found them,' and Tyson's voice was unchanged. 'They both got what they deserved. Ramrod McCall and Ben Tyler got the same, and I'm not complaining.'

'You will be,' Joe muttered. 'We found that herd of Lazy L white-faces yore crew had vented the brands on. Mostly all long three's and four's!'

The man with Tyson spoke up quickly. 'Like you know, I am the United States Inspector,' he began. 'Have you any proof of what you say?'

'Just a minute, Joe,' Reynolds interrupted. 'I'll handle this without help.'

'Sorry, Reynolds,' the Inspector
answered bluntly. 'The law comes first.
You heard me, Button. Have you any
proof?'

Griff Tyson smiled and balanced easily on his handmade boots. Texas Joe
unbuttoned the front of his shirt and
reached down inside. The smile faded
from Tyson's face when the lanky cowboy brought out a piece of green hide
and threw it to the government man.
Joe Bailey caught it and stared for a
minute.

Griff Tyson frowned and glanced at
Roaming Reynolds. The Inspector held
the piece of hide up to the light and
made a long examination, and when he
lowered the skin, his face was grave.

'Originally Lazy L,' he announced
firmly. 'With a long Diamond added,
and two curls top and bottom. The brand
has been vented!'

'That's the way I read it to old Lafe

Lassiter,' Reynolds said soberly. 'You can always tell a vented brand if you look through the hide, and must be upward of two thousand head blotted that-away.'

Tyson waved his left hand carelessly. 'About your claim to being gun-boss,' he said softly. 'Yore error!'

The Inspector moved to the side and watched both men closely. Both were broad of shoulder and superbly confident of their ability with the tools of their calling. Joe Bailey could read all the signs, and he made another attempt to postpone the issue.

'The Government comes first,' he stated bluntly, and watched Griff Tyson. 'Old Lafe will sign the complaint.'

'It ain't signed yet,' Tyson remarked softly.

'And it won't be,' Reynolds added in the same tone. 'I don't hold with putting a man behind the bars to rot away.'

Griff Tyson smiled again. 'I appreciate the sentiment,' he murmured. 'I knew nothing of this brand venting, but I suppose I am responsible for the acts of my men.'

'That's good figgering,' the Inspector remarked dryly. 'And you can tell it to the Judge in the District Court.'

'Later,' Tyson answered with a shrug. 'Right now I have some other unfinished business.'

'Which you won't get done,' Texas Joe sneered.

Tyson ignored him and turned his eyes on Reynolds. 'You said you was gun-boss!'

Roaming Reynolds smiled coldly, but now the fires were smouldering in his blue eyes. Straight as a tall pine, there was no tremble in his deep voice when he answered.

'That's my bet, Tyson,' he said slowly. 'You calling?'

'I'll see you and raise,' Tyson murmured, and both men forgot Texas Joe and the Inspector. 'You can tell Ramrod McCall you made a mistake when you see him.'

'Tell him yourself,' the tall buckaroo snapped. 'You and him was pards as long as he could do you some good, and right now he's waiting out on the dim trail. Waiting for you to ride up and tell him howdy. Waiting to say what he thinks because you left somebody else to do the things he figgered you would do for him!'

'Meaning the funeral?'

'What else? You were afraid of the shadow of death?'

Griff Tyson frowned as though he were thinking. 'It wasn't that,' he muttered. 'I paid the bills, and I'll do the same for you. I just don't go to funerals.'

'Yo're about due to go to one soon,' Texas Joe sneered softly. 'For the first … and the *last* time!'

Griff Tyson closed his lips tightly. The topaz of his eyes barely showed through the slitted lids while he fought against the blinding anger that swept over him. He was no longer handsome when a scowl twisted his dark face.

'Easy,' the soft voice of Roaming Reynolds warned. 'Getting mad slows up a gent's hand. I ain't asking for any edges!'

Griff Tyson steadied and opened his eyes a trifle. The tall figure of his opponent was blurred and hazy, and then he drew a deep breath and shook his head.

Gradually the smile returned to his face, and Texas Joe sighed with disappointment.

'You had him then, Roamin',' he muttered harshly. 'He couldn't see for looking!'

Roaming Reynolds frowned. 'The code,' he said slowly, 'it calls for an even break!'

'Which he wouldn't give you,' Joe snarled. 'And he had a hand on his gun!'

'You wouldn't know,' Tyson interrupted coldly. 'You ain't lived long enough to season.'

'I have,' Reynolds interrupted. 'Before you draw, Tyson. Chances are I could have settled this rustling and rode on out. But that was before I found Bobbie Zander at yore house. She told me what you said ... what you did!'

Griff Tyson fell into a crouch. 'So what?' he demanded softly.

'This,' and Roaming Reynolds drooped his shoulders. 'Make yore pass!'

Griff Tyson waited a few seconds while his eyes narrowed and changed colour. Then he ripped into sudden action with hand slapping down to the handle of his balanced Colt. Down and up with scarcely a pause to separate the two movements, with the muzzle hissing against worn leather like ice in a camp-fire.

Roaming Reynolds rippled the muscles in his shoulders with a jerk that plunged his hand down in a fl.ashing blur of speed. He stepped forward like a boxer to throw the scabbard down and away from his his long leg to gain a precious fragment of time. His boot hit a buried bull-post just showing above the dusty ground, and he plunged forward when Tyson's gun-barrel was tilting up.

The tall buckaroo twisted and threw a shot while he was hurtling forward. He felt the tug of Tyson's lead against his vest while he was falling, and a strangely savage voice snarled offside while he was looping into a roll.

'My turn, Tyson! You killed my pard on a sneak and I'm calling the turn!'

'The Deuce of Diamonds owner thumbed back his hammer while he was whirling to face Texas Joe. The lanky cowboy was completing his draw, and his thin face was contorted with anger and grief. Roaming Reynolds rolled up and shouted when his tall body came between the tilting guns.

Griff Tyson stomped his boot with surprise showing on his dark face. Never before had he taken more than on shot, and his smoking gun levelled up with thumb slipping the heavy hammer. Roaming Reynolds got his own shot away even while his narrowed eyes saw the firing pin hitting the shell, and the two shots blended together in a savage roar.

Reynolds was leaning forward with the bucking gun high for a follow-up. Griff Tyson staggered back a step and caught his balance. Tried gamely to raise his arm in one last, mighty effort of will. An effort which failed when he died on his feet.

Th gun sagged slowly with the passing of life; dropped suddenly when the Deuce of Diamonds swayed too far and crashed down without moving his polished boots. While the gun echoes rattled away and died out entirely.

Texas Joe stared down and started to tremble. Then he seemed to see his companion for the first time, and rushed across with a hoarse shout tearing from his tight throat.

'You leaded bad, pard? He get you hard?'

Roaming Reynolds shook his head and jacked the spent shells from his gun. 'Never touched me, Joe,' he answered gravely. 'But his second shot would have settled the ruckus if you hadn't cut in on the play. I felt his slug when I tripped over that damn bull-ring yonder.'

'At that, you beat him to the shot,' Texas Joe shouted excitedly. 'Reason I horned in and called for show-down was because I was afraid he'd get you while you was down.'

'He might have done it, pard,' the tall gun-fighter admitted soberly. 'I owe you one for siding me that time, but I don't know whether it was according to the code or not.'

'The code,' Joe sneered. 'You mind what I told you on the way down from Boot-Hill. He grabbed every edge, and he even started first for his gun.'

'You took advantage, Joe,' Reynolds chided softly. 'You hoorayed him until you got him to fighting his head.'

'You had him beat nohow,' the Button insisted. 'I didn't know it at the time, and my old gun started out of leather when he swapped ends to face me. Then you jumped between to take his lead. Don't reckon I got what he called seasoning yet, pard.'

'You got plenty of it,' the tall buckaroo praised softly. 'But yonder lies a brave man, Joe. And the fastest with a hand-gun I've met in all my travels!'

'And now he's all ready to go to a funeral,' Texas Joe sniffed. 'Just like that buzzard told him. I mean Thomas Kirby,' he corrected generously.

'Look who's coming,' Reynolds said quietly. 'Like the devil was riding their coat tails.'

Old Lafe Lassiter and Ely Zander were rushing around the side of the, Agent's office. They slid to a stop with eyes staring down at the prone figure in the dust. Old Ely tightened his over-sized coat and minced forward.

'You beat Griff Tyson,' he whispered. 'You beat the Deuce of Diamonds!'

'I had help,' Reynolds corrected soberly. 'I tripped over that bull-ring yonder just as I cleared leather. Tyson missed me with his first shot, but his second would have tallied if Joe hadn't cut in on the play.'

'You mean Joe …?'

Lafe Lassiter shook his head. 'Tyson would have beat me, Lafe,' Texas Joe muttered. 'Then Roamin' came up and jumped between me and Tyson. The

Inspector will tell you the same thing.'

'That's right,' the officer put in. 'And Reynolds missed death himself by the wink of an eye. Never saw so much fast work in so little time in all my life!'

Roaming Reynolds had forgotten the Inspector, and now he turned to nod his head. 'Obliged to you for staying out like you did, Bailey,' and his deep voice was calm and steady. 'You still got that hide?'

The Inspector nodded and turned to Lafe Lassiter. 'Reynolds tells me the Deuce of Diamonds vented close on to two thousand head of yore beef, Lafe. Looks like you owe them two something pretty, for the work they done!'

'They'll get it as soon as I sell the herd,' old Lafe Lassiter answered promptly. 'What you make of that venting job?'

'I gave my answer before Tyson made his last fight,' the Inspector answered. 'She was originally Lazy L, with a diamond and two wings added.'

'That's what I told Jim Telford,' Lassiter growled. 'He's a cold-blooded cuss, and he stood ready to buy from either

376

Tyson or me. What become of old Ely?'
'Fogged it behind the corrals,' Texas Joe
spoke up. 'Looks like he can't stand to
see a corpse.'

Lafe Lassiter smiled wryly. 'He's
looked on more than one of his own making,' he remarked quietly, and turned to
Joe Bailey. 'How about them critters in
the pens, Inspector?'

'I'll pass the herd under your own
iron,' Bailey answered promptly. 'I'm
declaring that Deuce of Diamonds brand
vacant so's you and your hands can clean
up the range. That-away you and old Ely
can settle between you for the stuff he
lost, and from what I can find out, Griff
Tyson didn't leave any heirs.'

'That finishes our work, boss,' Roaming Reynolds told Lafe Lassiter.

'Whoa up a spell,' Lassiter murmured,
and pointed up the street. 'Yonder comes
Manny and Bobbie Zander. Reckon me
and the Inspector will root on over to the
One Spot for a drink.'

Roaming Reynolds glanced at his
horse and saw that he could not escape.

Manny Lassiter was grinning happily, and Reynolds walked around the corner of the building. Bobbie Zander might get upset if she saw the body in the dust. The big cowboy slid down and came forward with hand outstretched.

'We heard just now, Roaming,' he almost shouted. 'Bobbie and me wants to tell you how glad we are you won.'

Roaming Reynolds nodded and studied the face of Bobbie Zander. Now there was a different expression in her brown eyes, and she sidled up to Manny and curled a hand under his arm.

'And we wanted to ask you and Joe to stay for the wedding,' she whispered. 'Just a week from today.'

'I don't deserve her, but I'll try all my life,' the big cowboy said seriously. 'You'll stay, pard?'

'Well, yuh see,' the tall gun-fighter murmured. 'We just can't cut 'er, Manny. Me and Joe has got to see a man over the hill about a dog!'

'Dog?' and disappointment showed in the girl's pretty face. 'I don't understand, Roamin'.'

'Aw, he's hooraying you,' Texas Joe growled. 'Yonder comes Lafe and Ely back again.'

Roaming Reynolds shuffled his feet and twitched his wide shoulders. A black wagon pulled up behind the office and Thomas Kirby climbed out. Came straight to Reynolds and spoke softly.

'Knew it all the time, Roaming,' he said solemnly. 'I'll do the work I was paid to do.'

'Fly at it,' the tall buckaroo muttered, and turned his back until the wagon had rattled up the street. Bobbie Zander moved closer to Manny Lassiter and clung to his arm, and Roaming Reynolds walked over to his horse and stepped across the scarred saddle.

'*Adios*, folks,' he muttered. 'Me and Joe . . .'

'Yeah, I know,' old Lafe chuckled. 'You got to see a man about a dog. Take care of yoreselves, and don't ride too fast on account of the load them hosses is packing.'

Roaming Reynolds stared for a moment. 'We always travel light,' he said slowly.

'You don't this time,' the old cattle-man chuckled.

'The buyers done made me an advance on them shippers yonder, so Ely slipped ten per cent in yore saddle-bags. You earned it and more, and Hidden Valley is still open back yonder if you changes yore mind.'

Roaming Reynolds stared at the bulging saddle-bags behind his cantle. 'Don't argue none with me,' Lafe Lassiter shouted. 'Unless you want me to get up my mad and show you who is going to be gun-boss of Summit Valley from now on!'

We do hope that you have enjoyed reading this large print book.

Did you know that all of our titles are available for purchase?

We publish a wide range of high quality large print books including:
Romances, Mysteries, Classics
General Fiction
Non Fiction and Westerns

Special interest titles available in large print are:
The Little Oxford Dictionary
Music Book, Song Book
Hymn Book, Service Book

Also available from us courtesy of Oxford University Press:
Young Readers' Dictionary
(large print edition)
Young Readers' Thesaurus
(large print edition)

For further information or a free brochure, please contact us at:
Ulverscroft Large Print Books Ltd.,
The Green, Bradgate Road, Anstey,
Leicester, LE7 7FU, England.
Tel: (00 44) **0116 236 4325**
Fax: (00 44) **0116 234 0205**

Emily Bragg, captive of the Comanches, has been with them for years. When a new prisoner is brought to the camp, she befriends and protects her. But when a Comanchero promises to ransom both women, Emily is not sure she wants to leave ... When the Penateka Comanches discover the creatures ridden by the invading Spaniards, they wonder if they too could mount them ... And a fugitive on a stage bound for Indian territory finds out that his fellow passenger is a U.S. marshal...

THE WELDING QUIRT

Max Brand

A young boy invades a camp of slumbering outlaws, and manages to create so much havoc that he routs all but one of them … Sleeper and his chestnut stallion Careless are rescued from a flash flood by a man named Bones. When Bones is captured by a sheriff's posse for killing two claim-jumpers, it's time for Sleeper to return the favor … Driven from his hometown, Snoozer Mell chooses the life of a gambler. But he has to return — and his past will pursue him …

HOUSTON'S STORY

Abe Dancer

George Houston's line of work carries with it infamy and danger, and it's not long before his peaceable ride through Utah is cut dramatically short. After a bank robbery and the killing of one of its leading businessmen, the town of Bullhead is angry and wound up. But Agnes Jarrow believes it's not the work of the young hothead who breaks free from the town jail — so Houston sets off on a perilous search for Billy Carrick.